MIRIAM UNFINISHED

HJ BRENNAN

Oakland

HJ BRENNAN

Printed Worldwide
First Printing 2026
First Edition 2026

ISBN: 979-8-9960293-0-3

10 9 8 7 6 5 4 3 2 1

Interior Book Design by Walt's Book Design
www.waltsbookdesign.com

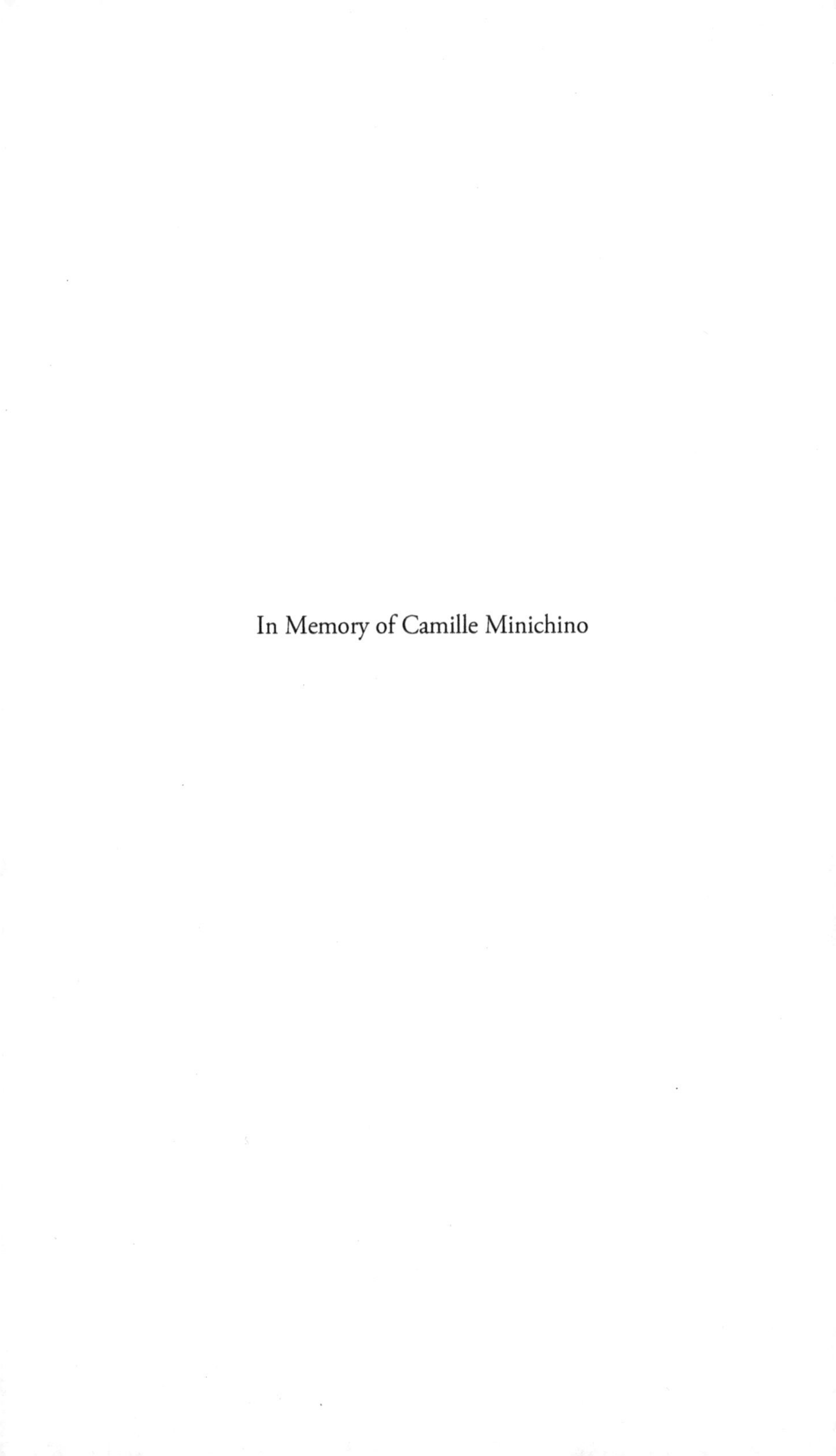

In Memory of Camille Minichino

ALSO BY HJ BRENNAN

Fathers' Day

This Then is What Counts

PART 1

Miriam

1

Long After the Hurt, October 2017

The small woman walks the six blocks to her gallery and arrives promptly at 10:30, Wednesdays through Sundays. Her entry to the building is up one granite step from the sidewalk where she unlocks the single-paned, heavy oak door and, daily, admires the original nineteenth-century hardware—the dark brass, low-relief doorknob, the vintage lock below. She twists the key for a quarter revolution and meets resistance. Light pressure, first in her thin, pale fingers, spreads to her wrist, her elbow raised slightly, the key moves the heavy mechanism like ascending a hill, crests the top, then descends swiftly and a solid brass *click.* She climbs the long, narrow flight to the second-story landing and another glass-paned door, this with gold-leaf lettering—*M. Pastor Gallery.*

The bell above the door *bings* as she enters. First things first. She turns off the alarm—21457, her birthday—a code that, had she had it in Manhattan, this might all be different. Then to the thermostat. Being an old building with high ceilings and tall windows to the street, balancing the temperature is, well, a balancing act. Next, cross the scarred wood floor past the flat file cabinet commanding the middle of the generous space, to the far back corner, and the door to the workshop. The shop glows burnt orange and smells like ancient, freshly polished shoes. Vertical racks house scores of canvases from past shows to be presented to clients having expressed interest in a particular artist, subject, style—or, less nobly, color and size.

A creature of habit and organization, she fits her Tupperware lunch into the small fridge, then hangs her shoulder bag, hat, and long coat on the door hook.

Her phone.

It's Irvin in Seattle. He has a buyer for the Lautrec lithograph—the Yvette Guilbert—and does she still have it?

She does.

She should send it.

She will.

"You okay?" he asks.

"Sales are slow."

"Time of the year."

"Yes, it's the time of the year," she says, "but you found someone for the Lautrec."

"Japanese collector."

"You've done well in that market."

"Yes." He pauses. "So, then."

"Wait. How was your morning? How's Destiny?"

"I've just opened. She's fine, Miriam. I have someone here."

"Of course."

"Thanks for sending the print. FedEx overnight. Gotta run."

"Bye, Irv." *I miss you.*

Her Diary:

Who buys art? One assumes it's the rich, and it often is. But not exclusively. I've read of a retired postal worker and his wife who had collected dozens of notable works in their small Brooklyn apartment. Upon their deaths, it was discovered they'd been collecting for seventy years, and long before the artists had become known. I've met a retail clerk who shared that he and his wife had saved up to replace their weeping refrigerator, but at the last minute decided on an Irving Penn portrait of Truman Capote. Those works, tucked away and loved in private.

2

The Visitor, 2017

B*ing!* The bell above the door. From inside the shop, she peeks out to the gallery. A large man, possibly her age, his hands in the pockets of his black wool overcoat. He stares at the small sculpture in the corner. She doesn't recognize him. She tucks a short strand of salt and pepper behind her ear, enters, and offers good morning.

"A Kehinde Wiley," he says.

He's familiar with this. "Yes. *Louis the Sixteenth. The Sun King.*"

"This is a treat. I didn't expect this."

"Hmm . . . " She folds her arms. "And what had you expected?"

"Well, the Bower exhibit—the trees."

"Of course." She acknowledges the bold watercolors on the back wall.

She says she was about to boil water for tea and would he like a cup.

He would, thank you.

In the shop, and the single hot plate at the window, she watches the water simmer. The steam, its droplets clearly defined in the raking light, rises with a memory—

Her dress had a spot on it near the hem, but it was a busy flowered pattern, and her mother said it wouldn't show. Across from her little brother in the back seat, she smoothed the dress on her thighs and felt the liquid gloss of her slip. At the wheel, her father had been irritated. They would be late for church. Her mother had calmed him. It was a warm fall day, but her mother said they couldn't put the windows down because of their hair. Their hair and her brother.

She pours the cups and places them on a lacquered tray—napkins, tiny spoons, and a miniature porcelain bowl of sugar arranged just so. She stares down to the street.

Her little brother, Nick—her adopted brother. It was obvious from the start that he and she would never connect, his every edge serrated, moving, and hot. Her father had locked the rear door on Nick's side of the car and removed the handle. The boy wouldn't be escaping at the stop sign *this* Sunday.

She carries the tray to the gentleman. He takes a cup, stirs in two spoons of sugar, and thanks her. She crosses the gallery and lowers the tray to her desk. With her cup, she joins the man in front of one of the Bower watercolors. "Such control," she says, "and lightness."

He says he appreciates the subtlety of color in what, at first glance, appears to be black and white.

"Not unlike the artist." She asks the man if this is his first time to the gallery.

He says it is. He says he's here for a week—maybe two—and considering moving from the city.

"Philly?" she asks.

He tells her he's from New York and he's heard that this small city, in the midst of Pennsylvania's rural splendor, has held on to a great cultural heritage—and this gallery comes highly recommended.

"Yes, a rich history—logging, Little League, the Repasz Band."

"Band?"

"Daniel Repasz." She turns to the windows and wonders whoever would have told him about this small city, this gallery? Still to the windows, "Our collectors are few and far between—as are our sales."

He replies that his guess is that most galleries operate on thin budgets. "Unless you're the Whitney."

A brain stutter, then, "Yes." She excuses herself to the rear of the gallery and into the shop.

Back against the door, her eyes trace the workbench, the clock, the windows to the street. *Twenty years.* She'd found this space for her gallery, directed contractors unaccustomed to physical requirements for the display and care of visual art, assembled her mailing list from the lists of the local library, colleges and orchestra donors, and hired two smart, capable student interns to help out. That was easy, and of her nature. The hard part had been her stoic surrender to the Whitney's board and suffering the museum director's suppressed smile, abandoning an ascendant career, leaving her staff, her circle of influence, New York's social scene, and the cooling crucible of youth. Here, and twenty years ago, she had started over—moved in with her ailing parents and gathered her morning-after dignity starkly alone.

They'd had their investigation and found nothing. Nothing but suspicions born of loose associations and conveniently misshapen histories. The police and the board had run their fingers down the menus of Irvin's and her lives and chosen only what would satisfy their appetite for retribution.

She glances to the clock. Minutes have passed, and she hasn't heard the bell. *He's still here.* She releases a deep breath and collects herself. *Step back, Miriam.* A likely coincidence. And why jump at the mention of, "New York, this small city, this gallery, the Whitney?" She takes a shorter breath, turns, and reenters the gallery.

His cup is on the tray. He's about to leave. He turns to her. "Ah, good. You're back." He's glad he's seen the Bowers in such a sophisticated environment—the mounting, the lighting, the surrounding empty space she's invested allowing each piece and the viewer to breathe. Uncommon in regional galleries, in his experience. The bell *bings*.

"Would you like to leave your information? For our mailing list?"

In the doorway, he thanks her, but he'd rather not right now. He says he'll be back—that he's been struck by two of the Bowers and has to give it some time. He plans to do some local fishing, cast his line into the nooks and crannies of the area. That's when he does his best thinking—fishing. Maybe up the creek at Powys. "It's near Trout Run, and it's stocked, right?" Meanwhile, he's staying a block away at the grand old hotel.

Alone again, she stares across the vast, bright, gallery space. Rubber soles, she crosses the open floor—so solid, having once supported heavy machinery—the pock marks of puttied bolt holes beneath its polyurethane finish. The large man and the Whitney resonate in the quiet, and she realizes she hasn't turned the radio on. At the flat files, she runs her fingers down the drawers to "L," and stops.

The sounds of light traffic on the street below.

She slides the drawer open, and a sterile fabric smell drifts up. There, on top of a shallow stack, is French cabaret singer Yvette Guilbert, her epically portrayed profile diffused through time and the protective sleeve. Fluid, alive, a spontaneous composition. Great art? Perhaps. Surely a great illustration—and, unquestionably, Lautrec had a thing for Ms. Guilbert, though she had her detractors. "*There she is! Long leech, sexless! She crawls, creeps with hissings, leaving behind the moiré trail of her drool . . .* "All these years from her academy studies, and Maurice Lefevre's moldering criticism of Yvette Guilbert remains fresh in her memory. Quotations she can remember, numbers not so.

The Whitney. That man. The radio. She leaves the drawer open, moves to the desk, and snaps the knob. Chopin.

Back at the files she slows, slips her fingers into thin, white cotton gloves, and pulls the archival folder from its drawer. She carries the print with both hands, chest-high, and crosses to the shop. With one hand, she holds Ms. Guilbert as on a serving tray and lingers over one of the watercolors near the door. She fumbles the latch. Inside, she lowers the folder onto the table and turns to the less glamorous work of the art business—the packaging, and call FedEx for an afternoon pick up. Then it's off to Seattle.

Seattle. Irvin's known there—full gray hair and the build of an aged athlete. The municipal parks, green and alive, the mist off the ocean, low clouds playful over and around concrete, glass, and steel, wet sidewalks, ferry horns, and the market. Opulent galleries, young international faces, and a city bursting with wealth. Irvin would have been there twenty years now. He had known a woman—someone he could move in with until he got back on his feet and maybe open a small gallery. He said it had taken a year of hot showers to get New York out of his hair. She still sends him birthday cards.

She never wanted to rinse herself of the city. She went back as often as she could, primarily for the art. Catching up with the street—murals, graffiti on the trains, pop-up shows in deserted first-floor offices, bank lobbies, and Brooklyn apartments. In one of those third-floor walk-ups, there in the shadow of Pratt, she had been witness to small works in an intimate space cleared of furniture, rugs, and last night's take-out—small, clean and prodigious pieces, some pierced, some folded, graphite on vellum and Arches paper. She had asked the artist, a young woman from Tempe, if she could show her work at her Pennsylvania gallery. No surprise that a few years later the artist rose in the international scene. On return trips to the city, she never went to the museums—and surely not the Whitney. No, she confined her visits to the smaller, emerging galleries—the galleries that wouldn't know her.

3

Square One, 2017

FedEx has come and gone. She stands at the window. On the radio, Brahms. The man in the black coat remains in her head, and she wants to call Irvin. To get his take on it again, his reassurance. She finds respite in his resolute denial. That, and to hear him tell about his morning, the day's news, his coffee. He always goes on about the coffee—one addiction replaced by another—the beans locally roasted and single-cup brewed. Mid-mornings, his is a chocolate croissant from across the way at La Boulangerie. Then his noon stroll through Pioneer Square and up into town, a salad at the lunch counter, and his playful chat with the mayor and the rest of the regulars. They've made good lives for themselves—he in Seattle and she here—smaller lives. His gallery is doing well. Now settled, he's lived with a smart, adventurous, and beautiful woman younger than him for the last twenty years. He seems happy, blissfully unaware—and that's why she won't call, won't bother him about the visitor, about her suspicions. Anyway, she is probably being paranoid.

Back at her desk, she turns down the music and smiles at the incandescent sounds of schoolchildren on the sidewalk below. Another field trip to the goldsmith's shop.

That last day at the Whitney, the director's explanation had been long. He'd gone on about his delicate situation, the intricacies of the moment, and a landing so soft she wasn't sure what to do. Was he asking her to resign? Should she stay, or should she go?

"You must go now, Miriam."

When she'd returned to her office, she found folded boxes and a roll of packing tape on the floor, and Jacquie from security in the corner. How thoughtful. Jacquie had watched while she packed—and so quickly it all went—her years into boxes. She followed Jacquie to the elevator. Jacquie pushed the cart. Total awkward, total silence—neither had known what to say. Jacquie's hands locked onto the cart handle as they descended, her eyes locked front. The elevator's indifferent lights exposed the naked, the cast out.

The director's assistant had arranged for a van at the curb to take her books and things over to her apartment. The driver—unshaved, unkempt—had told her stories. She hadn't heard most of it—something about his life on a kibbutz.

Her things in boxes. Things on which to refresh tired eyes from spreadsheets, budget constraints, last-minute cancellations, scheduling. Things with histories. American artifacts from a thousand years ago—and some from yesterday. The ancient Miwok baskets, a 1978 World Series ball signed by *The Yankees,* including Reggie Jackson from the back-to-back series years of '77 and '78, and the Barbie prototypes collection. Her small, silver-framed Polaroid of Shirley Chisolm and her—and who had she been back then that she was not now? Dreams. Aspirations she'd had back then—and this day, there were none. It was four in the afternoon by the time the driver stacked the last box in her living room. She tipped him, and he left.

In forty years, she had never felt the failure and abandonment of that day. Leaving the lights off, she'd poured a tall glass of Bailey's Irish Cream and, wrapped in her coat, curled in the chair at the window. It had been a dark fall day—and darker in her apartment. Outside, the lights were coming on. The usual traffic, the usual people passing on sidewalks and busy with their lives—so busy with their lives. She took the empty glass to the kitchen sink. In the bedroom, she slipped out of her shoes and, still in her coat, crawled into bed. She slept twelve hours.

Miriam had awakened with a headache, rolled over, swung her feet to the floor, and realized she was fully dressed. She felt gross. She was starving. Shower first, or eat something? She stood cautiously, gained her balance, and followed the path to the kitchen—water on for tea, bread into the toaster, a trail of clothes to the shower. Standing in the tub, she twisted the shower knob progressively up to near-scalding. Yesterday's caustic veneer melted in the drain.

Barefoot and raw, she sat in her robe at the table, the benevolent cool of the floor easing its way up through the fire. She stared into her cup. There was a saucer next to it and a slice of toast with Mom's strawberry jam.

She called her mom.

4

The Large Man in the Black Coat, 2017

The large man was back in his hotel room. He'd had lunch at the microbrewery across the street, and he needed a nap. With some difficulty he removed his coat—he oughta drop a few pounds—slid the mirrored door aside, and hung the coat on a squeaking hanger. On the shelf above was an extra blanket and an iron, and it reminded him of the times they'd travelled with the kids—requesting two queens and a cot. Limping farther into the room, he saw the message light on the phone. He checked his cell. Gail.

Their grandkids were visiting this week, and Gail would be loving it. With him gone, she could fully release her inner child, and the other side of that thought was sad. He knew he was holding her back—that he'd become a frump. Retired from the force and feeling disconnected from the action—from the life—he wasn't very interesting. He was mostly tired, and Gail wanted to travel—Barcelona, Lisbon, Rome. This was their chance, she'd said. Get out, see the world, have a little fun. His preference was to sit in the chair in his corner and read.

He crossed the room to the windows and moved a sheer curtain aside. Out there were nineteenth- and twentieth-century Pennsylvania rooftops buttressed for the dark winter's approach. Silent steel tracks wound through the rusted scraps of the city's once-burgeoning industries, and, beyond, the sage backdrop of the Appalachians communed with the Methuselah of rivers. Not that he'd do it justice, but he should have brought a sketchbook. He pulled his phone from his pocket and called his wife.

"Hi, Babe!" The phone nearly jumped from his hand. Kids screamed and laughed, and a voluminous Wurlitzer pumped out The Beatles, *Ob-La-Di.*

"Gail, what—"

"We're at Central Park! The carousel. Can I call you back? Whoa! Hold on honey. This thing's fast!"

"Gail, I—"

"Are you okay?"

"Yeah, I—"

"Love you!"

His fingers searched behind him for the bed, and he sat. They'd done plenty together back in the day—the concerts, the bars, season tickets to *The Jets.* That trip to San Francisco, and Gail leaning out over the front of the cable car at the top of the hill and yelling, "Let er rip!" Yeah, they'd had some fun. They all did—the cops from the precinct and their others. Years had slipped by, he'd made detective, some of the men and women he worked with got transferred, shot, died in their sleep, or were simply worn down from the hell of it all.

She must not eat at the brewery, he thought. The small, attractive woman with the chestnut eyes—Miriam. Looks like she pays attention to diet. He'd have to open up to her eventually.

5

Her Brother's Keeper, 2017

T*he man in the black coat* . . . She stood at her desk holding her phone, and did she want to get into it again? Was she her brother's keeper? She ran fingers up the back of her neck, into her hair, and across the scar. If she called Nick, what would she say? "Hi, Nick, remember me? Your sister? There's a large man in a black coat, and he seems suspicious of my time at the Whitney, and he says he's going fishing at Powys—near your place? I thought you should know?"

Twenty years ago, and six months from New York, her father died. At her dad's funeral—*their* dad's funeral—Nick had shown up at the cemetery late and loud in a brand-new, red truck and stepped out slim as ever. Slicked hair, cowboy boots, and a new suit showed the hanger crease at the knees. The irony was surely intentional. Their dad could never get him into a Sunday suit. That day, Nick kept his distance, stayed out on the wet grass beyond the edge of the canopied gathering. From the corner of her eye, she'd seen him flinch as the casket was lowered. Was it satisfaction or regret—that flinch?

Following the service and back at the small parking area, church members chatted beneath the maples and hovered around her mom and her—touching them, some awkward, others needy—before turning to their cars and leaving. When the congregation had thinned, she saw Nick coming their way. Unnerved, she hurried her mom into the back of the car. "I'll just be a minute." She closed the door.

He crowded her space, hands in his back pockets. His breath, whiskey dressed in mint, he grinned canine teeth. "Finally."

She took a step back. "You didn't have to come, Nick. No one expected you."

He stared.

"I wish you hadn't."

He glanced at the car, then back.

"I'm taking care of Mom. I've moved back in with her. My old room. Sometimes things work out for the best."

He moved his head to the side and spit.

"What about you, Nick? When did you get that truck? And those boots? You don't make enough selling screws. Is it drugs?"

"I'm set." He smirked. "To the fuckin nines."

"So, what now? No more Dad to blame. What will you—?"

"Too bad about your fancy job, and all. Too, too bad." He blinked what could have been mistaken for a smile and moved away.

That day at the cemetery, Nick was gloating—so full of himself and his new truck. He'd said more to her that day than he'd spoken to her in years—poisoned words.

She wouldn't call him.

When I was growing up in the sixties and seventies, there was such pressure on my parents to appear perfect and as seen in "Family Circle." People dressed for church. Back then, I visited a friend's home occasionally, and they all seemed so happy to be together, she and her four brothers there in that clean house. They'd ask me to stay for dinner. They called supper, "dinner." The mother and father dressed nicely, spoke politely to the children, and they were lovely. Fresh peaches sliced over vanilla ice cream for dessert. Thin ginger cookies on the side. How many families are like that?

6

The Large Man in the Black Coat is Back, 2017

She stood at the window and saw him coming up the walk. He was heavy on the stairs. So he was serious about the Bower paintings?

Bing. She crossed the gallery. "I'm glad to see that you've returned, and I apologize for not knowing your name." She extended her hand. "I'm Miriam."

The man nodded, and they shook. "Brian. Brian Beaufalont."

"Well, that's better. And where will you hang your painting, Mr. Beaufalont? Please, not over the sofa."

He laughed. "I have a reading room on the third floor of our home—high ceilings, white walls, and filtered light. I hang the work I love there—watercolors and pencil studies. Mostly twentieth century."

"A discerning collector. May I suppose you have a blue-chip artist or two?"

He blushed. “I do—exactly two. A small Homer etching and a Hopper pencil study. Big-time collector, right?”

“That’s impressive. Why that era and media?”

“They’re not as complicated . . . as life’s darker subjects.” He unbuttoned his coat.

A satin lining similar to Dad’s on those bright Sunday mornings, and we were off to the church, and the snow, and the ice on the narrow country road, and . . . “Indeed. And a reader. What do you read?”

“I never guessed in my retirement I’d get hooked on histories—art histories. I don’t think anyone would’ve guessed.”

“Because?”

“Well, I was a cop. Detective. NYPD.” He didn’t blink.

She folded her arms and held her elbows. “Yes, who would have guessed?”

“Anyway . . . ” He walked over to a painting. “I think this is the one.”

NYPD, the Whitney, Trout Run.

“Good choice?” he asked across the room.

She took a breath, slid her palms on her hips, and joined him. “We can ship.”

“This is the best price?”

“I’ll pay for the shipping.”

“Done.” They shook. He stuck his hands into his coat pockets and stared at the painting. “Miriam, you’re a nice lady. I like you.

But there's another piece of business between us." He focused down on her, and his words were from a Steelcase file cabinet with names, dates, and they were ordered. "We have to talk about the Whitney."

A bolt up her back! *Now what?* A tremble ran her legs, and she had to remain poised.

"The statute of limitations petered out a long time ago," he said. "Back in the day, Detective Nettles didn't suspect you of direct involvement, and I'm not sure why. Not a great note taker, that woman. Then the court gave you a pass, and everyone moved on to other issues. The insurance company brought in an expert—Scotland Yard—to investigate. You talked to him."

She took a few steps away, then turned. "This is bizarre. Old news, Mr. Beaufalont." Arms crossed, her jaw tight.

"Yeah, but he also passed on you. Went high—went after big-time art thieves, crooked dealers—and came up empty."

"And you're bringing this up because?" Adrenalin-weak, choked.

"The insurance company paid Ms. Brigitte Bardot six million dollars for her loss, but the company's new leadership wants the Warhol back. They've hired me to find it. No offense—I'm going low. I think you know where it is."

She pulled a stuttered breath, leveled her shoulders, and regained herself. "Mr. Beaufalont, or I should say, 'Detective.' All these years. Look at me. I'm sixty and barely paying the rent."

"You gave your code to your brother. What I don't know is why?"

"Because he asked!" She spun and whipped back to her desk. She braced behind her chair and faced him.

"What?"

"I didn't give my code to anyone! What's the matter with you people? Is nearly everyone in law enforcement inept? And I thought you were retired."

He pulled a hand from his pocket, formed a fist, and raised a thumb. "First, I checked into who did this sort of thing—robbed museums. Were they still on the street?" Now an index finger. "Then I riffled through the city's files of skinny white guys who worked the burglar scene in that part of town. Ronald 'Cash' Hazzard made the top ten. He lived alone in the Bronx and tended bar. Guess where. The Whitney staff's old hangout, the Ramona, of all places" He added a middle finger. "So we go down that path—make a big assume it was Cash and another small man or woman."

"Or woman!" she snapped.

Bing. She closed her eyes for a moment, then looked to the door. It was the building owner.

"Hey, Miriam. Letting you know we'll be shutting the water off for about thirty minutes. All good?"

"Yes, all good. Thank you."

He waved. *Bing.*

The detective approached her desk. "Anyway, a little further digging and we ID'd your brother, Nick, at the Ramona about a week before Cash quit. The current manager—nice lady, tall, good-looking woman—remembers locking Nick in the Ramona's office on Cash's instructions. Said Nick was pretty out of it at the time.

Then a few weeks after the heist, the boys go out and buy brand-new expensive vehicles. Nick closed The Screw Shop nine years ago—his only source of income—and I don't know what took him so long. It still sits there, abandoned and falling in on itself every time it rains. How's he continue to eat, Miriam?

"Why are you asking me? Ask him—or Cash."

He folded his arms across his chest nearly doubling his girth. "I don't know exactly where Nick lives, and you're the smart one in the family. Nick's—and, excuse me here—the nimrod with a list of bad choices and misdemeanors as long as my arm. And less than a year after the theft, Cash drives his brand-new Corvette into the side of a cement bridge, and that's that—for the car and him. But you know all this."

"I didn't know about Cash."

"That leaves you and Nick. Your code and Nick."

"And the engineers and electricians?"

"Journeymen—and not their thing." Hands back in his pockets, and his attention taken by the Bower paintings, "They really are special, aren't they."

His eyes back on Miriam. "My guess is Nick knows as much about art as you do about carburetors. But you—you were wired directly to the world's finest museums, biggest galleries, international collectors. It's a huge market of obscene wealth and never enough. Maybe you were presented with a chance to have a small piece for yourself. Must have been exciting. If I'm wrong, let me talk to Nick."

She sat at the desk and ruffled her hair. "It sounds like you're making a movie—Brad Pitt and a car chase. I'm sorry, detective, but in this gallery, in my small life, this is a bit much."

He went over to a window, his back to her. "The insurance company made it financially worthwhile, and we all hope it's a short-term thing. I thought maybe it would revive the spark—that it would get me off my butt, and Gail would like that."

"Your wife."

He nodded. "Fifty-one years, grandkids, and I put a new hole in my belt each year. Look at that—three cars backed up at the light." He turned to her. "Where's Nick live?"

Her back stiffened. A series of loud *clunks* from somewhere deep in the building, and they stared at each other until the noise stopped. "I don't know where he lives."

"He's your brother."

"Estranged brother."

"And you've never been to his place?"

"Years ago. Mom told me how to get there. It's in the boondocks. I could never find it again."

"Somewhere near Trout Run," he said.

"Somewhere."

7

His Hairball Idea, 2017

Retired New York police detective Brian Beaufalont crossed the hotel parking lot on a wet, predawn Friday. Mercury-vapor lights muffled in the haze. His gait was crooked, his rubber shoe covers tight, the toes of his left foot numb. This sciatica thing had started on the drive over from the city. He unlocked the rental car, took off his overcoat, folded it twice, and squeezed it between the door post and the headrest and onto the back seat. He should have rented a four-door—a midsize four-door. Wedged behind the wheel—The car was the size of a toaster!—he wiped the mist from his eyes. Another few blocks toward the river, then onto the beltway.

It was his hairball idea to simply knock on the door and ask about the Warhol—that is, if he could get someone to tell him exactly where Nick lived. He was betting on the element of shock. A knock on the door, and, after twenty years of wondering if someone was on his tail, the guy might be relieved. Statute of limitations—tell me where you unloaded the art, and no one's the wiser. No hurt, no foul, and you're free to go. Here's ten grand for your trouble. The cash was in his coat.

The defroster was at capacity and useless. He lowered his window enough to see the fog crawl up from the river, cross the beltway, and descend into the city like it was hungry. Glancing up at the last second, he saw the lit, overhead sign pointing north.

The Whitney had done everything right by immediately contacting the police. And the police had done a credible job of locking down the gallery and interviewing everyone who had been anywhere near the print in the previous forty-eight hours. In twenty years since the theft, there had been no word of the missing print from the FBI or Interpol, and he had ten grand saying Nick knew where it was.

He signaled to the big rig that had been on his butt and blinding him for the last five empty miles and took the exit to Trout Run. The semi did too. Approaching the intersection, he backed off the gas and thought he had moved his left foot to the brake—a habit Gail always cautioned about—but his foot was numbly unresponsive. Searing pain shot from the back of his leg, up through his ass and into the middle of his lower back. He should have removed his wallet. His back wrenched, vision doubled, a clapped-out pickup drifted broadside into his lights, and—*Pow!*

The sun had risen behind low clouds, and the padded mist cast everything in a thick, flat, morphine shade of slow. An EMT wheeled the detective's gurney past the semi's carbonated fizz of colored lights and the walrus climbing back into the cab, past the llama in the Smokey Bear hat, a few waking locals in bathrobes—

and a skinny, Mad-Max character with whiskey breath who leaned into his face and advised, "Go back to fuckin New York, dipshit!"

Retired New York police detective Brian Beaufalont thought he might be paralyzed and on his way to going blind. He couldn't move his head. Rainbow halos pulsed from two streetlamps beyond which everything was up for grabs. He'd read that when one of the senses fails, others become more acute—and right now he was smelling burned rubber, diesel exhaust, and, strangely enough, sweet patchouli oil.

There was a metallic snap behind his eyes, and he was levitating, then slid like a mound of dough into the crisply lit stainless bay of an ambulance. Pressure in his ears as doors *moofed* shut, and a few seconds later he was being rocked side to side. A young paramedic tore open paper envelopes and tugged at his sleeve. She had lovely, luminous skin and a great haircut. Rubbing alcohol, she gripped his wrist—and a poke. She had the profile of a Pre-Raphaelite ingénue, and he wondered was she happy? He wanted to tell the young woman how much he liked her hair, but his tongue was heavy, and he was so sleepy. Gail would love that hair.

8

Global Warming, The Moron and The Yankees, 2017

Frost on the sidewalk this morning, and the stairway to the gallery hadn't grown any shorter. Part of her daily workout, Miriam jogged up the steep flight and caught her breath on the landing. The bell *binged* as she entered. She punched in her birthday code and dropped the morning paper onto the desk. Back from hanging up her coat, she flipped the radio on—Mozart, *Andante 21 in C*, third movement, *Elvira Madigan*. She opened her laptop and settled in. The music slowed her breathing—the flat files, her desk.

It would be closer to noon when the first visitors would make their way up the stairs—curious college students, artists, couples on their way to a Saturday lunch at the microbrewery, and folks from surrounding boroughs searching out the unique crevices of the old downtown and thrilled to find the goldsmith, the bookstore, her gallery.

The front page of *The Gazette* stared up at her—The Tubbs fire was raging in Santa Rosa, California with dry conditions and devastating winds attributed to global warming. Those poor people. Here, it was pounding rains, flash floods, and climate denial.

Secretary of State Rex Tillerson said he has no plans to resign and will not do so, denying reports that Vice President Mike Pence had to urge him to stay in the job, and sidestepping questions about whether he called President Donald Trump a moron.

Moving right along to *Sports—The Yankees* had a terrible time with *The Indians*, managing three hits and losing zero to four in the Division Series opener. *Geez, guys!*

She flipped to the *City and Local* section and a large photo of yesterday's early-morning crash in Trout Run—a small car resting on its trunk up the side of a utility pole and a smashed red pickup truck diagonal across the intersection. Police cars, an ambulance, and a trailer truck bracket the frame. *That looks like Nick's truck!* The one he'd showed up in at their dad's funeral.

9

The Prince Awakes, October 2017

Retired New York police detective Brian Beaufalont traversed the last bridge of his dream and stepped down into the near dark. Floating above him and to each side, as far as peripheral vision would allow, he caught flits of multi-colored reflections that chirped and hummed, and maybe he was still dreaming, and he probably was. Compressed limbs—and as much as he wanted them to move, they wouldn't. Toes. At the far ends of weighted legs, he thought he successfully wiggled his toes.

Muted conversation from the distance. A background of comings and goings, and, in the foreground, a door clicked open, light fanned across a hospital room, and a tall slender man appeared at his shoulder.

"The prince awakes." The young man reached across him and did something to a monitor. "I'm Jeremy, and I am your loyal attendant for the next nine hours, m' lord."

Moving only his eyes, Brian did a slow assessment of the situation. "Where am I? What happened?" His cheeks and nose were numb.

From across the room, Jeremy returned and checked a drip tube hanging next to the bed. "You're on the third floor in intensive care, but we'll be moving you to the royal suite in another hour or so."

"Brooklyn?"

"Say *what*?"

"I'm in the hospital? In Brooklyn?"

"*Hell* no m' lord. You're but miles from where you plowed your beanbag-of-a-car into a truck, cracked your head, broke a couple ribs, pierced a lung, and separated a clavicle. Might have meant huge consequences for an older, less fit individual. But royal blood and those daily visits to the gym paid off. That or dumb luck."

He wished Jeremy hadn't mentioned his clavicle, and suddenly it hurt like hell. "Sorry, I don't—"

"I'm sure you don't," Jeremy smiled. "It'll all come back a little at a time. Right now, we gotta get the easy stuff back in order. Get you mended so you can go steppin with that fine damsel drove four hours to get here and's been waiting for you to wake up."

"Gail?"

"See? You remember."

"She's here?"

"I'll send her in." At the door, Jeremey turned and bowed at the waist.

10

She Takes the Plunge, 2017

Phone to her ear, Miriam stood at a gallery window and watched the heavy sky descend. She hadn't called Nick in years and didn't know if this was still his number. The call dropped. She tried the two hospitals. He hadn't been admitted. She called the paper and asked for the photographer credited with the photo and left a message. How, in the twenty-first century, could she feel so out of touch? It was Saturday and as busy a day as the gallery would see. She grabbed her coat and locked the door behind her.

11

This is a Quiz? 2017

He didn't know which was worse, lying down or partially sitting up like this. His left arm was immobilized, he could barely breathe, and everything hurt. At least the new room got magnificent afternoon light, and he had a great view of the hillside's fall colors. Now if he could keep this oozing pasta salad on the fork long enough to reach his mouth.

Gail dabbed at his lip with a napkin.

There was a tap on the door frame and a young, fit guy in one of those new *Cuckoo's Nest* haircuts entered. "Detective Beaufalont. Good to see that you're up. I hear you've been through a lot."

Nearly to his mouth, the pasta slipped off the fork and landed on the sheet. "Fuck," he whispered.

Gail sank back in her chair, the napkin in her lap.

The kid was tan in October and dressed like a fashion shoot. He projected impossibly good vibes. "Travis McGowan." He approached the bed and offered his hand.

Brian shifted his eyes to Gail, then to the oily fork in his grip. He lowered the fork to the tray.

"Garden State?" Travis said.

"This is a quiz?"

"Garden State Insurance, and we heard about the accident? I'm here to see that everything's okay and check in on the status and all?"

"Status." Brian shifted his eyes to Gail. She gave a small shrug.

"The Warhol?" Travis said.

Gail rose and stood across the bed from Travis. "Mr. McGowan, thank you for your visit. We're still recovering from quite a shock. Perhaps you could check back in a day or two?"

Travis first seemed disappointed, then embarrassed. He thrust his hands into his pockets. "Oh sure, of course. How about tomorrow then?"

"Let's try that."

Brian's eyes ping-ponged between them, and each time he moved his head ever slightly his collarbone yelled.

"Great!" Travis rebounded. "See you tomorrow. Glad you're doing okay, sir." He spun and left.

"Who the hell was that?"

"Eat your pasta, Babe."

12

Miriam Reaches Out, 2017

Miriam drove slowly, hunched over the wheel on the narrow, forgotten, forest road, and watched for the turnoff. Could she ever find Nick's place again?

She drifted past a black mobile home set back from the road—*That's not the one.*—with all the shades pulled, in front of which was a large sheet of plywood spray-painted with, "We don't call 911." The people out here sure liked their privacy. Probably had guns for personal protection, not trusting the government, the police, or each other.

She'd only been out here once to drop off a box that Mom had left to Nick, and he hadn't let her in. That day was brittle and overcast, the trees bare, and she stood on his stoop waiting and knowing he was in there.

"Nick!"

The box was heavy, her fingers raw. He was probably getting a real charge out of this, and it was so juvenile. Tormenting her again. That or he was dead drunk. It was, after all, past noon.

Supporting the box with her raised thigh, she knocked again. "Nick!" She waited. *Alright then.* "There's a box here by the door, Nick. Mom wanted you to have it—her bowling ball."

Now, with the leaves in fall's full bloom and everything grown over, Miriam wouldn't be able to see Nick's trailer from the road.

This caring about Nick didn't make any sense other than he was all she had left of their family.

She passed a row of mailboxes shot full of holes, a federal crime if anyone cared—which they apparently didn't. She bore left on the narrow dirt strip toward the creek and, tentatively, waded in and out of gullies and over roots and rocks for the next five minutes. Jostled about, she was afraid her little car might lose a wheel.

At a slight break in the dripping undergrowth, she edged into two puddles that feigned to be the start of a driveway. Finger-nail branches screeched against the sides of the car. Around a slight bend and into a bit of a clearing, she stopped behind the truck. The same truck that had shown up new, resplendent and loud at their dad's funeral—the truck in which Nick had cried at their mother's funeral. It showed its age—rust-rotted, fogged glass, and a peeling Trump/Pence bumper sticker. The truck in the paper wasn't Nick's.

Out of the car, she slipped past the heap, up three steps, and onto his little deck. *Okay then.* A last breath, she knocked.

There was a creaking inside, padded thumps approached, and the door cracked open.

"I seen you comin. Seen you through the trees way out by the road." He held the door nearly shut. He'd been drinking.

"Hello, Nick. It's a relief to see that you're okay."

"I'm good, awright. Damn good."

"There was an accident in Trout Run. The picture in the paper. It looked like your truck."

"I seen it. I was there. Told the dipshit outta-stater to go back where he came from."

"How thoughtful of you."

"Yeah, I'm thoughtful, awright. Like thinkin about all the money I made off'n you."

"I guess that could take a while. It's damp out here. Mind if I come in for a minute?"

Nick squeezed out and closed the door behind him. "Out here's good."

"You don't want me in your home?"

"Nobody goes in there but me."

"What are you hiding, Nick?"

"Not hidin shit," he scanned the darkening treetops, "and here we are this fine day." He pulled a pack of cigarettes from his shirt pocket and tapped one out.

"I tried calling, but—"

"I seen you did." He lit the smoke.

"I was concerned."

"Why?" He tossed the match.

This is ridiculous. She started down the steps. At the bottom, she turned and threw her hands into action. "Oh, for a number of reasons, now that you ask—we grew up together, you're the only family I have, and I'm a fool."

Smoke up his face, he squinted, and folded his arms. "I used you good."

"Abused, Nick. The word is 'abused,' and all of your tricks and little jokes were certifiably cruel. It was difficult being around you, and you made Dad's life hell."

He grunted. "I got you better'n you even know."

"I think I do know, Nick. How much money *did* you have? I hope it was worth ruining two careers." She headed off to her car, stopped, and spun back. "By the way, there's a big guy in a black coat here from New York looking for you."

"You say."

"Yes, Nick, I say." Fists at her sides, she stomped back up the drive, stumbled, and regained herself. "I say he's looking for you, and he's smart, and he's serious, and he's a cop."

"Bullshit."

She climbed the steps. "You know what's bullshit? Do you, Nick? That I'm here. That I cared. That for years I've suspected you were involved in the theft, and I refused to believe it. That I'm sixty and alone, and I live hand to mouth, and eat cold leftovers at my desk, and I was a curator at the goddamn Whitney, Nick!" She shoved him, and he hardly moved. She shoved him again. "Move!"

He dropped the smoke to the deck and stepped on it. "Fuck'r you talkin about?"

"When I shove you! Move!"

He laughed once, shrugged, and went inside.

She heard the lock. She stared at the faded door, the dull louvered window. All her weight in her shoes, and her heart raced. Behind her the sound of the creek bubbling small around rocks and fallen limbs. She was weak, sweating. A cold wind at her neck, the rain moving in.

Her knuckles hurt—fists screwed down like vises. Willing them to ease, her fingers uncurled, and blood flowed to her extremities. She bowed her head. *Why?* Why had she . . . ? She stood rejected at the door of this single-wide *Deliverance,* and she'd done this to herself.

13

What She Should Have Said, 2017

She didn't reopen the gallery that Saturday. On the drive home through the buffeting, deranged frenzy of the storm, she hardly noticed the road. All the things she wished she'd said gathered in the furry between her eyes, and why hadn't she demanded flat out, "Why?" How could he? And where is the goddamn Warhol?

Back in her apartment, she'd made tea, stared into the cup, then dumped it in the sink. She hugged her mom's doll and stood at the window. The double-paned glass muted the drubbing of basketballs on the cracked-and-puddled playground across the street two stories below. It was truant teens and chronically unemployed adults who were apparently oblivious to the rain and claimed the place twenty-four seven.

The thumping on the courts took her back to Nick in his bedroom, pounding his fists on the wall. He'd kept the family awake deep into the night that first time he was sent home from school.

Her mother had encouraged her to help the boy with his homework—ever-organized perfectionist that she was—and she'd tried. At the beginning of each year, and starting with a fresh slate, he would accept her help. But a month in, his attention would fail and give way to unimaginative classroom disruption, fighting, and worse.

She'd had to save herself.

14

If He Met Brigitte Bardot . . . 2017

Retired New York police detective Brian Beaufalont's shoulder and ribs were killing him, and where was the nurse? If he sneezed again, he'd ask to be euthanized. Otherwise, his memory was starting to take shape. He was in this Pennsylvania town to get the Warhol print back from the redneck who stole it and return it to the insurance company that was paying for this whole debacle.

He still didn't know how the young Travis fit into the big picture, but he was amused by the boy's verve, and if he had one more daughter he might have introduced them.

That the insurance company sent Travis to check on "the status" of the investigation telegraphed the faith anyone had in ever seeing the print again. Come to think of it, what did that say about him? Central Gallery Prague and Brigitte Bardot, especially, deserved better.

His thoughts leaped to retrieving the print and personally presenting it to Ms. Bardot. If there was time, he'd definitely drop twenty pounds first. He'd need new slacks, a sport coat, and a light-blue button-down shirt. Probably new shoes. He wouldn't go as far as young Travis with his haircut, but it would be professional and contemporary.

The ceremony would be in Paris and the Eiffel Tower in the background, and there would be photographers and an accordion, and champagne. Probably a tripod and a French documentary filmmaker—a big burley guy in a nubby sweater and corduroys. It would be shot in black and white. Ms. Bardot would smell of lavender bathwater, and her hair in a French braid with wisps floating come-hither free in the French breeze. She would embrace him, kiss him on both cheeks, then deeply on the lips. He would hug her—at first, politely, and her breasts pressing into his new jacket and button-down shirt, and . . . Of course, Gail would be there.

"Detective Beaufalont." The kid appeared at his door.

"Travis."

Travis crossed and settled into the chair at the window.

"You've done something else to your hair," the detective said.

"Supercuts."

"Super."

Travis bent forward, elbows on knees. "Can we talk more about the Warhol?"

"Shoot."

"Huh?"

"Go for it."

"Oh." Travis took the lead. "What good news can I relay to the office? That you're getting close? Made a contact and you know where the print is? Can we send someone to pick it up while you're in here? Should we—"

"Travis, you make a lousy investigator. When I get out of here, I'll continue my pursuit. You can tell them I have a plan, and I'm following it."

"They want to know about the ten thousand dollars you withdrew from the account."

The retired police detective stared at Travis for a long few seconds, then moved his gaze to the window and the autumn hillside. His coat in the back seat.

Fuck.

I move and breathe between narrow brackets here—between mountains and the river, between the comfortable and those who struggle. The gallery is a brisk fifteen-minute walk from my apartment in the summer. The worst days of winter's ice and snow stretch that to twenty or twenty-five. Living downtown, I have easy access to the impressive arts center for performances, the library for books and talks, two colleges for their cultural and sporting events (The small four-year school has a decent baseball team.), and there is a limited variety of ethnic restaurants and delis. During those fifteen-to-twenty-five-minute walks, I get glimpses of the larger life in and surrounding this city. There are times of the year that pickup trucks pass through with recently shot white-tailed deer draped over their fenders or hanging from their open tailgates. Schools are closed the first days of deer season. Other times of the year it's fallen bears on display. There are rifles on racks in rear truck windows and bumper stickers frequently announce the confrontational-to-combative predispositions of the drivers. There appears to be an innate distrust among much of the citizenry for "flatlander elitists"—anyone who doesn't work with their hands.

15

Breakfast, February, 2018

Dippy eggs, crisp bacon, and a double order of white toast, Nick sat in the general-store-and-breakfast place. It was a sizzling, loud, and familiar place on the way to other places, and Baxter, the plumber, was at the far end of the counter having the usual. They all had the usual—the trades guys on their way to their first call—HVAC, electrical, new construction or digging a woman's ring out of her sink. "I had to ask her to please stand back, and let me do this. Her perfume!"

Their trucks and vans were parked on the frozen, rutted gravel out back. Kathy kept their mugs filled between flipping home fries, bacon, and eggs on the grill. Another regular, an eccentric retired professor, would be showing up any minute now. Professor Bill's daily order was a three-cheese scramble, whole wheat toast, and—still mirror-eyed from the night before—a Bloody Mary.

Kathy had just cracked eggs into a stainless bowl as a large man in a black overcoat entered. No one paid attention to the man, as was their way, but they all paid attention. The place slowed to quiet. Kathy clicked a fork through the professor's eggs, and, head down, her eyes strolled past the big guy. Everyone knew she had no liquor license, and, from where Nick sat, he could see the vodka bottle between a couple loaves of bread beneath the counter.

This big guy looked state—Liquor Control Board.

The back door slammed, and they heard the professor stomp off his boots. Little guy, he had the spread-legged walk and energy of a spider. "Gentlemen, Kathy, wei hångt es? And I see you've saved my seat, thank you." He straddled a stool and beamed his scatter-toothed grin around the room. "Gentlemen, here we are again, and a new day ahead of us. Ah, that we could dally, and who knows what interesting tales we might hear. Dragons, kings, Vikings, near-death struggles and—"

"Your order will be right up, Bill. I'm afraid we're out of tomato juice, though." Kathy exaggerated her eyes and tilted her head toward the big guy.

"A bloody outrage!" The professor slapped the counter and rose an inch. "How can one begin his day without tomato juice?"

Kathy dropped his slices into the toaster, then confronted the big guy. "What can I get you?" She splashed coffee into his cup.

"Oatmeal."

"You got it." She went back to the grill, tended to Bill's omelet, glopped oatmeal into a bowl, and set it in front of the man. "Not from around here—that accent."

"Nope. Looking for a guy to give a big insurance check to. Guy named Nick. Then, I'll do a little fishing and head back to Brooklyn."

No one at the counter blinked. Nick slowly plowed home fries around his plate with his thumbnail.

"Must be talkin ice fishing," she said. "And Bill, I think I found some more tomato juice."

Huh, Nick thought. Sounds like Miriam's fuckin cop. What took him so long?

~ ~ ~

Retired New York police detective Brian Beaufalont had driven around the block and seen all the trucks and service vans—Harer Electric, Baxter Plumbing, McDermott Roofing & Gutters—parked behind the only breakfast place in the area. The drivers probably knew how to back out of those deep ruts, though, by the shape of some of the trucks, a few attempts may have gone sideways. In a rented midsized four-door sedan, he parked out front. He stepped from the car to the smell of maple-sugar bacon on frosted air, and his stomach did flips.

It was warm inside and eggs-and-coffee humid. He scanned as he moved into the space. Corners clear. About a dozen guys at the counter, truckers hats, no one talking, lady behind the counter in the open kitchen moving efficiently—and it was probably her place. Big flat-screen, Fox News cranking away, and no one seemed to notice when he entered. He took an open stool at the counter. Not a peep, but he knew they were all aware of this big-city stranger in the black overcoat and no hat. He picked up a laminated menu, and—damn—it looked good.

Are you kidding? Trout?

There was something going on a few stools down with the little old guy who had just come in—something about Vikings and tomato juice—and here she came.

"What'll you have?"

"Well, it all looks good." He lowered the menu. "But hearing my wife and the doc in the back of my head, I'll go for the oatmeal, nuts, and raisins, please."

"You bet." And she was gone. It was like she had eight arms the way she ran that counter and kitchen. Not a shy bone in her, she asked where he was from and what the hell was he doing here.

He said he was from an insurance company with a check for someone around here named Nick Pastor, but he didn't know exactly where he lived.

She showed no reaction. "Good luck with that. More coffee?"

Backbones stiffened around him as everyone stared into their plates.

Someone at this counter was feeling wary as a Pennsylvania Ruffed Grouse and sitting stone still.

Irvin and I started at the Whitney Museum of American Art as curatorial assistants in 1984. Meeting him for the first time, I was diminished. He fills a room. I first thought of his bearing as self-confident. Weeks later, arrogant. Now I know it as the kid who was bullied. We have similar academic backgrounds having coursed through Stanford, he as an undergrad and grad student and I in pursuit of my PhD. We have significantly different lives otherwise. My early impression was that, having been offered the Whitney position, he had "arrived," and this was "it" as far as he was concerned. Knowing him as I do, I'm sure he accepted the Whitney position and kissed his PhD goodbye in the same breath. Not so for me. Between my appointment and working on my doctorate, I saw this as the next rung on the ladder to director.

16

The Beginning of the End, 1997

Stomps up the stairs from the galleries, around the corner, and Miriam's door flew open. "Do you believe it? The friggin gestapo?" Irv's bleached hair, always groomed and pressed like the rest of him, was rattled.

She got off the phone and pointed.

"What?"

She pointed.

"*That's* what I should care about?" Middle and ring fingers of his right hand in splints, he pulled up his fly.

She couldn't help herself—it was funny.

When he first showed up in a cast months ago, all he said was, "Racquetball."

She suspected Irvin had another life, nocturnal, possibly straining innocence, but in thirteen years she never pried, and he never offered.

He was pacing. "They're insinuating I had something do with the print walking out of here. I'm not answering another question until my goddamn lawyer gets back from whatever beach he's on. They're checking phone records. They've been to my place. They want to know about my hand."

"And you told them what?"

"I was changing a flat."

She raised her eyebrows.

"What?! And they want to know about you and me." Tall, athletic build, and beyond handsome, he ran his good hand through the blond tangle. He was doing half laps of her office, and now he picked up the cup on her desk and took a sip. "What *is* this? It's awful!"

"It's good for your complexion. Irvin, please." She rose, came from behind her desk, and placed her hand on his arm. "I am sorry. Sit. Let's talk."

He dropped into a chair. "All I said was I hope whoever took it knows how delicate it is. Cotton gloves, that they wrapped it properly—and I had nothing to do with it." He raked his hair. "They're coming for us like the goddamn cavalry. Minds made up, put a ribbon on it, and a neat little parcel. Perps caught and chain em to a wall until they break." He checked both armpits. "Look at this. Look at me." He sniffed. "I stink!"

"Perps," she said.

"The cops don't give a shit about the Warhol—they're just paid to tighten the screws. It's the board that wants it back. Prague and Brigitte Bardot have them by the balls, and whatever you thought the print was worth a week ago, it's just doubled. And who wants to be the next putz to loan something to the Whitney?"

She stood and considered the print on her wall—a crisp Weegee photograph of a former black-and-white New York. Arthur Fellig, aka Weegee, probably used that word, "perps."

Turning to the window—cabs, tourists, buses, squad cars, and an ambulance four floors below. Everyone late for something. Two people on a bench—an elderly couple—beneath a gray sky and, it appeared, not in a hurry late in life. Behind her, Irv was still going off—something about plastic spoons and Rikers Island. Tens of thousands of pieces are stolen each year, she thinks. Billions in black market dollars. Most of the works never seen again, thieves never caught. Part of the game, isn't it? Part of what makes it all so precious? That it would be stolen?

"You and I?" she asked.

"What?"

"You said they want to know about *us*."

"Yes, the two stunning specimens we are. And I'll bet the detective—you've met her? The terrier in tweed? She's thinking movie rights. Like maybe I'm the Raymond Fernandez in all this, and you're Martha Beck."

"Serial killers? Irv, please. Shall we get some air, take a walk? Let's go over to the Ramona for a drink."

He launched to his feet. "We can't be seen together, and I shouldn't have come in here. Exactly what they want. You're only my boss, right? We're not *seeing* each other. If they ask—when they ask—we're not."

"We're not."

"Right."

"But Irv, we're not."

"Right." He was at her door. "And you really have to dump whatever's in that cup." He left.

She went back to her window reverie—the bench empty, the elderly couple gone. *Were* they a couple? Married fifty years? Or brother and sister and wondering what to do about Mother?

Had the police been to her apartment? They'd have to get a key from Mrs. Greene, and Mrs. Greene wouldn't go down easy. She would ask her tonight. She moved the few papers from her desk to the file drawer and locked it. And why had she done that? She'd never locked it in the past, and there was surely nothing of judicial interest. She unlocked the drawer. She sent open folders back to the ether and shut down the Mac.

What to do? How to feel? A couple days ago it was shock. How? Who? This was a bad dream. It had been an unplugged Saturday morning at home when she got the call from the assistant director. The way he put it was, "Miriam, we need all staff in here immediately. I've left a message for the director, and where the hell is he? Call Irvin and get his ass in here now! Shit has happened."

She'd scrolled for Irvin's number. As it dialed, she imagined large men in Halloween costumes—a bear and a zebra—racing their van across the George Washington Bridge in a 4 a.m. reverse commute. New York plates. The Warhol wrapped in a moving blanket. Had they pulled off in Paterson? Were they in Ohio by now? A zebra? Get a grip, Miriam.

The heavily framed print had floated dramatically in the gallery entrance. There, in the dark, Warhol's small work had been subtly lit. As Miriam approached the gallery, the head of security, the director, the assistant director, two board members, and Irvin stood like carved stone at the tape barrier. They were flanked by a small woman and a large man, both in suits, neither of whom she recognized. Arms crossed, no one talking, they stared at the once-taut, invisible lines that had suspended the work, now obscenely twisted and curled. Someone had simply walked in, cut the filaments, tucked the Warhol into their bag, and left? The small woman said something to Irvin, and she, the director, and the big guy followed him from the gallery. As they passed, Irv rolled his eyes.

It had been Irvin's idea to bring the Warhol from Prague's Central Gallery to the Whitney. "It'll be a sweet historic juxtaposition to our emerging artists' ambitious soliloquies. Plus I might get to rub shoulders, or nether somethings, with the sexiest woman of my youth."

Miriam grinned. Irvin had a way of keeping things grounded.

17

Where Would She Sleep? 1997

The police *had* been to her apartment, and Mrs. Greene was required to let them in.

"There were two, Miriam. White guys in cheap-ass workout suits and a warrant. I went in with em, kept an eye on em. Made em leave everything where they fuckin found it."

Miriam told her there was nothing to find and thanked her.

"That's right, Miriam, and they left with nothing. Snooped around and left empty-handed. If there's anything I can do . . . "

Miriam thanked her again and closed the door.

This was a violation. It was as if someone had been inside her clothes. She hadn't taken another step into the room. She wanted a cup of tea and to sit in her chair in the corner by the window. But strangers had been in her kitchen. There were two of them. They had opened her drawers and cabinets. She had all of her account numbers, phone numbers, and passwords taped inside a cabinet. They had walked across this room, this rug—the bottoms of their shoes on her rug—and touched her things. Her mother's doll was on the sofa against the wrong pillow. As a child, her mother had rarely been allowed to play with the doll. It was brought out for an hour or so on holidays, then returned to its box and locked in an upstairs drawer so it wouldn't get soiled. Later in her years, Mom had given her the doll. "Keep Missy safe, honey." The delicate fabric of Missy's dress and leggings had tinted with age. Most of her eyelashes gone, there were fine cracks spreading in her cheeks, and a stranger—someone with thick fingers and maybe a smoker—had wrapped his fingers around her body and lifted her off the sofa.

She wanted to take a shower, wash her hair. And how could she undress? They had touched her towels, her pillow.

Where would she sleep?

18

She Hadn't Slept, 1997

Miriam hadn't slept. She sat alone in the director's office. Her slacks, blouse, and blazer—natural fabrics—understated grays, white, neutral. She was reminded of perception—perception and entitlement. This was a spacious, sparsely appointed room in which huge sums of money were casually discussed—a nexus of the art world, and she aspired to this office as hundreds of current art history majors aspired to hers. Beverley Sills, Lee Iacocca, or any number of the Vanderbilts had likely occupied this chair across the low glass table from a former director. In the chair next to her, a comfortable board member would have reposed—but a quick glance at his watch—and eager to escort Bubbles, Lee, or Gloria to lunch as soon as the check was signed.

Behind her, the door opened, and lowered voices ended abruptly. The director entered and closed the door.

"Miriam."

She stood.

"Please." His long arm motioned to the chair.

She sat.

"Coffee . . . no, it's tea, right?" He was at the serving table beneath a Rauschenberg monotype. He turned to her. "One lump or two?" He cat-smiled.

"I'm fine, thank you."

"Coffee for me, then." He poured a cup from the carafe. "Black." He took a sip and lowered onto the spartan leather sofa across from her. Fine Italian wool knees—and he kept his jacket on.

Distance, formality.

"Thank you for coming in early, Miriam. This is so unfortunate for all of us. Sad, so sad."

She nodded and fixed on his cup. It appeared to be part of his body—his skin a polished translucent white. The cup—contemporary Japanese porcelain of perfect proportions—was tall enough to be interesting, its delicate handle placed in the lower two-thirds, and steam curling an inch above the rim disappeared into this privileged space. The director was probably saying something important. She should be listening.

". . . the media storm you stirred a few years ago before my arrival. But the museum grew from that, and we'll survive this."

Storm I stirred? They'd talked about that. He said he knew it was the former director's disproportionate ambition, his pet project—how when it failed he'd laid it all at her feet. Right?

"Harrison Davies—our esteemed chairman—and Detective Nettles from NYPD will be joining us in a few minutes." He checked his watch.

His watch had a thin profile, the leather watchband matched his shoes.

". . . the board and Dr. Davies?" His knee bounced. "We'll want to discuss next steps."

Next steps? Behind her, the door opened.

"Ah, Harrison."

Ford, she thought. Harrison Ford came to mind, and she was having trouble concentrating.

The director shoved up from the sofa and nearly ran around the table to greet Dr. Davies. She stood and watched the hearty handshake, the director's stretched and glowing Cheshire smile, his affectionate shoulder grip on the older man. She felt overweight.

A small, elegant woman in fitted blue tweed and a tie appeared and rapped on the open door.

"Detective." The director released his grip and waved her in.

The director introduced Miriam to the detective. Miriam stood and watched as the three of them milled about the office, to the coffee service, examined the art, and found seats around the low glass table. The director and Detective Nettles settled on the sofa, and Dr. Davies in the chair next to her—his collar open, loafers polished. His sport coat smelled new and expensive. The director's coffee had cooled.

"Harrison, Detective, Miriam," the director began. "We're caught in the tragedy for which we've all prepared." He cracked his knuckles. "It has always been a matter of when, not if."

Was she hearing an ever-slight tremolo in his voice? A Dire Straits reverb? In Dr. Davies' presence, the director had dropped a spot on the food chain.

"Miriam, we've asked the detective to interview anyone on our staff who has had the least association with the Warhol." He peered into his cup and placed it with soft deliberation on the table. Finger in the cup's handle, his sights in her direction. "Somehow, someway, someone walked in here and took it." He sat back.

Now the detective leaned in and reached for her coffee. A size-zero pedigree Whippet in short black bangs, full lips, and long, tan, manicured fingers perhaps deceiving—stronger than they appeared. The detective stared at her through brown cat's-eye glasses that matched her heels. "Yes, someone or a couple someones," the detective said.

Texas, Miriam thought.

The detective relaxed into the sofa and took a sip holding her cup in both hands. Owning Miriam, she hadn't released her stare. "The 'someone' and 'somehow' are interesting. But, from y'all's perspective, I'd have to guess the 'somewhere' is more important. Where is the Warhol?"

"Amen," Dr. Davies said.

"The department's someone-and-somehow team has checked for leave-behinds—something they dropped, slip of paper, snagged fabric. Believe it or not, a couple months ago a thief left his wallet on a nightstand. These guys aren't your everyday brain surgeons. Our people have dusted for prints, checked the locks and videos, and taken a hundred photos." She glanced at the director. "Thank you for the floor plans."

The director ran his fingers down the edges of his tie, anchored his palms on his knees, and nodded.

The detective was back to owning Miriam. "The video shows two skinny hooded yahoos in a foot race through the building, going straight to the gallery, punching in your passcode like they were on a game show, and they were out of here and through the loading dock in less than ninety seconds. New white Lexus up the street, New York plates, and we can't see the numbers. What we *can* see is that one of them handled the art carefully. At the car, they sandwiched it in what looks like foam board and bubble wrap before it went into a backpack. Did I get that right?"

The director nodded.

My passcode? She'd rarely had to use it, and when she did, she was likely to need two tries to get it right. Against protocol, she'd written it in reverse on the back of the medical card in her wallet. She'd wished they would have allowed her to choose her own code—something she could remember—a birthday or something sequential like prime numbers or a rhyme. *Columbus sailed the ocean blue in fourteen hundred ninety-two.* And wouldn't someone need an outside key to get into the building? She didn't have a key. Irvin didn't have a key. Maybe the director did. There were security boxes at the entrances containing building entry keys for fire and police, but you'd need a key for those, too.

And now she'd missed whatever the detective had been saying. The three of them were looking at her, waiting. She sat straighter. "I'm sorry. I didn't get much sleep." To her right, she could almost feel Dr. Davies frown.

The director spoke. "Miriam, this is going to hit the papers. Harrison has used his influence to delay things, but our time's up." The director nodded and smiled toward Dr. Davies. Back to facing her, "I might have advised against bringing the Warhol from Prague for the very reason we're here today. But you and Irvin had things in motion long before I arrived."

The director's forehead was shining now. His eyes intensely dark, the pupils like dimes. Was he on something?

"We need some answers and—"

"Whoa there, big fella!" The detective shot off the sofa as from a rodeo chute. She flashed a lovely smile. "How about Miriam and I have some alone time? Nice to meet you, Harrison." They shook. She offered her hand to Miriam. "C'mon, girl, let's take a walk."

19

Mind if We Close Your Door? 1997

As Miriam led the way, the detective's stiletto heels struck the museum floor like steel on flint, and Miriam imagined a fan of sparks in their wake. "This is it," she said. "My office."

"Great. Is there a ladies' room?"

Miriam pointed down the hall, and the detective excused herself.

In her office, Miriam picked a bird's nest basket from its shelf—so tightly woven that water couldn't escape. The police had been to her apartment and to Irv's, and they had interviewed him. Was interview the right word? Now it was her turn. She replaced the basket and drifted her fingers along the rows of Barbies, straight and lifeless—stiletto heels. The detective, on the other hand, Irvin's "terrier in tweed,"—

"Sorry," the detective stood in the doorway. "I'm up at three and in the office at five. By then I've had four cups, and there's always a fresh pot at the duty desk. They change it on the hour. Mind if we close your door?"

"Please," Miriam said.

She offered one of the chairs in front of her desk, then chose the other. The detective moved hers to face Miriam.

"Your director's not a patient man." The detective was small for the chair—bronze skin and perfect nails on chrome armrests.

"He has a lot of responsibility."

"Does he ever unwind? Take a break? Vacation?"

"Not that I've seen." Miriam released a breath and settled farther into the chair. Steel and leather—it was more comfortable than it appeared.

"You're not from the city," the detective said.

"It shows?"

"I'm not either. Small ranch outside of Austin. Horses, cattle, Dad and two brothers. You?"

"Preacher's daughter, small town, Pennsylvania. One brother."

"Shit damn! I had preacher's daughter down cold. Preacher's daughter named Miriam Pastor. That had to get some laughs. And a brother you say? Younger?"

"Yes."

"Preacher's daughter suggests a girl who hits her teens, shaves her head, and joins the circus. Not in your case, though. Am I right? Girl Scout Gold Award, high school volunteer at the shelter, scholarship to Pratt, Masters at Columbia, and a Stanford PhD. Want to hear how it looks so far?"

Miriam blinked, and tried to catch up. "I'm sure it's suspicious—my passcode, and all."

"Y'all should be in P.R.," the detective smiled, "Suspicious." She did a three-sixty scan of the room. "You're the bottom of the executive pecking order with personal code access. Irvin doesn't have it, nor do the junior curators, interns, and the list goes on. The electricians and engineers have it, being first in, last out, and we've talked to them. Nothing there. With Harrison being an old-school newspaper guy and the director being, well, the director—who doesn't take vacations and is wired tighter than a drug-addled thoroughbred—and me being an intuitive type, you and Irvin have captured our imaginations. I smell coffee. Is it one of those carafes?"

"Excuse me? Oh, yes. I hope it's hot." Miriam rose. "They bring them up each morning—coffee and hot water. I don't know who. I never see them. Cream, sugar?"

"Milk, if you have it."

Miriam supported the weight of the carafe in her fingers and wrist. She was weak. She needed to be strong, alert—this interrogation. That was it—the word she was looking for. The spoon sparkled against porcelain. She handed the cup to the detective.

"Thank you. Why that Warhol?" Fingers laced around the cup, the detective sipped and looked out over her glasses. Arresting, green eyes—her gaze was different now. Soft.

Miriam sat. "Well, it's . . . I'm sorry. What do you mean? Should we be talking about this here? Should I have a lawyer?"

"Of course, you can have a lawyer, but you're not being charged, and this isn't an interrogation. The fact that we're chatting in your office without a lawyer says something. It's not how my associate operates—Detective Ciccone. You saw him in the gallery—big guy in the bad suit? If he or anyone else from PD contacts you, call me." She handed Miriam her card. "But you and I? We're just chatting."

Miriam held the card in her lap, stared at it without seeing, then back to the detective. "Then I shouldn't be concerned?"

"Mmm, that might be a stretch. If you'd like to reschedule this conversation, I can come back later—to meet with you and your lawyer."

"I don't have a lawyer." She turned her head away, and this was crazy—in this situation—but she had to stifle a yawn. "And I don't have the faintest idea who might have taken the print. Honestly, if I did, I'd—"

"What's so compelling about that piece that you had to go all the way to Prague to get it?"

"There's only one. We were required to meet the owner at Prague's Central Gallery."

"Brigitte Bardot."

"Yes. She acquired the Warhol in her divorce with Gunter Sachs."

"Who's that?"

"Playboy art collector."

"Whose idea was it? To bring it here—the Warhol."

"You've spoken with Irvin."

"*We're* speaking now—you and I. Good coffee, by the way."

"I wouldn't know, but I'm glad."

"Why that Warhol?"

"Why . . . what?"

"Aren't there tons of Warhols? Why the one somebody just had to have?"

"We heard this unique piece might be available, and it was perfect. It would punctuate our planned exhibition on race in America. Warhol had used a controversial photograph of a police dog attacking an African American man in a peaceful, sixties Birmingham protest. We would feature the work at the head of the gallery which we had planned to juxtapose with—"

"You and your frog?"

"I'm sorry?" Miriam asked.

"You said, 'We. We heard, we would, we planned.'"

"Irvin and I have worked closely for years."

"Closely."

"Professionally."

"Of course. Tall, smart, single handsome guy, but not your type."

Miriam felt a tension release. "He is a close friend—a best friend. We tried to date a couple years ago. It was a disaster. One false start after another. It's something we share fondly, something we can laugh about."

"It's worth a lot. More than the rest of the gallery combined." The detective placed her cup on the corner of Miriam's desk and crossed her leg.

"It's a special relationship. Irv and I appreciate and respect each other." She tucked an auburn sprig behind her ear.

"No, the Warhol. I meant the print."

"Oh."

The detective uncrossed her leg and scooted forward. "So y'all get the piece here from the other side of the planet where it's resided safely for thirty years, then Irvin's boss's and best friend's passcode is used to steal it. Dang, Miriam! Why do you have to make this look so easy?"

"I don't—" She realized her fingers were doing a gentle inventory of her lips. She lowered her hand to her lap.

"Okay, relax." Detective Nettles sat back. "Sometimes I get ahead of myself. The lieutenant says, 'Nettles, rein it in, take a powder.' So, let's pretend that *why* this seems so easy isn't important. Once in a while we all do things that aren't completely thought through—like the time I straddled the climb-over ladder and peed on the electric fence. I was only ten, but *wheee doggies*, and that sure as hell wasn't thought through. What a pisser, right? Who has your code?"

Electric fence? Miriam felt the searing sting, the cramp in her gut, and shuddered. She saw it as a Beardsley drawing—a farting, laughing sultan and a masked, goat nymph peeing on . . . an electric fence? Her code?

"I don't . . . No one. No one has it. I don't know. Security? IT?"

"Nope. Security has their own eight-digit code, and IT's puckered up tighter than a bull's ass."

Another visual.

"And a coded entry," the detective said, "to that gallery. None of the other galleries have a passcode. Why that gallery?"

"The owner required it."

"Brigitte Bardot."

"Yes."

"Let's try and wrap our heads around an incompletely considered breach in museum security, Miriam. Let's say it might involve you and a slip of the tongue—or worse. You didn't write your code down somewhere, did you? We have so many passwords anymore. I need a password at the bank to write myself a check, to pay the cable company, my phone bill. When I can't get into an account and I call for help, they want to know my password. If I knew my password I wouldn't be calling in the first place. So maybe you wrote your code down somewhere, and—I have to give you the benefit of the doubt, here—someone picked it up?"

The detective stood and was checking out the Barbies. "What's all this?"

"Barbies."

"I get that, but why?"

"Art imitating life imitating art."

"Like those carnival mirrors where you see images of yourself repeated smaller and smaller forever?"

"Close enough," Miriam said.

"What will you do next?"

"Next?"

"After the Whitney."

"I'm sorry?"

"When you leave here. Then what?"

"I don't have plans to leave, and I guess I never thought about it. Why do you ask?"

"My gaze at the horizon shows a storm blowing in. Dark clouds moving your way fast."

"But you said maybe someone took my passcode, and I had the benefit of the doubt."

"That's what I think. Not what the director thinks—the director and the board. Nope, they have this drama all tidied up, and where do you want the flowers sent? I'm guessing there's going to be a smoking hole where you sit, and the DA's office won't have a thing to do with it. Business decision. For the good of the institution. Action was taken."

Fired? Miriam gripped the armrests and attempted to stand. Her legs weren't having it. Fired? She was being fired?

"So who got your code, Miriam? Did you write it down? Give it to someone?"

Miriam wished her legs would work, and this was so Kafka. She had to get to the restroom. She tried again to stand.

"You okay?" the detective asked.

"I . . . " There was a lapse between thoughts and speech, and her speech stalled awaiting instructions. She shook her head.

"Here, let's get you up, move around some." The detective helped her to her feet.

Miriam motioned to the door.

The detective supported her like helping a new foal. "Okay, there. Easy, girl. Step at a time."

20

She Wasn't Holding Air, 1997

The detective had left the building, and Miriam needed to be alone. Her door closed, she sat at her desk, head in hands. Breath short, her seams rent and she wasn't holding air. It was preposterous how life could jettison its orbit and strike out into this hysterical, insane trajectory. Surely they knew she had nothing to do with this. Had she *ever* done anything out of line? Ever? Shave her head and join the circus?

When she went off to Pratt, Mom and Dad didn't have much to help with her room and board, theirs being a small country church. So hers were ten-hour days of classes, studies and studios followed by five hours as restaurant hostess at Tommy's Grotto. Tommy was terminally constipated, and he hated you—whoever you were—for how you placed the forks. He was reviled by all who worked there, and the wait-staff turnover medley played allegro. Tommy would not allow her to sit or lean. Her lower back and feet ached just thinking about it. But she got a free meal each night, and the cooks were kind. Then, at Columbia, she was awarded a paid internship at the Whitney, and her course was set. Was there anything in any of that to suggest a life of crime?

She needed sleep. She called the assistant director and left the message that she was going home, and she'd be in early tomorrow. She said Irvin had also checked out for the day. She called her favorite curatorial assistant and gave her the same information.

"I'm so sorry, Miriam."

Miriam thanked her and said that this, too, would pass. She'd see her in the morning and invited her to lunch, ". . . off-site."

I haven't had a day like that day ever. The police and the director. He seems to have a thing for me—not a good thing. His eyes never look directly at mine. More like my eyebrows, or lips. Irv said the same. A disconnect. As though we are the children the director inherited in his new marriage to the Whitney. Unwanted twins, both started as ACs long before he'd arrived. Twelve years before. Nettles, a strange bird. Suggested that I was going to be fired. "What will you do next?" What would I?

21

There's Something About the Car, 1997

So you wrote it down." Detective Nettles sat next to the antique doll on Miriam's sofa. Bent forward, elbows on knees, she held Miriam's medical card—those nails. "Backwards." She looked out over her glasses. "Clever."

Miriam stood in the kitchen doorway with a plate of cookies. Not that she'd thought what she had to say was so important, but she'd called Nettle's a week after being forced from the Whitney.

Miriam entered the living room and placed the cookies on the coffee table. She took a seat across from the detective.

"It was when we first began installing. I could never remember it."

The detective lowered the card and took a small cookie. She examined it front and back. "How many laps around the high school track do you represent, my little biscuit? How many minutes on the stationary bike?" Eyebrows arched, "What do you think, Miriam? Is it worth it?"

Miriam reached for her second cookie.

"Where was Irvin when you called him about the theft?" the detective asked.

"I don't know. Home, I suppose."

"How long did it take him to get to the museum?"

"I don't remember. Why?"

"Try, Miriam. Try and remember. After you got off the phone that Saturday, how long did it take you to get there? Did he arrive before you? Before lunch? Where do you think he was when you called him? Was there background noise?"

"I honestly don't know. Maybe a coffee shop."

"He didn't say where he was? You didn't ask how soon he could be there?"

"I . . . "

The detective was up and checking out the bookshelf. "You like Anne Tyler. Life in Baltimore, right? Look how we live, Miriam. Attractive single women in our own apartments with cabs waiting, air-conditioning, two weeks of vacation each year, and cookies between meals." She took a bite. "Mmm, almond flour, dark chocolate, and sea salt. Perfect."

Miriam relaxed some.

"There's something about those yahoos and the car," Nettles said.

"Lexus."

"Right. By the way, I'll be back down on the ranch all next week and catching up with my brothers—a working vacation. Dad's not getting any younger, and there's heavy lifting to do. It's going to kill my nails. You can call me anytime if you think of something, anything—an unusual phone call, something you overheard, a new security guard, repeat visitor spending too much time near the print." She took a bite. "Ever string fence in horizontal rain? Try to get a clairvoyant sow into the back of a truck? There's easier things in life." She took another cookie. "Like being police detective. You know the codes start with the same number, right? Nine? Like the last one you wrote on your card? Anyone would know that was the first in the sequence."

Miriam dropped her hands to her lap. "No, I—"

"Hey, and I'm sorry about how it went down with the board. That had to be awful. If it was me, I might be on a raging bender. But look at you, here, a week later and baking cookies."

Miriam stood and went over to the window. Dozens of miniature birds blew in like smoke and lighted in the trees lining the street below. "It hurts," she said to the window. "And I guess it confirms what's been there all along—in the back of my mind. That I was a lucky imposter and never deserved to be there. I was keeping someone better, more qualified, from the position."

The detective stood close behind her. "Preacher's daughter. That original sin thing."

"Maybe. When I left, I felt so worthless. That the theft *is* my fault, and there's nothing I can do to make it right."

"So you went down without a fight. Disappointing, but I get it. It's just too easy for white men to do whatever they have a mind to. Your pal Irvin, though—I hear he made them pay. Stood tall in that director's office and calmly ripped him and Dr. Davies a new one. I hear he told them his lawyer would string em up by the balls. Gotta love that." She patted Miriam on the shoulder and returned to the sofa.

Miriam turned and smiled small. "Of course he would."

There was a fitfully-suppressed fury in Irv, and his initial response to things could appear confrontational. Or was it competitive? His blown-up reaction that day in her office was all passionate brushwork and surface treatment below which were layers of dark and somber underpainting.

The next day, following the detective's interview, and after the direction all this was taking became obvious, she'd met him at the Ramona for a drink—she had one, he'd had a few, a lit cigarette on the ashtray, and he was already in that scotch-driven, offshore hurricane and planning his land-touchdown revenge. Whenever he got like that there was little she could do to deflect him, and it was difficult to watch. She told him so—that she was so sorry she'd dragged him into this.

He told her to forget it, that it was simply high-octane drama for the new, coke-snorting director, throwing his weight around and showing the board what a hard-ass he is, and one of these days he'd be taking him down. "Stay tuned, Miriam. He's going down."

She'd chalked that one up to the scotch, leaned into him, and kissed him on the cheek.

He put his hand to his face and said having his boss kiss him, he felt better already, and ordered another drink. There was a new bartender at the Ramona.

"Security herded Irvin from the boardroom and out through the building," the detective said. "They say he never stopped talking. That he stood out front on the walk, faced the doors, and calmly continued his summation for the jury. Drew a crowd."

"Irv's big on concept, vague on execution. It seems to work for him—for us—with me there to clean up his brilliant messes." Miriam returned to the chair.

The detective extended an arm across the back of the sofa and stared at her. "Really."

22

There's Something You're Not Telling Us, 1997

The phone. She ignored it. She'd been on her sofa going through her finances and wondering how to approach Mrs. Greene about breaking the lease. Miriam was moving home—to her childhood home.

It was her mother's suggestion that first morning she'd called, "Come home, Miriam." Maybe that's what she needed—a restart. Away from all the reminders of who she was not, and she saw how everyone on the street seemed to know she didn't belong. That she'd been told to leave, and why was she still here? Also, Mom said Dad wasn't doing well.

And Irvin. They'd taken him, too. It was her code, so why Irvin? Maybe it was as he said—the new director flexing his power for the board. But Irvin? Of course, with her gone, how long could he have lasted? Would anyone else have the patience? He came in late and left early—or didn't show up at all—but she'd put up with it for good reason.

They'd revived a staid institution, he and she. And he was one-of-a-kind brilliant—some ways helpless, hopeless, but an ideas-from-left-field genius. They hadn't talked of what he intended to do next. She knew he was on the outs with family. He down-played holidays, seemed to have no sentimental ties. There was a woman out West, but that was about all she knew of Irvin's recent life.

The phone again. It buzzed on the kitchen table. She went out and answered.

It was Detective Ciccone, NYPD. Could she come over to the station this afternoon to help him fill in a couple details for his report?

She asked if she should clear this with Detective Nettles.

He said Nettles had asked him to call. That while she was on her cowgirl vacation, all of a sudden the lieutenant wanted a report in the morning, and it was in his lap.

She wondered could they do this over the phone.

"No."

"Oh."

"Three o'clock."

"Well, okay then."

23

How Well Do You Know Irvin? 1997

It wasn't a tiny room with a single light and no windows as seen on TV. Miriam was in a conference room with one wall of glass. Notable was that the room had nothing notable about it—no landscapes, seascapes, or motivational posters. No credenza. What appeared to be rented furniture—nubby-upholstered armchairs—was scrunched shoulder to shoulder on both sides of a forlorn table that mimicked wood. A nothing room, the air—discarded gym socks.

She faced the glass and watched as what she assumed to be detectives and administrators popped up from their cubicles sporadically, and others, some with stacks and boxes of paper, passed the window. Perhaps the copy room was next door.

Two men in white shirts and ties approached the door—one large, the other small. They entered, and she recognized Ciccone from that first morning at the gallery. He nearly filled the doorway. He grinned, and, for such a large man, he had small teeth.

"Good afternoon, Miriam."

She nodded.

With clumsy effort, the men extracted two full-size chairs from compact-only spaces and sat. Ciccone opened a manila file, shoved it a few inches forward, and spread his elbows on the table. "Nervous?" He grinned again. His fists looked swollen.

"You wanted to clear up a couple things for your report? It's due tomorrow?" she said.

Ciccone and the other guy glanced at each other, then back to Miriam.

"Yeah, that's right. A couple things. Maybe a few things. First, how well do you know your buddy Irvin? Guy's a piece of work, right?"

Her attention was briefly drawn to the smaller man who was fussing fingers through his jacket pockets. "Irvin and I have worked together for thirteen years, and I have never known him to be anything but upright, intellectually curious, and brilliant." She rubbed cold palms on her thighs and wove her fingers in her lap.

"Yeah, I'm with you on that brilliant part, " Ciccone said. "Brilliant storyteller in *my* book. So you guys dated, right? Maybe shared some secrets?" He shot a look at his partner. "Will you sit still?"

The man had found his pen and showed Ciccone. Ciccone nodded, then was back at Miriam.

"And you dated?"

"We dated briefly. It didn't work out. That was two years ago."

"Didn't work out. Maybe cause you found out you didn't like some of the stuff he was into?"

"We dated twice. We remain close, possibly best friends. Why is this so important?"

"Movin right along." He checked the file, then was back at Miriam. "Nettles thinks somebody got your passcode, Miriam, and that's a fact. The only what-if in this is how. There's two possibilities—well, three, actually, but let's start with two. You gave it to someone, or somebody got it some other way. The second possibility is a longer reach than the first, so let's start with the first and easiest, as old man Occam would say." He leaned farther forward. "Who'd you give it to?"

Ciccone's head was nearly halfway across the table, and it was huge. A trickle of sweat ran down the small of her back. Maybe someone could open the door?

"Oh, I'm sorry." He leaned back and relaxed. "You look like you could use some water. Would you like some water, Miriam?"

She nodded.

He asked the other guy, "Would you get Miriam some water?"

The man nodded, squeezed out of his chair and left the door open on his way out. Cool air rushed in.

Ciccone loosened his tie and, chin raised, undid his top button. He leaned back, hands on hips. "So while we're waiting for Henry, maybe we can get to know each other. You ever run track?"

"I'm sorry?" she said.

"You know, being trim and all. Were you a sprinter? You have that toned look—maybe you go to the gym. Maybe a personal trainer? Am I right? I wrestled—90k Olympic contender—which you probably guessed."

"I hadn't."

"It's the big ones like me—hitting the gym, the weights, doing the supplements—we get slowed down with joint problems. It's the skinny ones that're fast, like those two guys—at least we think maybe they're guys—on the video."

Detective Nettles never mentioned that the two thieves may not be men. Had she and Ciccone discussed that? Did they really think she would use her own code? Where's that water?

Ciccone's elbows back on the table. "So until Henry gets back, let's recap what we got so far." He ran his finger down a page in the file, then focused on her. "First, we got you and Irvin dating, and you've been together for—what'd you say—thirteen years?"

"I—"

"Then some skinny, toned sprinter dudes—or dudettes, or dude and dudette, maybe—race through the museum like pros in brand new running shoes, use your code to gain access to the gallery, and steal a six-million-dollar artwork owned by Brigitte Bardot, but you never ran track. Am I right?" He pulled a pen from his shirt pocket and prepared to write in the file. Not raising his head, he asked softly, "Am I right?"

"I—"

"Where the hell's Henry?" He stretched around and yelled, "HENRY!"

It shook the glass and went through her like a shot. Heads popped up from the cubicles, some with amused looks. She grabbed the edge of the table, then dropped her hands back to her lap. Red and damp, Henry appeared with a bottle of water, handed it to her, and edged back around the table and into his chair.

Ciccone took an impatient breath and backhand motioned with one finger to the water. "Please, have a drink. We'll wait. Henry, close the goddamn . . . please close the door and pull the curtains."

She twisted the cap, took a swallow, screwed the lid on, and placed the bottle in front of her.

"All done?"

She nodded.

Better?"

She nodded.

"It says on top of page two that Nettles thinks maybe there's something you're not telling us. Do you agree with that, Miriam? What it says on top of page two?"

"There's nothing else to—"

"Ah, so I gotta guess." He grinned. "Is that how we do this?" He checked in with Henry. "I gotta guess."

Henry smiled and nodded.

Ciccone moved back to her. "I gotta guess it's something about you and Irvin 'working together' for the past thirteen years. Then you guys figure how to get this six-million-dollar Warhol to show up from somewhere behind The Iron Curtain, and then you hire a couple guys, maybe, and give them your code, and make it look like they stole the art *and* your code?" He was waiting for an affirmation, his pen in the writing position.

She was feeling faint, and did Detective Nettles really give her okay to this?

He slammed the pen on the file. "OR WAS IT YOU WORKING ALONE?!"

Fear struck. She had to move. She twisted off the lid and took another drink. She sat the bottle aside, uncapped. She lowered her head and took a long breath. Fists beneath the table, she regrouped.

Ciccone held his pen in the writing position, a confession on its way.

Seconds like hours, head lowered, her voice a near whisper, "Detective, you know as much about this as I. I've told Detective Nettles what I know. May I go now?"

In the cab, she didn't remember getting up from the table, walking to the elevator, going down to the first level, or leaving the building. And she was shaking—uncontrollably shaking.

24

This Scares Me, 1997

Back at her place, Miriam kept the lights off and left her shoes by the door. Water on for tea, she took a shower. Hair buffed, and in her robe, she closed the shades and switched on the lamp by the sofa. She brought her tea and phone in from the kitchen and curled next to mom's doll. Ciccone had bullied her—rattled her. In the shower, she'd somewhat cleared her head. She checked her phone. Irvin had called.

She hit "talk" and waited. *Come on, Irvin, you called fifteen minutes ago.*

He answered. "Fucking Ciccone! Did he call you?"

"Hello, Irv."

"Yeah, hello! Did he?"

"Yes."

"Goddamn it! He *said* he was going to bring you in. What'd you say?"

"I told him I told Detective Nettles everything I know and asked to leave."

"That's it?"

"What else is there?"

"Right, right. Sonofabitch grilled me, too. Wanted to know about our sex life, the twisted shit."

She couldn't help herself—she smiled. It was great to hear his voice. "And?"

"And what? I said it was like dancing with a nun in work boots."

She laughed. "Best to tell the truth. He was trying to get me to say we schemed together to steal the painting, or that I, alone, had done it."

"That's a load of crap. Why would you use your own code?"

"I don't think he's gone that far in his speculation. He's not a thoughtful man."

"Take *that* to the bank."

"But he is relentless," the nerves were back, "and, Irv, it scares me."

"Fuck him, we're innocent."

"Innocent people are convicted every day. This scares me."

25

This is Screwed! 1997

"Why didn't you call me? I told you to call me, Miriam. This is screwed!"

Miriam had just answered the door and Detective Nettles brushed past and was in the middle of her living room. She spun and faced Miriam.

"We had it under control, step at a time, and now Ciccone has the lieutenant's ear, and she's wondering what's taking so long. You should have called."

Miriam gently closed the door and crossed to the window. "He told me it was your idea that I talk to him."

"Where are the cookies?" The detective was in the kitchen.

"Tin on top of the refrigerator." Miriam moved to the corner of the sofa and sat.

The detective opened the tin, and sat across from her. She put the lid on the table between them and, tin in her lap, aggressively chomped a cookie. It sounded like she was marching on gravel.

"Things aren't good." She picked through the cookies and chose one.

"Ciccone?"

"Right. He has your file, and I've been taken off the investigation."

Miriam Ruth Pastor—a file.

"Politics, and it could be bad. You saw for yourself the guy's an earthmover." Last of the cookie into her mouth. She picked another. "I can't talk to you, but if I feel that I have to, I will. And we have to keep that between us, off the record—like I'm Deep Throat."

"This is a mess—my life."

"The lieutenant likes simplicity. She doesn't do complications. Did Ciccone mention Occam?" Another cookie.

"He did."

"There ya go. Listen, Miriam. That y'all—most of the staff—were out of the office, the next day being Saturday, kinda complicates things for Ciccone. Any one of you could have met up with the two yahoos and exchanged the print for bucks. But Ciccone has you at the top of the list, and the lieutenant likes that."

"I'm thinking of leaving—of going to see my parents for a while. Is that legal?"

"Sure. Looks bad, but it's legal. Pennsylvania, right?" Another cookie.

"Dad's not well."

"I'm sorry. Serious?"

"We don't know yet."

"How soon are you leaving?"

"As soon as I can get things packed and in order. I have to speak with my landlord."

"So more than a while. You're moving." The detective put the tin on the table and replaced the lid. "Miriam, I have to stop with the cookies and get something off my chest." She rose and went to the window. "It's been weighing on me since we first met in the director's office—so heavy it was difficult to stay on point." She returned and sat next to Miriam. "You remind me of someone—someone I lost years ago." She folded her arms.

The room had stopped breathing. Miriam waited.

Nettles crossed her leg. "My older sister—a high school senior. I was eight. Her murder. It was . . . ," she took a breath. "It's unsolved. When I was old enough, I had to get out of there. Way out. It's why I'm on the force."

"Oh . . . detective, I am sorry."

"She was my hero. Everyone was attracted to her—men and women."

"I . . . Well I don't—"

"You don't have to say anything. I just wanted . . . You bring her to mind."

They both faced forward. Neither moved for the next few minutes. The sounds of the city through the glass—a garbage truck five floors below—and it had never seemed this loud. The truck moved on. The apartment gone quiet. Curious thoughts arrived from corner shadows, brushed shoulders, looked confused, and wandered off as time carefully felt its way back into the room. The detective was first to speak. "You probably don't have coffee."

"I . . . No, but I can make tea if you'd like."

"Would you?" She pointed to the tin. "Those little suckers dry you out."

26

Ciccone Is Beaming, 1997

The morning after Nettles was taken off the investigation, there was someone at Miriam's door. She checked the peephole. Ciccone and Henry stood in the hall. Blood rushed to her gut. She opened.

"Hello, Miriam!" Ciccone glanced side to side as if he was addressing the entire floor. "May we have a few words?"

She backed a step. "Please, come in."

"Thank you." Ciccone beamed.

She was quick to close the door behind them.

"Nice place. Very neat. You clean it yourself?"

"How can I help you, detective?"

"May we all have a seat? This could take a while."

"Please. Would you like water or tea?"

"I think we're fine right now, Miriam. But if you'd like something, by all means . . . "

She moved her mother's doll from the sofa and offered them seats. She sat across the room.

Ciccone's nostrils flared with a deep breath, then relaxed. "There are people from the museum that were hesitant about going to bat for you, Miriam. Spotty record, and all. Not following protocol. Evidently the place took quite a hit and operated at a loss as a result of one of your follies. Couple years ago? Possible misuse of funds?" He stretched back, opened his suit coat, and sank deeper into the straining sofa.

She stared.

"Doesn't ring a bell? Then there's something about fraternization, which we've already discussed, and, shall we say, a loose management style?"

"Is this an employment review?"

"Heh, heh." Ciccone slid his arm out across the back of the sofa and tapped Henry on the shoulder. "Cute, huh?"

Henry nodded, smiled, and moved an inch from the paw.

"No, Miriam. I assure you this isn't an employment review. But the little things do add up, and, all of a sudden, we have one big messy situation. That's when Henry and I get called in to hit the old reset button. Isn't that right, Henry?"

He nodded.

"Are you here to arrest me?"

Ciccone crossed an ankle over his knee. Argyle socks. "Well yes we are, Miriam. I had planned to work up to that slowly, but now you've spilled the beans. We're here to arrest you under suspicion of First Degree Grand Larceny, New York Penal Law 155.42. Henry, would you please illuminate Miriam regarding her rights? And no fucking ad . . . Please relate the rights exactly as written."

Henry had thin lips. Watching Henry's mouth as he recited her rights, Miriam was deafened by a laser-pitched drill boring a hole at the back of her skull.

Moments later in this scripted farce, Miriam was back from the kitchen with her purse.

"Henry will carry your purse." He pointed. "Purse, Henry."

Now she stood in her living room with her wrists being secured behind her.

"Protocol," Ciccone said. "Sorry." He grinned those tiny teeth. "It's what we gotta do to get you down to the station for photos and prints. Hey, cheer up. This ain't a conviction, just an arrest."

She was numb. Out-of-her-body numb.

"Okay, here we go, and I'll hold your arm for support on the stairs."

They were through her door. A final *click* behind her and they started down the hall.

"What the fuck?!" Mrs. Greene stepped from her apartment.

They continued to the stairs.

"Uh-uh. This ain't happenin to Miriam in *my* building."

They were down a few steps, Mrs. Greene right behind them. "What are the charges?"

No comment.

"I said, 'What are the fucking charges?!'"

No comment, second landing.

"Are white people all of a sudden deaf? Miriam, what are the charges and where are they taking you?"

"Grand larceny," her voice flat. "To the station."

"Nineteenth precinct?"

Down three landings, Miriam glanced at Ciccone. No response. She looked to Henry. He nodded.

"Yes."

"Bitch inspector in charge over there. I'll make a couple calls—this shit ain't happenin!" Mrs. Greene stopped on the landing. "Let em have their student council, census bureau booking crap, and they'll let you go, Miriam." She called down the stairs, "Make em give you fuckin cab fare back here! And you two fools keep your hands to yourself—sorry-ass perverts."

Miriam was back at the station, hands restrained. This was medieval. She was being searched—deeply searched. She watched herself from above as the prisoner provided her vitals including social security number, finger prints, and she stood for photographs. The air dead and cold in the bowels of the building, she was given a voucher for her purse, watch, earrings, phone, and wallet, and taken to a cell. She was allowed three calls from the payphone in the cell. Did she want quarters from her purse?

"No."

She couldn't have dreamed this. She should have left for Pennsylvania yesterday. Her father ill at home, she wouldn't tell him about this, ever—nor her mother.

When she was young—before Nick—her father and mother had taken her with them to a Sunday service on a prison farm. She remembered it being dry and crackling with heat. Her dad delivered the sermon in the shade, the prisoners at picnic tables beneath a pavilion. Dad said it was an island of repose for lives of depravity and sin.

Where was Nettles? She should have contacted a lawyer yesterday when Nettles told her she was off the case. *Should* she call someone? Irvin? He had a lawyer. Who would have taken the print? Almost anyone. Anyone in IT who knew her code, or anyone who got it from one of the IT staff? The director. It would have been the director who threw her under the bus. Was he that insecure?

What got Ciccone so worked up about her? He loved making her squirm, and he was good at it—which was as much her fault as his. What comes next? They said something about arraignment.

It had to have been hours of inaction, and what were they doing out there? How many prisoners were they processing? Where was she in the queue? She would be here all night, possibly days, in unfamiliar water—a riptide of bureaucracies. The Whitney's and the New York criminal justice system. No one knew she was here. No, that wasn't right. Mrs. Greene.

A key, a grating noise, a slide, and the door opened. She was told where to go to retrieve her possessions. There, she was handed a small box containing her things. She hurried everything into her purse and handed the box back. The officer gave her a desk appearance ticket. He explained that she would be required to appear in court next month.

"You know how lucky you are?" Ciccone boomed up behind her like a freight. "You got a friend at the sixty-third precinct. Friggin captain. Claimed you're family. Asked us to go easy and give you that appearance ticket and cab fare." Ciccone awkwardly pulled his wallet from his back pocket, cricked his neck, extracted a couple tens, and handed them to her. "Said he'd pay me back double. My lucky day. Be seein ya around, Miriam." He backhanded a wave like shooing a fly. She was about to pass through the steel door when he called, "By the way, you're lookin at twenty-five years if the DA brings charges."

27

Politics, 1997

Mrs. Greene stood in her doorway and watched Miriam come up the hall. "They give you cab fare?"

"Yes."

"Good. I told Mikey to make sure they give you fuckin cab fare."

She stopped at Mrs. Greene's door. "Mikey?"

"Captain Michael Greene, sixty-third precinct, Brooklyn. My brother-in-law."

"Thank you, Mrs. Greene," they hugged, "thank you." She collapsed into Mrs. Greene and let her emotions run. "They said I could get, tweh . . . twenty-five years!"

"It's okay girl. It's okay. It's . . . Go on there." Mrs. Greene held her until she was done.

Wrung out, Miriam stepped back and spread mascara with the heels of her hands. "I'm sorry."

"You think they got anything on you?"

"No. But that doesn't seem to matter."

"Politics."

"Yes."

"If they got nothin, the DA will see that. They gotta convince the DA, and the DA's a busy fuck. There's eight hundred arrests a week, and this week there were three assassination attempts on the mayor. You think the DA's got time to screw around with you, and no record, and no evidence?"

28

Maybe She'll Die in Prison, 1997

It was humiliating, Irvin!" Everything spinning, she couldn't sit. Miriam leaned back against the wall between her windows, arms crossed and tight. Early evening's long shadows from a single table lamp.

"The being searched?" Irvin's arms spanned the back of the sofa.

"All of it. I was required to verify who I am, and they questioned everything I said. I was locked in a cell!

"But you're home now. I left a message for my lawyer. We'll set something up."

"Do I look the same? As before I was in jail? Tell me I look the same, because I don't feel the same. Do I look like someone who's had a woman in a badge and latex gloves run her hands up between their legs? Under their arms, under their breasts?" She retightened the fold of her arms. "And this is just the beginning. I'm supposed to appear in court next month."

"Mrs. Greene said maybe the DA won't make a case."

"That's right, Irvin. Think about it! My future hangs on, 'maybe.' Maybe she'll go to prison for twenty-five years. Maybe she'll be raped in prison. Maybe she'll live out her sentence, or maybe she'll die in prison. A few weeks ago we were on top of the world."

"There's the other maybe, and, considering the odds, my money's on, Maybe it's not as bad as it looks."

Miriam sprang off the wall and crossed the room. "Maybe's not good enough right now, Irvin! You're calling it from the cheap seats. I'm in the batter's box." She lit the other lamp.

A tap at the door. Miriam checked the hole. "Oh . . . " She opened.

Detective Nettles stood in the hall like she didn't know what to do next.

"Detective?"

"I guess I was passing by and—"

"I don't have cookies."

"What?"

"If you're here for cookies, I haven't baked."

"Right."

"Would you like to come in?"

"Yes."

"Then do."

The detective entered the apartment slowly, saw Irvin, nodded, and made her way to a chair. Miriam closed the door and joined Irvin on the sofa, the antique doll between them.

"This is lopsided," the detective said. "I shouldn't be here, but I am. And nice to see you again, Irvin."

He grimaced.

"Miriam, this should never have happened. You don't take someone through the wringer without good reason, and it's my opinion there's not good reason."

Hands behind his head and looking comfortable, Irvin asked, "You didn't intervene?"

"No, Irvin. I didn't. I was kinda busy and unaware. Now that we're talking, where were you while Miriam was being tagged like a calf?"

He cleared his throat.

"Never mind, I don't want to hear it. Miriam, I'm here as a friend."

"What happens next?" Miriam asked.

"They'll present your file and their position to the DA. The DA will decide whether to take the case—and you—before a judge. The judge will hear the case, and there will be a date set for trial. If it gets that far, bail will be established, or you'll await trial in jail."

Irvin folded his arms, his middle finger still in a splint. "But it won't get that far, right?"

"Stranger things have happened."

"Some friend."

"We have to be aware. Prepare. Now would be a great time to talk to a lawyer."

"I've got a call in to mine," he said.

Miriam stared into her lap. "I'm being erased."

29

The Halcyon Days, 1992

Before all of this—the theft, the dismissal, the arrest—Miriam's life glittered. Her pulse and place in the marvelous city. Well-dressed young people popping in and out of cabs, the rumpled newsstands, an embroidery of language, food, and double-decker buses. Eclectic and alluring neon displays, and, "One Night Only!" The bustle of traffic, and sidewalk hustlers, and—just over there—a man with a cello.

She occasionally stopped by to chat with Small Sal at his pizza shop—three pies under glass, heat lamps, and a buck a slice. There was always a line. Next to Sal's, Ulrich sulked in his brass-instrument-repairs emporium. In contrast to the searing heat from Sal's ovens and the brilliance of his toppings, Ulrich's was a dimly lit, sleeping-and-alkaline space scattered with miniature tools, soldering supplies, and stacks of aged sheet music. You had to knock to be let into Ulrich's.

She dropped in on Mrs. Greene from time to time, her kitchen a hot bouquet of mac 'n' cheese, fried cabbage, and collard greens.

And her career—the discovery and acquisition of historic and emerging American art, studio tours, the pomp of openings, celebrities, and the press. Beyond the pitch and swirl of the museum were her own evenings and weekends, and she frequently slowed between strides to remind herself, *This is me*! There were dinners, and theater, and *The Yankees* in summer. *Giants* games puffed in earmuffs and down mittens, and she had gone with an array of attractive, ambitious men—though nothing approached serious.

Then, there was Anthony.

They'd met at the Sampson Gallery during a crowded fundraiser attended by many of the city's beautiful people in expensively dressed-down casual. She'd waited for Irvin beneath the covered entrance in the hammering rain, and he hadn't shown. Another Irv moment.

Inside, it seemed many of the wealthy were tall, and she was, as Irvin always said, "A Lotus among Buicks." Through a crowded doorway and looking for familiar faces, she was bumped from behind and jammed, full-body press, into a black Adonis.

"Ola!" he said. "Fancy meeting you here." His arms folded around her.

"I, I'm sorry. Do we know each other?"

"No, but perhaps we should."

She backed out of his arms. He smelled great.

The crowd surrounded them shoulder to shoulder—the heated bodies in flowered conversation. The room steamed and dripped like an over-planted terrarium. He presented his hand, "Anthony Williams, and you are either a collector, a sponsor, or lost." He sparked his smile.

She shook the hand—a buzz at the back of her neck. "I'm Miriam, and you are right. I am currently at a loss."

"Follow me." He guided her through the melee like a tight end leading a running back. "Red or white?" he asked at the bar.

"Chardonnay, please. And Mr. Anthony Williams, you are a collector?"

He laughed.

He laughs easily. It's real. Jamaican?

"I wish. I am loosely associated with the gallery and Doctors Without Borders. I'm the face in the video Mr. Sampson produced. I'm an actor."

"You must be quite an actor to work with Larry."

"Oh, ho, then. You know him as Larry."

"Our paths have crossed." They clinked glasses.

"Actually, I worked *for* Mr. Sampson, and it wasn't easy." He leaned down. The softest cotton, his voice touched her ear. "That man has some strong opinions and is quick to let you know them." He stood back up. "But this could be the break I need. The spot's being distributed worldwide with subtitles."

"You're not multi-lingual as well as charming?"

He took a step back. "Can you tell I'm blushing? I get by with Spanish, English and some Rasta thrown in. We did two prints—English and Spanish. Beyond that, it's subtitles and dubbing."

She scanned the room. "Is Larry here? I see Aby's leaving."

"Mr. Sampson left earlier. He said he might be back, but I doubt it. You like jazz?"

She blinked. Now *that* was a tectonic shift. Did she? Had she ever thought about it? "Well, yes, I—"

"Let's go, then." He gathered their glasses onto the bar and took her hand. "This way."

"Wait, I . . . " Why was she following him, allowing herself to be swept along? Down the stairs, through the lobby, and they were outside through the rain and into a cab. Had her wits left her?

He gave the driver an address. As they sped away, he told her about the small club, and it belonged to one of his Jamaican schoolmates, and had she ever heard the world's foremost double bass, Ron Carter, and he meant, like, up close and personal?

"You're from Jamaica."

"In Jamaica I was a hungry boy, and my family lived on the jungle river near Ocho Rios. Daddy and Madda always singing, and"—he wove his fingers in the air—"there was music in her walk. Daddy raised ganja and goats, and we sold the ganja from beneath a blanket in the market to the tourists from the ships. You must not let the police see,"—he shook his head and his finger—"no way. Madda carved figures from cedar and strung them with wire and painted them so bright. Have you ever seen a green leopard?"

The rain had stopped. The sounds of tire spray filled the cab and multi-colored drops, like living jewels, raced across the windows.

"The boys and I—before the sun—we fished each morning when we swam into the dark ocean with our spear guns. Big strings of fish we took to the side of the road, and we sold them in an hour.

In Ocho Rios there is music in the streets, and it shouts from speakers as big as busses, and the tourists who were bold enough to leave the walls of their resorts were lost and stunned because Jamaica is hot and loose and loud. We followed them—the tourists. I wanted to be like them and be rich and have their clothes and a beautiful woman and a big watch and a Ferrari and listen to the Rolling Stones."

Anthony's power—he's like the tide.

His friend Edmond was her size and twice as animated as Anthony. They had arrived between sets, and Edmond came from behind the bar cackling. "It is the Guzzi Mon, everyone! Anthony-the-Guzzi-Mon Williams!"

They hugged and Anthony lifted him off his feet. He lowered him and introduced Miriam. With a huge, gap-toothed smile, Edmond spread his arms and approached her. Miriam moved back too late. Edmond held her in a waltz and was on his toes as Brubeck's *Three to Get Ready* tinkled like a chandelier from the sound system. She looked wide-eyed over his shoulder to Anthony.

"I think he likes you!"

Edmond backed away from his partner and bowed. "Thank you for a lovely dance, madam. Please allow me." He took her arm in his and led them to a corner booth with a "reserved" sign.

"Thank you, Sir Edmond. A chardonnay for the lady and one of your healing fruit concoctions for me, old friend."

"A fruit concoction would be good for me, too," she said.

Edmond held two fingers up to his bartender and expanded his cheeks. "I need one minute. And Ron will want to say hello." He disappeared, and a few moments later a very tall, slim man squeezed in next to her.

"Ron, mon," Anthony said. They bumped fists.

"Brother Anthony."

"Miriam, meet the inimitable and nice guy, Ron Carter."

Ron gently shook Miriam's hand and hers was swallowed in his. "It's my pleasure," he said. His smile, embracing.

Delighted, she looked back and forth between the men as they caught up.

"Miriam may be at a loss, Ron." Anthony winked at her.

"Yes," she said. "This evening spins quickly."

Anthony asked Ron, "You are teaching?"

"Always—teaching, learning, playing. There are a couple students with us tonight. And I heard about your new spot. People say you're irresistible—a sensational new talent."

"Am I the thorn between two roses?" Miriam asked.

"Our apologies," Ron said. "How do you spend your waking hours, Miriam—beautiful young woman, marked by sophistication and intelligence?"

"Well, that's a lot to live up to. I'm a curator at the Whitney."

"Boom!" Anthony exploded his hands.

"I'd love to hear more about that." Ron checked his watch. "Please excuse me, and it is an honor, Miriam. See you in the next set." He slid out and was gone.

"You let me go on about myself, and you don't tell me I am a goat, and you are the goatherd?" Anthony said.

She laughed and laid her hand on his. "You are not a goat, and your story is lovely—incredibly colorful. And your energy."

Edmond was back with their drinks. He raised his eyebrows at Miriam and disappeared.

The drummer edged around the bass on the tiny stage and tucked in behind his kit.

"That's Tony Williams," Anthony said. "He and Ron played with Miles when Tony was just seventeen. This is going to be special."

In such an intimate space the music filled her pores and was as profound and transforming as the most provocative visual art that was her world. The quartet seemed to revolve around Tony, and the dynamics, and the scale and colors advancing and receding, the release of power, and the punctuation of rests between phrases. The music *lived* in the time it created.

They shared a cab back to her place, and they exchanged numbers.

"Thank you for this extraordinary evening." She touched his arm and stepped out to the curb.

A thoughtful pause, and he blew a kiss.

She closed the door and waved as they pulled away. She stood for a moment and recounted the night. Had Irvin shown up, none of this would have happened. And Larry had already left the event, and there was no pressing reason for her to stay at the gallery, and from the very start there had been a palpable magnetism between them.

He'd sent a kiss.

She thought she loved jazz. She loved waltzing with Edmond and sampling his healing fruit concoction. Tonight, the cab rides were transcendent. The rain had left the streets shimmering, everything in fine focus, and the traffic lights glowed brighter than she'd ever seen. The air—so fresh after the rain with its tiny negative particles riding fat and happy oxygen molecules—and it was like the hippo dance and Shostakovich conducting *Fantasia*.

She took in a long, new breath. A light-headed exhilaration. Would she call him? Tonight? Would he call her when he got home?

30

Barely Dressed? 1992

They had both exercised discretion and restraint, and her every nerve stood on end. It was three days later, he called. There was a Jamaican street fair in Flatbush Sunday afternoon, and would she like to go? Kids, food, music, and dancing, and it would be muggy and hot and loud and the men finely dressed and the women barely dressed, and it would feel like every night in Montego Bay.

"Barely dressed?" she asked.

He stuttered for a moment, then said it would be *some* women—*other* women—and that the two of them would be an exemplary demonstration of tasteful decorum.

She laughed. "Okay."

That Sunday was the beginning of a new portrait of her life in the city. Anthony's palette was fearless and rich, and they danced to a music she hadn't known. They saw Ron again as well as other jazz greats, and Miriam hadn't roller-skated since youth fellowship outings from her dad's church. In a few weeks, with Anthony's help and encouragement, she was skating backward with confidence. His skating was of his nature and fluid. He spun and whirled on one skate, his head nearly to the floor, then rising up and his arms like wings as he slowed and sped in the current of the music and the colored lights—a black swan on wheels. Over the next six months they were together nearly every leisure moment—he at her place or she at his.

Anthony loved record shops and pulled title after title from the bins featuring his recording friends at Tower Records. On their second trip there, a gravelly baritone behind them grumbled, "Look, don't touch, cause lookin I don't mind."

Miriam turned. Anthony eased the LP back into place and, keeping his fingers in the stacks said, "Pay no attention to the old hippy quoting Little Feat from *Representing the Mambo*, Miriam. You will regret encouraging him." He turned and bumped fists with the man, both of them laughing. "Miriam, meet Russ Solomon. He owns this joint, and you would think he'd have it cleaned once in a while."

"Fuck you back, Williams. And nice to meet you, Miriam." They shook. "By the way, Anthony, I saw that doctor's spot. You're getting better." He winked at Miriam. "And to think this is where he got his start."

"He made me the man I am," Anthony said. "Gave me my first job in New York and for low pay, long hours, and no benefits. I couldn't wait to leave, and that was his gift to me."

"Hah! It was here he was discovered, Miriam. A fashion photographer friend from Japan walks in here, sees this disproportion-ately beautiful Jamaican, and the rest is history. You think it was an accident my friend came in that day?"

Anthony put his arm over Russ's shoulders. "And now Russ has two hundred stores in fifteen countries and his hamster-cage-of-an office in Sacramento."

"Roots, Anthony. Never forget your roots."

31

Guzzi Mon, 1992

Anthony got Miriam started with her own small jazz library after talking her into esoteric stereo hardware. "No digital, only vinyl. And not the biggest or most expensive, but high quality," he said.

So now she had a modest stereo system and the start of a growing jazz collection—*Kinda Blue*—"The first and most essential."—Herbie Hancock's *Maiden Voyage,* Coltrane, Ella and Louis, Lee Morgan, Brubeck, and Art Blakey's *Moanin'.*

Some weekends they stayed in, removed from the all of it, and Sunday mornings Anthony spoiled her with his perfect, freshly baked croissants.

She curled at one end of the couch with a book, and he spread out on his back with his fuzzy socks in her lap as he combed through *Backstage.*

She closed her book. "Guzzi Mon?"

"Yes?" He lowered the magazine.

"Edmond called you 'Guzzi Mon.'"

"Oh, that." He raised the magazine.

"So 'guzzi' is patois? Maybe it means cozy? Like, you're Cozy Mon?"

"Ha! 'Cozy Mon.' I like that. No, Guzzi is Italian—Carlo Guzzi. He started a motorcycle company about a hundred years ago on Lake Cuomo—Moto Guzzi." He folded the corner of the page.

"And?"

He lowered the magazine. "I found one as a boy—a Moto Guzzi, overgrown and lifeless in the jungle. I hacked away at him and freed him from his tormentors. I hacked more and made a clearing around him, and for two years I tore into my great fortune right where I found him. I begged for tools, took things apart, cleaned and polished, replaced chewed wires and the cracked battery. My friends and I borrowed a battery from one of the resorts. That Guzzi ended up with a lot of resort parts. Tires were a problem, but my uncle knows a guy in Kingston, and one day he showed up with two tires and spark plugs. Long before I proudly rode my motorcycle into Ocho Rios, I had become Guzzi Mon—always a joke. I was fifteen, and after that ride down the middle of town and through the crowded market there was no more joke. Guzzi Mon is a hero." He raised the magazine.

"Geez, Anthony!"

He'd been picking up television work, each role more significant than the last since the airing of the Doctors Without

Borders spot. Recently he'd landed a role on *Law & Order.* She was so glad for him and feared what would likely be their end.

It was a Saturday morning at eleven when he said, "I must go to LA."

"Of course."

"It will be a couple months."

She rose from his bed, wrapped the sheet around her, and went out to the kitchen.

"Miriam."

"I'll make you coffee." She put on a pot of water and snatched the bag from the cupboard.

He was in his pajama bottoms at the kitchen doorway. "This is big. I will go to LA, and I will call each night. Then I will come home."

She counted the tablespoons into the French press. "One. Two. Three. Four."

"Marco will be here, and he will know where I am every minute."

Her back to him, she simmered. A long minute, and the water boiled. She switched off the burner, grabbed a dish towel, and poured the water onto the grounds. "You're shuffling me off to your agent?"

"Miriam. No. You are angry, and this is not fair."

She stirred the coffee, topped it with the plunger lid, pulled the sheet tighter, and leaned back against the counter. "What isn't fair, Anthony? That you are going to leave, and we won't see each other ever again? You say you're coming back, but I can't help feeling this is the end for us."

"No. We will be together. This is one job, then I will be back. We will go skating."

"May I say something I think I have never said?"

He slipped his hands into his pajama pockets and leaned his shoulder on the doorframe. He nodded.

"Bullshit!"

And she was right. As intimate and wonder-filled as their short life together had been, it tapered away. The nightly calls dwindled to weekly, then occasionally, then nothing. LA scooped him up like its newest flavor, and he was a star, and he had a celebrity agent, and there were awards shows, and his portrait on the cover of *Rolling Stone,* and he lived on Mulholland Drive with a Ferrari.

I couldn't take time from work when he left, or I might have gone to LA with Anthony. It might all be different if I had. But you can't force these things, can you? Love? I had invested so much of myself in him, in us. For months, I was emotionally lost, then overtaken by self-doubt. I wasn't grand enough, tall enough, sexy enough. I didn't deserve him. I didn't deserve any of this. He is large in life, so comfortable in the world. It appears that he is living his dream. I hope he's happy.

32

A Pot to Piss In, 1995

A couple years after Anthony left for LA, Irvin and Miriam tested the dating waters, so to speak. Of course she'd always liked him, was amused by him—appreciated his smarts, talent, and humor—and they'd been a great team. She, his senior for eight of the past eleven years.

And he kept her in stitches over his daft stories—some more believable than others—like conning his way through the attainment of his master's degree and his studies in Paris. At least the parts of that raucous Paris semester he could remember. Over drinks at the Ramona, he gave Paris the Irvin-over-the-top spin—his rumpled sheets and those come-to-Jesus mornings.

"I had an attic room six stories up. Unheated. The last flight, I had to grapple the young lovelies up a friggin ladder. And did I mention there was no running water? Walk to school in the snow? Hah! I used a butane bottle to boil ravioli and warm my hands."

He said he'd shared a first-floor toilet with six others and, in the middle of the night, had to race the stair lights down each flight because they were on timers. That, or piss into his ravioli pot.

"Geez, Irvin!"

He took a sip, slid his glass farther back on the bar, snuffed out his cigarette, and parked on forearms and elbows.

"I knew people who knew people who hung out at Les Bains. It's a nineteenth-century public bath where the likes of Proust and Manet used to unwind."

"I've read of Manet at the baths."

"Yeah? Well, in the seventies, it was redone as a sexy night club for celebs and other fops." He pulled his glass back in, took a hit. "The place was thirty-percent provocation, thirty-percent figuration, thirty-percent art, and ten-percent insanity. The Gazolines played once in a while—non-binary—with their giant penis-of-an emblem. The wetter, the better at the baths, right?"

A trio of squad cars passed the Ramona, sirens screaming. "See? Some aberrant shit going down as we speak.

I carried a discreet Leica in my jacket and snapped a lot of smut at the baths. This one night, Karl Lagerfeld shows up in heels and earrings, a revealing one-piece, and all his junk flopping around. My friggin Master's Review Committee went ape shit over *that* shot."

33

Prague, 1995

Perhaps it was their trip to Prague—and the indelible, if less-than-romantic experiences they shared—that had been proximate, if-bruising, cause for a shift in their relationship.

They were in Prague to meet the director of the Central Gallery, and the Warhol's owner, Brigitte Bardot, and to sign for the loan of the print.

At the hotel, and it hardly seemed like a hotel, the driver had taken their bags from the back of the van, through the tired arched doorway, and into the small registration desk. He exchanged a few polite words with the young woman there, tipped his cap, and left.

Long, graceful fingers took their passports. The woman spoke English as clearly as she likely spoke four other languages. She wasn't what one would call glamorous. Her physical attraction, which was abundant, was squared with professionalism and self-confidence. She was probably an accomplished skier, an expert shooter, and could handle horses.

"It is a fifteenth-century building, this boutique hotel—very restful, attentive personal service, and a small dining room west of the bar should you choose to dine in—five tables."

Irvin mouthed to Miriam, "West?"

The woman smiled and pointed. "That way. Please call down for anything you will need from the bar or the kitchen as late as midnight. Emile will bring it to you." She was busy at the keyboard, then asked, "This is business travel?"

"We're here to meet with staff at the Central Gallery tomorrow morning," Miriam said.

"You have chosen your hotel wisely. Central Gallery Prague is a ten-minute walk, and you will pass interesting sites along the way." She presented tourist maps from beneath the counter. "Two of my friends are curatorial assistants there. Everyone thinks they are twins."

Rows apart, they had been confined on the full plane for ten hours. In her room, Miriam's release was complete as she flopped back onto the bed. Fresh flowers on the dresser, a mirrored armoire in the corner, and beyond the broad, curtained window, the hushed thribbing of small cars on the narrow, cobblestone street one story below.

The air was different here. The smells and sounds low and resonant as in a lute's shell. She closed her eyes and imagined lurid tales from within the walls, lusty laughter, and loamy song from the tavern below. This room—its clean, contemporary surfaces hiding centuries-old, and massive, ax-hewn posts and beams. She nodded off.

34

Math Camp, 1995

She woke in the near dark. *Phew.* She checked her watch. Little power nap. Unpack, freshen up, and meet Irvin downstairs in thirty.

How could he be so attractive, even from the back? Her entry to the lobby had been silent down carpeted stairs.

The receptionist was in the middle of explaining something, and it appeared they'd been talking for a while, and that Irvin's mojo was working. He leaned across the counter, their faces nearly touched.

". . . so there are two tickets available." The woman looked up. "Oh. Here is your dinner date."

Irvin spun around. "You look refreshed."

"Tiny nap, and I'm starving."

"Good. Gabriella's made a reservation. It's a short walk and a place you'll love—garlic soup and cold beer."

"Hmm. Well then, and thank you Gabriella," she said. "Shall we?"

The narrow, stone walks sloped away from the buildings to the cobbled street, and Irvin mentioned that walking home from a bar could be an issue. Silver and gold exchanges, antique shops, a tobacco emporium, ice cream, and cafes—the street was storybook intimate, with most structures reaching up three stories. They passed beneath rings of light cast by heavy bronze sconces that may have been from the eighteenth century.

"August in Prague, Irv." She slipped her arm into his. "Isn't it romantic?"

He patted her arm. "Yes, boss."

She leaned into him. "Not for us, of course. But isn't it? Romantic?"

"You're sure, 'not for us?' This is the place."

"Bohemian folk mannequins?" she asked.

"Too funny, right? Gabi said it was kitsch, but the food's good."

"Gabi?"

"Gabriella—at the hotel."

"Of course."

They entered what appeared to be a Disney version of Bohemian life in the nineteenth century and found menus in six languages. There were more mannequins, murals, and garlic and onion clusters hung from the ceiling. The place rattled and chattered, and the diners seemed to be enjoying themselves. Irvin found a table on the patio.

"You'll try a beer, right? When in Rome?"

"If I must. I thought we had reservations—there's no host."

"Reservations? Figure of speech. The Czechs aren't big on fancy schmancy. They think it slows down what we came for—food and drinks."

Two pilsners showed up, and they ordered two bowls of the famous garlic soup.

Miriam was startled at the beers—their size. "Is this a quart?"

"Liter. Cheers." Irvin lofted his.

She sniffed hers.

"Stop that!" he whispered. "You want to get us thrown out?"

She raised her mug with both hands and they *clicked.* She took a sip. "It's not so bad."

"Miriam, to the Czechs, this is their finest wine. If anyone asks, it's fabulous—absolutely the best. The Czechs drink more beer per capita than anywhere else in the world. The second-most country is a far-distant second." His mug was a half-liter low.

"Right, right. I'll be a sport. And I'm sorry this had to be such a quick trip. The director—you know?"

"I wouldn't want your job," he said. "It's great to have you between him and me. I'd never be able to suffer his hisness the way you do. I'd last ten minutes."

"Speaking out of school," she said, "he doesn't show a lot of interest for the institution, but makes quite an investment in self-promotion. Is anyone home at the board? I mean, he's great at working a room, accepting praise, but fiscally . . . Enough about work."

"Please!" When did we become these adults having to be so serious all the time? I mean, do you ever let your hair down, short as it is?" He took a drink.

"Well of course, I've dated."

"In the last few years?"

"There was Anthony."

"Couple years ago." He lowered his mug. "What about high school? You have any fun?"

"Debating club, president of the student council, and I was in the band."

"Whoohoo! Now we're talking. What about the prom? Stay out all night? Carnal steam in the backseat?"

"I was prom queen and came home immediately after the prom. I had to work at the shelter the next day."

"A teenage trollop."

She crossed her eyes. "Okay. What about you? How did the young Irvin spend *his* summers?"

"Math camp." His mug was empty. A buxom server in a puffy-sleeved blouse replaced it seamlessly.

"Math."

"Yep. Nerdy kids from the Northeast and me. My parents made me go, and I mostly hated it—off to the Poconos every summer with humidity, bugs, and it included a trip to an amusement park. The counsellors gave us each a roll of tickets, and told us to forget math for the afternoon, and have some fun. Were they nuts? For most of those whack-job kids, math *was* the fun. At the end of the day, a lot of them still had all their tickets. Some had given theirs to me, being the social, charismatic one in the group. It's easy to pick up girls with a couple rolls of tickets."

"Sorry I asked."

"There's more. Up for it?"

"I'll stop you if I can't stand another word."

"I took a girl to the senior prom who punched way above my weight. She dated college guys, but she didn't have a date to the prom, go figure."

"She was also into math?"

"Not even close. She was the beautiful, long-legged drum majorette for the band and famous for leading them up blind alleys. All of a sudden, a hundred marching musicians playing *Lady Marmalade* to a dumpster."

Miriam laughed. "What did she wear?"

"Majorette stuff—boots, big furry hat."

"To the prom."

"Oh. White and pastel, I think. Probably satin, and—hell, I don't know. She could march, but she couldn't dance, so we didn't, and it was my first and worst prom. The band played *Get Down Tonight,* and that song makes my lungs shake and my legs twitch. I wanted to dance and get loose, but she wouldn't. Also, I was using a cane from a game-saving football injury, but I was faking it. We went back to her place after the prom where her mom changed her into a chastity belt and jeans for the after parties."

"Geez, Irv."

"Yeah. Good night, Irene. Meanwhile loads of my mates were having the nights of their lives. Some consummated the evening and are married to this day. I dropped her off at her place at four, went home, and forgot about it. Lift a colorless benchmark of your life over your head, shake it, and it's a blank Etch-a-Sketch."

"Where is she now?"

"She married a square-jawed rich guy who raises sheep, had a couple daughters, and she's herding little woolies over cliffs."

"You are so full of it."

"Neighbors are alarmed at their plaintive bleats."

Conversation shifted with the arrival of the steaming soup and Irvin's third beer. The soup was soulful, thick, and complex, and like nothing she'd imagined—she said she could live on the aroma alone.

Satiated, they reposed in the glow of that Czech-garlic-soup stupor and watched the comings and goings beneath the clusters of allium vegetables.

Snapping out of his languor, Irvin suggested they continue their stroll and walk off that totally gut-stuffing meal—he didn't mention the three liters of beer—and see what they could see. They headed toward the river and Lesser Town.

35

Why? 1995

It's like New York, or anywhere else, isn't it?" Irvin said.

"What?"

"Prague. I mean, look over there—McDonald's. How long until Starbucks shows up on every corner?"

"I guess I'd rather overlook that. Surrounding that McDonald's it's all Prague."

"Uh-huh. Wake up tomorrow and everyone's eating what the Colonel cooks."

They crossed an expansive plaza with a cloud of weed in the air and a trio of buzz-cut young people running about with nets on poles.

"Were we like that, *ever*?" Irvin asked. "Free to get high and frolic about in the park? And shouldn't they be doing homework, or something?"

"There were others around us who were happy and living in the moment. You and I were too driven."

"You, for sure. I made my own fun, especially in college, and I made a lot of money doing it, as if that mattered. Got caught on few snags, but came out clean except for my Destiny."

"Your destiny."

"Yeah, fate can get serious. My Destiny hung upside down naked on a brass pole and winked at me. Crazy, right?"

"You're losing me."

"The woman who stole my heart. Her name was Destiny—a pole dancer."

"I guess I don't want to hear why you were in a strip club and a dancer winked at you."

"Curse of these tight g-genes, you know?" He ran his hands down his sides. "Tall, smart, handsome to a fault—"

"Please stop!"

A little farther down the walk and, "Are you and Destiny still together?"

"I've skated through a lot, got away with plenty, but Destiny finally said she'd had it with my betrayals and left."

"Why do you do that?"

"What?"

"Betray."

"Nature of the beast. And, *why* is a useless question. *What, where, when*, those have answers. *Why* is a crap shoot."

"*Why* is not useless if it leads to further questions."

“Thank you, Sherlock. Hey, look at this.”

They stood at a three-way intersection before a sandwich board chalked in English. There was jazz downstairs tonight—Geri Allen, cocktails, and Guinness on tap.

A cab moved in close and slow. Did they need a ride? Irvin smiled and waved him off.

“Check it out?” Irvin asked.

“Absolutely!”

36

Geri Allen, 1995

It was like a small New York bar—or better yet, Paris—with its low, vaulted ceiling, eclectic furniture, and a confusion of wall trappings. Whoever did the decorating had conflicting tastes. Behind the bar were two young hip bartenders, lit bottles, and the sound system played mellow jazz. The room was easing into what would be a long night according to a small sign hung from the ceiling, "Serving until 3 a.m."

Irvin led to the bar. "Sit for something refreshing before going downstairs?"

"Should we see if we can get a table first?"

"Not a chance," the bartender approached—cute young woman with multiple piercings and straw hair piled high and pinned as if accidently. "Right now you might be able to squeeze in and stand at the back."

"Can we take a drink down?" Irvin asked.

"What would you like?"

Downstairs they edged into a back corner beneath a low ceiling. The audience sat shoulder to shoulder and across from each other at three rows of banquet tables running the length of the dark room, and, at the far end were stage-lit drums, keyboard, and a bass guitar. Miriam sipped her soda. Irvin swilled scotch.

Seated at the middle row of tables, two American couples sat across from each other and seemed well into their evening—which may have started at noon. The women blinged in mega jewelry and were loud. The large men also wore mega jewelry and were loud and sported faded-orange, "Hook 'em Horns" T-shirts that did little to hide their bellies. The couples, with a few pitchers of beer between them, glowed cadmium red and looked like, come winter, they could heat the place.

Applause rippled front to back. Geri Allen had taken her place at the keys. The drummer and bass player were queued, and the trio went right into it.

Allen led the way with ferocious rhythms and counter rhythms from Zimbabwe to Detroit, the bass player's eyes never left her, and the drummer stitched her lyrical syncopation over, under, around, and through. The small room shook with feral intensity. Five life-changing minutes later there was that bottomless moment when everyone remembered they hadn't been breathing followed by an eruption of cheers and applause. Geri Allen acknowledged her audience, nodded, and smiled into the mic. "It is an honor and a pleasure to be here with you tonight and to experience this music together . . . "

To Miriam's left, there was a shuffling, scratching, and bumping commotion as three heavily mascaraed, buzz-cut-and-giggling young people tumbled down the stone steps and into the room. They wrestled a large cardboard box. The standing crowd in the back was further smooshed as the three lowered the box to the floor and opened it.

PIGEONS!

The room exploded. Tables toppled and screams screamed. Panicked patrons and petrified pigeons launched in every direction. A feathered projectile rocketed at Miriam. She ducked, it slammed into Irvin's shoulder, did a quick midair tumble, and changed its flight plan.

Startled stage lights lit dust rays and feathers, and someone shrieked, "Get it out!" A woman flailed as others tried to disengage a terrified avian from freaked-out hair. Across the room the drummer quickly broke down her kit and got the pieces stashed. Geri Allen and the bass player were long gone.

Above it all a man yelled, "Got ya, ya little pecker!"

Miriam and Irvin were pinned in place as the surging mass made for the exit. In her panic, a corpulent woman jammed Miriam's face into the stone wall, and, "Ahh!"—her hand to her eye.

Miriam and Irvin stood alone with the settling, pecking and gurgling birds as the last of the crowd escaped.

37

She Didn't Sleep on Her Back, 1995

Upstairs, the police were escorting the three young anarchists to their evening's lodging. At the bar, Miriam held a bag of ice to her eye. Irvin held a scotch.

This was awful. They should have gone back to their hotel after the garlic soup. They should be asleep right now. They had an important meeting in the morning, and they had to be charming and sharp. So why were they sitting at a bar in Prague, and Irvin was ordering another drink and obscenely flirting with the twenty-something bartender?

He could be her father.

And what if she started showing signs of enjoying his quips, his lilting stories, his lovely profile? Would he invite her to his room? Across the hall from hers? Not a bad bet. Then, in the morning, would the freshly showered young woman, skin aglow and her hair in a damp braid, join them for breakfast? Really, Irvin?

Concert cancelled, the manager apologized and offered another round on the house—Irvin was quick to raise his glass.

There was three-deep-and-soaring twaddle at the bar reliving the episode that would be told and retold in multiple languages over the following decades.

The dozen pigeons would grow to hundreds, and a story emanating from the Netherlands holds that a few birds remained and propagated—that feathers continue to float down from the lights and land in drinks to this day.

Marketers that they were, the bar's owners would add a special martini to their selection—"Squab Drop." It would be distinguished by a small white, finger-rolled turd of feta and minced olives in the bottom of the glass, and available in gin or vodka.

The manager felt horrible about Miriam's eye and drove them to their hotel.

Her head throbbed. She took a couple aspirin and went to bed. Her eye hurt and everything was tired—her feet, her ankles, and those cobbled stones.

Tomorrow was Friday. They had a 10:30 at the Central where they'd meet the director and her staff, tour the museum, and lunch with Brigitte Bardot. The Bardot piece was troubling. She imagined one of the world's most famous women to have been pampered all her life and to be impossible. That they would be required to coddle her would be keenly embarrassing and morally eroding. She guessed the woman could care less about the art and was using this opportunity to advance her animal rights foundation. Fine. Miriam was authorized to pay homage, and she had a check for fifty-grand for the cause.

Following lunch, there would be a little chit-chat, a light dessert, and a late afternoon flight back to New York.

The pillow, soft as it was, hurt her face in every direction. The least painful was flat on her back. She never slept on her back.

38

This Isn't Good, 1995

She woke with a stunning shiner. Her eyelid puffed and bloomed purple, blue, and red, and there was nothing in her makeup bag that could handle this. Three hours. She had three hours to do something about her eye before the meeting.

Showered and dressed, she tenderly slipped on sunglasses and went down to the lobby.

"Good morning, Gabriella."

"Madam."

"Gabriella, is there a store nearby where I can buy cosmetics?"

"There is, but they are not open until ten."

Her shoulders dropped. "This isn't good."

"Madam?"

Muriel raised her glasses.

"Oh! I am so sorry. Shall I call a physician? The police? How did this happen?"

"It was an accident, and it looks worse than it is. It was at a club last night. Pigeons."

"Ahh, U Malého Glena. The jazz club. I read about it."

"We have a meeting at the Central this morning, and I can't go like this."

"Have a coffee and breakfast. By the time you finish, my assistant will be here, and I will join you in your room. We will fix your eyes."

39

Central Gallery Prague, 1995

Following Gabriella's cosmetic and wardrobe adjustments, Miriam stood in sunglasses outside the hotel watching Friday morning on the narrow street. Locals bustled about doing the things locals do—picking up a basket of goods from the little shop with the red door, pushing the stroller to the park, waiting for the tram.

Irvin joined her. "Ready to rock?"

"You must be built from iron," she said. They started off toward the Central Gallery.

"How so?" He lit a smoke.

"You don't show any signs of the sopping despot you were last night."

"I like your shades."

No reply.

"Nice scarf. Bright for you. Decorative. Nipping at garish. Shades, scarf—trying a new look, I guess—barely within the realm of acceptable for chief curator at the Whitney. You know, maybe we should look for shoes while we're here."

"Thank you." She wasn't listening. She was focused. She'd forgotten about her bruises, the make-up, Gabriella's false lashes, and the scarf. At the Central Gallery, they would make a strong impression, sign the contract for the Warhol, suffer lunch with Brigitte Bardot, and leave. She'd barely slept.

"Central Gallery Prague makes quite a footprint," Irvin said. They passed through the public market stalls on their approach. "Which door?"

Miriam pointed. Minutes later, they entered a vaulted Renaissance archway and were into a busy contemporary space in contrast to the building's historic façade. Irvin drifted off to a gallery dedicated to Dali.

Director Anna Marie Novåk appeared from a nearby catacomb in a bowl cut, soft soles, and round, tortoiseshell glasses. She was followed by two side-by-side young men in trim, nearly matching suits and ties. They wore brown wingtips. Gabriella's friends, Miriam thought.

"And you are Miriam, here for the Warhol, and welcome." The director extended her hand. "You are alone?"

Miriam removed her sunglasses and they shook. The two lieutenants exchanged quick glances and raised their eyebrows ever slightly.

"It is a pleasure to meet you in person. Irvin's here somewhere. He wandered off down that hall," she nodded.

"Then he is deep into surrealism. Shall we find him as I show you around?"

"Please."

"These are my assistants, to whom I owe fashion advice, rapier criticism, and much of the recognition I receive. It is they who keep us on the edge of the razor—Anton and Andrej."

Deadpan, the two A's shook Miriam's hand after which they resumed their positions.

The four started off in Irvin's direction as the director related stories behind the artist. "It was at the London Surrealist Exhibition in 1936 that Dali nearly suffocated. He chose to give his lecture attired in deep-sea diving gear. Something went wrong with his air supply, and, as he gestured wildly in his panic, the audience laughed and cheered. Fortunately he was able to release the lock on his helmet and escape his death. If you would like more or less information, please tell me. Anton and Andrej agree that I can be talkative. I love giving tours."

The boys glanced at each other.

They rounded a corner, and there was Irvin, bent at the waist, his face inches from a canvas.

"And this must be Irvin," the director said.

Irvin straightened and smiled. "And you are Professor Novåk?" They shook. His eyes met Miriam's, and he didn't hide his shock. "I—"

"What?" Miriam said.

"I see you've caught me astonished at some incredible brushwork." He grinned.

"Infinitesimal strokes," the director said, "Dali's flesh feels alive. And Irvin, please meet Anton and Andrej."

The boys shook his hand.

An hour later, they were in the director's spacious, fourth-floor office. Her young lions had peeled off at their den with the iron cell door. Inside the director's office, her windows open to Old Town's spires and castellated charm, a chain rattled in the breeze. Miriam and Irvin were surrounded by terribly imaginative swords, pikes, axes, and two suits of armor. The ornately framed Warhol screen print perched on an easel behind her desk. Irvin stood at the window.

"Irvin, would you please sign this?" Miriam asked. "Below my signature?"

He signed the contract, then puttered around examining—touching—the weapons.

From out in the hall, one of the lieutenants beckoned the director.

"Excuse, please." She left the room.

Irvin was back at the window. "Red tile roofs for days. Our little hotel neighborhood makes Prague feel so quaint with its tiny shops and narrow streets. This is total urban sprawl. And who did your eyes, Jezebel?"

"Must you? You know—"

"Shall we meet Ms. Bardot?" The director was back.

40

With Brigitte Bardot, 1995

The director, Miriam, and Irvin enjoyed historied views through the tall, arched windows of a neighboring café as they awaited the arrival of their distinguished guests. The director and Irvin sipped pilsners, Miriam a Pepsi Max. Ms. Bardot would be arriving with Roger Vadim—friend, filmmaker, and former husband.

French. Miriam was hearing French as Ms. Bardot and Mr. Vadim approached from the hall and appeared behind the director. *God, she's still beautiful!*—Brigitte's entry as if on air.

The three at the table stood. Greetings all around, hugs and kisses, and Irvin took the opportunity for what was, by any measure, an awkwardly long hug. Stepping back from Brigitte, he kept her hands in his and nearly swooned, "Maintenant je peux mourir heureux."

Now he can die happy?

Brigitte smiled and responded in French. Irvin appeared confused.

"You are a beautiful man," she said in English. "I love you both already, and you may borrow my Warhol. Would you like to come work with me, Irvin? To save the animals?"

Irvin looked like he was considering it.

Roger addressed the director. "A clear day in your city, Professor Novåk. Brigitte and I have been enjoying the market this morning."

"Yes, and, please, I am Anna. Shall we sit?" She gestured for the waiter.

Brigitte placed two cigarettes between her lips, lit them and gave one to Roger. The wine arrived. Roger poured.

Miriam was distracted as Anna and Brigitte chatted in French. How was it that, at sixty, light fell so perfectly on Brigitte, and it was as if on the wide screen—the camera slowly circling and imperceptibly moving in ever closer, the advancement of years diffused through the slow motion of smoke drifting up from sensual lips as she spoke?

Anna laughed and turned to Miriam. "Brigitte wants to know if I have a fish, a goat, or a donkey. And would I like one?"

Brigitte lit two more smokes and, holding them between her fingers, continued in French. Roger snuffed his old one and reached over.

Brigitte asked, "And you, Miriam, do you have animals in your life?"

Miriam glanced at Irvin. "No, however, . . . " She reached into her shoulder bag on the chair back. "I have something for your foundation." She handed the check across the table.

Brigitte examined the check, smiled, and passed it to Roger. She rose, held her cigarette high and away, and flowed around to Miriam as though she'd rehearsed for weeks. She kissed Miriam on the cheek, carefully removed a tear from her own mascara, and returned to her seat. She spoke in rapid-fire French. Seconds later Roger translated.

"Brigitte says you are a gorgeous, young, and vibrant person to care for the animals as she does. The Dalai Lama has recently joined her foundation, and now you are joined with Dennis." He shrugged. "The Dalai Lama asked her to call him, 'Dennis.' She is serious about your handsome Irvin coming to work for her. And she says you don't need to paint your eyes as she does only because it is expected of her. Be yourself. Also, don't give your body away as frequently as she has." He shrugged again.

Miriam sat dazed.

Brigitte was wound up and selling another idea to Anna in French. Anna shared, "She would like us to meet tomorrow and visit an animal shelter. She will be alone one day as Roger leaves tonight."

Miriam regrouped. "Oh, I'm sorry, but we have a flight this afternoon."

"Maybe we could, Miriam."

"Irvin, our flight."

"I was meaning to ask if we could stay another day."

Miriam blushed and apologized to the table. "Would you please excuse us for a moment? Irvin?" She placed her napkin on her chair and went out to the hallway. Irvin followed.

Her arms folded, "What is this?"

He was a total fidget—fingers aflutter, then through his hair. Anxious linen slacks and he paced. "It's The Stones in Prague, Miriam. Tomorrow night, and we're already here. The Voodoo Lounge Tour, and I got tickets . . . from Gabi."

She leaned on astonishment.

His arms spread in plea, "It's just one more day, Miriam—you, me, and The Stones. This is friggin big!"

"Irvin we can't."

"We can."

"I'm not."

"I am."

"Must I draw the line here? Like, this is finally *it?*"

"No. C'mon Miriam. One more day?"

"I'm leaving in a few hours, Irvin. Going back to New York as planned and budgeted."

"I'll pay the difference," he said.

"And Monday morning when I show up for the director's meeting with a bizarrely colored eye and you're nowhere to be found?"

"I can fly back Sunday."

"You'll be in no shape Sunday."

"Tell them I got sick. Food poisoning. Garlic soup."

He wears me out. She adjusted her demeanor, turned, and went back to the silent table. Irvin arrived seconds later and slowly, sheepishly, lowered onto his chair.

"I will go to the concert with you," Brigitte said. She and Roger had fresh smokes.

"I . . . Wow!" Irvin said. "No, I'm sorry. I've upset this lovely lunch. I—"

"Our apologies," Miriam cut in, "this is embarrassing. We infrequently behave as children—and never in front of others. A small misunderstanding, and we're better now. We appreciate your patience."

Brigitte released a thin stream of smoke from the side of her mouth and backhand-waved her cigarette. Her eyes, those lips, all Irvin. "I have no influence—you will stay, or you will go. If you stay, we visit the shelter with Anna. Then we go to the concert. We won't need tickets. Do you want to meet Mick?"

For the first time, in maybe forever, Irvin was speechless.

41

Staying Inside the Lines, 1995

On the tarmac awaiting takeoff, Miriam raced through the last two days. The three college kids catching pigeons—now arrested—for a premeditated, preemptive strike on what? Middle-class? Texas? Maybe simply youthful fun. She lingered at Gabriella—back there at the reception desk, as professional and helpful as ever. They hadn't talked about Gabriella's personal life as she tenderly tended to her eye. The young woman was kind, gentle—and what would her life be like when she wasn't at work? A relationship? Husband? Wife? Poet-musician, carpenter? And the bartender at the jazz club with whom Irvin was ridiculous. Another bright, industrious person of whom they knew nothing—perhaps pre-law in her room this moment studying for exams.

Geri Allen. She hadn't gone into it with Irvin, but she was thrilled that Geri Allen happened to be playing on their one night in Prague, and that they had stumbled upon her. She had a number of Allen's LPs on her shelf at home—where Anthony's coals still cooled.

And here she was, on her way back to her New York bubble.

Irvin. Off to the concert with Brigitte Bardot—and his Destiny back home, a pole dancer.

By contrast, she was boring, color-inside-the-lines and right-as-rain Miriam—a Girl Scout for life and old before her time. Falling in with Anthony? An aberration. And, why *hadn't* she gone to the after-prom parties? The warp and weft so obvious from Dad's teachings—so easily accepted as a child and now unraveled. Miriam-the-compromised and living alone with a black eye.

She looked out her window, and there were the hard-working uniformed people on little tractors pulling all the luggage. Day and night and all the seasons, they pulled the luggage.

Rethinking, she took another swing at herself—a solid swing. *She* was hard working. And conscientious. Orderly, in control, and responsible to a fault. Miriam Ruth Pastor, chief curator at the Whitney.

She removed the seatback card in front of her and scanned the red arrows pointing forward, aft, port, and starboard, and checked behind her for the nearest exit. She slipped it back into its pocket. Irvin. Claiming illness might be the best path. Keep it simple. Couldn't fly. The garlic soup. But if honesty and integrity were her choices, she would have to defend him to the director, and it would be awful. The director's ego. The word of God. He so loved his position and his office, hearing himself speak—the status, the view from his condo, and his fashion awareness as chronicled in *The Sunday Times.* He would be quick to ask about Irvin—he always asked about Irvin.

She would have to mask her exposure and appear confidently relaxed in one of his Mies van der Rohe chairs before responding.

42

A Day in Central Park, 1995

Having returned from Prague, Miriam and Irvin found themselves in each other's company more frequently—she in his office, he in hers. They'd hidden the possible evolution of their relationship during working hours, trying to be less obvious than they were. But everyone saw it.

"Have you seen Irvin?"

"Whence goes Miriam, there, too, is Irvin."

It was *The Phantom of the Opera* that committed them to a date. Irvin had scored tickets, invited her, and it was an electric evening—dinner, the show, and a little après-theater karaoke bar. Those singers!

They'd shared a cab back to her building, and she asked if he'd like to see her apartment. She shouldn't have. Looking back, she'd sent the wrong message. They'd chatted for twenty minutes in her living room, he drank a lot of scotch, then asked, "Is this going to be a sleep-over?"

There it is, she thought. We're friends having a pleasant conversation and a lovely evening. You ask me what I'd be doing if I wasn't a curator, then that? I wanted to ask you, "What if *you* weren't a curator? Would you be a film-maker, a venture capitalist, a life coach? Do you read? What do you think of Paul Beatty? Have you traveled? Do you like the mayor? *Yankees* or *Mets*? What's your goddamn sign?" She'd called him a cab and spent the weekend trying to figure out how she felt about their date—about him.

By Monday morning she'd concluded it had been her doing—inviting him in and letting him open her uncle's scotch. It was that pair of unfortunate events that had ignited his compulsion and blown up the evening. Maybe if she'd waited until a third date—if there *was* a third date—it *would* have been a sleepover. She'd confront him after the director's meeting.

That Monday, Irvin sat in her office and listened dutifully as she replayed her point of view, though, when she got to the part about him having a screw loose, he rolled his eyes. He rebounded quickly and suggested a make-good date the next Saturday—drinks and dinner at one of the city's finest restaurants.

Really? She thought. Isn't this, *Here we go again?* She told him she had to think about it. The next day she agreed to a second date, but on her terms—lunch in a boat on the lake at the park.

Wasn't it everything they both needed—fresh air, sunshine, other happy couples and families lazing about? A Renoir afternoon.

His initial reaction had been, "You're kidding. Bugs? Sunburn? Fish?"

She said she thought it would be playful and transformative. He jumped back in with, "Of course. Let's do this. What should I wear?"

True to his magnified nature, Irvin met her at the boathouse wearing L.L. Bean's finest rendition of urban adventure—cargo shorts and an Australian bush hat. She thought it amusing and sweet that he'd gone to the trouble.

The kid at the boathouse had given Irvin a long once-over. Then he steadied the little craft as Miriam stepped in first with the picnic basket and settled amidships at the oars. Irvin followed, tipped the boat significantly, and the kid snapped, "Stay in the middle!" Irvin plopped down on his seat, his white-knuckled grips on the gunwales. The kid shoved them off.

As she rowed slowly and smoothly, the hollow sounds of the oars in their locks and the sun on her shoulders, she was taken back to her little-girl summers. Dad had taken her fishing for bluegills, and they were alone on that small Pennsylvania lake as they cast their lines into the shaded shallows. Everything about him loosened on those outings. Gone was the rigid posture of the preacher, his unyielding struggles with Nick and the devil. He relaxed. He told her stories of growing up in coal country, and the hardships they faced, and family loyalty. He also confessed that he knew he was obsessive, unyielding, and often a pain in the butt to be around—he'd actually said, "butt"—and that even *he* was a sinner. She hadn't known what to do with her father's confession, but she knew it was something special between them.

She checked back over her shoulder. They were still in the clear. Turning around, she saw that Irvin fussed. His hands jumped from their holds on the boat and tightened his hat tie. He quickly regained his grip. He glanced over the sides from left to right, and, with each movement, the boat tipped.

She asked what was wrong.

"Nothing. Shouldn't I be rowing?"

She said she enjoyed rowing and asked why he thought he should.

"Look around," he said. "You see other women rowing while the guy sits in back?"

She said she didn't realize how fragile he was regarding his masculinity.

"Not so," he said. "I'd just like to row a while."

She leaned forward, the oar grips nearly at his chest, spread her arms, and brought the tips into the bow behind her. She scooted slightly askance on her seat. She told him to stand slowly, keep his feet planted shoulder-width, and to shuffle baby steps toward her.

"Right." He stood—unsteady, bent at the waist with a firm hold on the boat.

She told him he'd have to let go and somewhat stand. He did, like heavy, greased machinery. His eyes were last to rise from the hull. They widened in horror.

A split-second and their vessel was head-on slammed. Two amped-up teenage boys, each hauling an oar, were going for the lake's speed record—and Irvin was tossed from the craft.

He floundered. He splashed. He choked and churned as he was sucked under. "Help!" he cried. "Help!"

She was about to dive in, then paused. She called for him to stand.

"I can't swim! Help!"

"Stand up!"

"What?" he sputtered. "What?" He stood.

He seemed so lost. She covered her mouth, turned aside, and nearly hid her laughter.

Little waves lapped at his belt. "It's shallow." He removed his sad hat, and he was white. "I smell like a goddamn carp."

43

Slacks and Loafers, 1995

They met the next afternoon on terra firma in SOHO. Irvin wore slacks, loafers, and a Polo—the city's most eligible bachelor. He appeared convinced that yesterday never happened. She waved from the table. He ordered a latte and joined her.

"You're looking great, Miriam. Probably up at the crack of dawn?"

"Early, yes. Sunday mornings are for escape—living the adventures of others." She patted the book next to her. "John Krakauer. *Eiger Dreams.* Pakistan, K2, and thirteen tragically lost in one summer."

"Wind-blown heroes?"

"Hardly."

"Probably pales to the bone-chilling work we do each day." He sipped.

She glanced around and whispered, "The board has begun a search for a new director."

He looked side to side, then leaned closer, "No shit. Where'd you hear that? How long have you known? What's it mean for us? Do we get to grill the candidates?"

"I overheard Todd on Friday, and it means instability, and hold on to your seat for the next couple years."

He sat back, hands on hips. "'. . . that there may be blood throughout all the land of Egypt?'"

"There may be blood."

It's impossible to express how my life had changed immediately after the theft. That it was as though I was in a small cage being poked with sharp sticks comes close. I was all nerves. I couldn't sleep or eat for weeks, and Irvin said I looked terrible. He is <u>so</u> dependable. As I dialed his lawyer, I had a shadow of hope—that, at last, I'd be in the care of my champion.

44

Her Day of Reckoning, 1997

Miriam signed in at the lobby desk, was given an adhesive pass for her lapel, and directed to the elevators. She carried a leather portfolio containing a comprehensive outline of the past two years' events leading up to the theft, a color-coded spread sheet, and copies of phone records, travel vouchers, plane tickets to and from Prague, meals, hotel bill, and photos of the beginning, middle, and end of the Warhol's installation. She had printed out emails and approval signatures from the director for each phase of the installation. In other words, this was typical Miriam stepping up to the plate and waiting for the elevator.

Polished granite, stainless steel, and glass—the lobby echoed with each footstep. Conversations overlapped, the elevator doors parted, and young professionals bubbled out recounting last night's game.

She emerged on the twenty-fifth floor and stepped onto thick, contemporary Chinese rugs edged up to formal wainscoting. Wing chairs bracketed sitting areas left and right illuminated by crystal lamps. An efficient-looking twenty-something manned what might have been a former Oval Office desk, and on the wall behind him was "Wilton, Speare & Wharton."

He smiled. "Hello, and you must be Ms. Pastor. Right on time. I'll let Mr. Speare know of your arrival."

She was due in court next week—and would Irvin's lawyer have time to prepare? Meeting with him today, at this late date, seemed suicidal. She couldn't eat, and sleep was a series of short slides to abrupt landings. Mr. Speare had been brief with her on the phone, distracted—just another day at the office—while she stared down twenty-five years in prison.

The admin led her past muted office suites and stopped at a doorway. "Mr. Speare's offices." He leaned in and announced, "Monica? Ms. Pastor."

Monica led Miriam through a short hall to Mr. Speare's private office. Following a curt introduction, Monica left.

"Please have a seat," Speare said. He didn't get up, but he appeared to be a very tall man with long hands. No smile, the skyline and multiple bridges through the window at his back, and, looking around, she scanned the shelves—photos, trophies, and a basketball.

"Yeah, I played ball. Georgetown. Coach John Thompson. A couple years in the pros. Traded, injured, and traded. It finally sank in—the lesson Coach Thompson preached. Freshman year he held a basketball in front of us. We didn't know it had a small hole in it. Coach said, 'Right now this is your life.' Then he crushed the ball. 'This is your life without a degree.' Years later, and fed up with the trades, injuries, and all the moving—I quit the pros and went back to Georgetown Law. What's your story?"

Miriam opened her folio and passed the outline, spreadsheets, and photo copies across the desk to him. He slid them aside with the back of his hand.

"Tell me in a hundred words or less."

This is crazy.

"Listen," he said, "Irvin gave me his take on things, so I have some background. Give me your version, but keep it brief."

Irvin? She folded her fingers on the empty folio and abbreviated the tale. When she finished, he checked his watch.

"Alright. Thank you. I'll meet you outside the courtroom fifteen minutes before they open. This shouldn't take long."

"What does that mean?"

"It means I'll meet you outside the courtroom, and I'll do the talking."

"But—"

He pressed a button on his phone. "Monica?"

Miriam had lost eight pounds—and she didn't have eight to lose. Mr. Speare met her at the court, and got them signed in and expedited. The judge seemed all business and perhaps antagonistic toward Mr. Speare, and Mr. Speare was showing the judge no love. Miriam's hopes dissolved by the second. There was legal sparring between Mr. Speare and the assistant DA which she didn't fully understand, a display of mutual irritation—obviously a bad history between them—and the judge issued an Adjournment in Contemplation of Dismissal. As long as Miriam didn't spit on the sidewalk or get a DUI in the next six months, her records would be destroyed.

Back out in the hallway, she wanted to hug Mr. Speare. He shook her hand, checked his watch, and left.

45

Coffee? In Your Place? 1997

"Did I fuckin call it, or what?"

Mrs. Greene and Irvin were in Miriam's living room putting a dent in her triple batch of nervous-relief baking. They were the cookies Detective Nettles liked, and there was her knock at the door. Miriam let her in.

The detective full-frontal hugged her and kissed her on the cheek. She gripped Miriam's shoulders. "Congratulations." She kissed her on the other cheek. "Sometimes the system works. It doesn't put Ciccone in a good place with the lieutenant, and that's icing on the cake."

The detective took a seat across from the sofa. "Coffee? I smell coffee?"

"Mrs. Greene was so kind to bring it."

"And please allow me to buy you a cup, detective. Cream, sugar?" Mrs. Greene asked.

"Milk if you have it, thank you."

Mrs. Greene headed out to the kitchen.

The detective whispered, "Did you talk to her about the lease?"

"She did and we're cool!" Mrs. Greene called.

"Sorry," the detective mouthed.

"It's hard to think that this whole thing is over," Miriam said.

"Well, I wish that was true." The detective chose a cookie. "They're not going to walk away from six million dollars. The department may continue with the investigation, but, more likely, the insurance company will pick it up. And they're not always as transparent as we'd like."

"So it's going to get worse?"

"It depends on the angle they take. They can be unpredictable."

Miriam went cold.

Mrs. Greene returned and handed a cup to the detective. "This city's done enough harm to Miriam. I'm glad she's leaving—takin care of herself and movin to the country. I got people bangin the door down to get into my building, and this is my chance to shuffle the deck. I gotta be movin downstairs, myself—'the old gray mare.' But I'm going to miss her, way out there in Pennsylvania. Bears, raccoons, and who the fuck *knows* what."

46

Pizza in the Dark, 1997

Irvin had come to Pennsylvania. It was for her dad's funeral. He showed up at the hospital an hour before her father passed away, and they prayed and waited in their exhaustion—Miriam, her mom, and Irvin. The pressure in the room ramped up to near crushing. Then, a plunge from a cliff, impact, and silence. Her mom held her husband's hand and wept without a sound. Miriam's arm around her mom's waist, the room at dead stop, she stared into the clock above the bed—the second hand still moving.

Miriam and Irvin left her mom, the nurse, and her father and stepped out to the hall. He embraced her, and she cried silently into his shirt. Life and death continued throughout the corridors, the cold whir of the hospital busy without them.

He released her and leaned back against the wall. "How?" His eyes were wet. "I'm so sorry, Miriam. There aren't words. Like, where do you go with this? Where did *he* go? All that energy."

Her hands behind her, she rested against the opposite wall. “He’s probably arguing with St. Peter about whether to let the next guy in—thinks there’s something not right about his story.”

A heavy man in a bouffant cap, scrubs, and squishy shoes pushed a cart of linens between them followed by what appeared to be a large family—the men and boys taken from whatever they had been doing an hour ago in hunting clothes and boots.

“Complicated guy—advocate for the poor and the oppressed, generous and kind, taking me along to work at the shelter.” She let out a breath held since she was a child, “Sometimes impossible at home and his war with Nick.”

“I haven’t seen my dad in years,” Irvin said. “I feel like I should visit. Of course, I’ve probably embarrassed him all to hell and back, being in the news. I wonder how he spins it to their learned friends.”

They paused as three *bings* repeated on the intercom.

“Your mom’s going to be a mess for a while.”

“These last months have worn her down,” Miriam said. “She’s aged. I’ll be with her day and night.”

“And who’ll take care of you?”

“This sounds callous, but taking care of Mom will be good for me. Get me out of my skin. Try to figure out what’s next. Maybe drag out the paints and brushes during her naps.”

“Pet portraits?”

“Shut up, Irvin.”

"Sorry."

"I think you should visit your parents."

"Yeah, I'll think about that. The prodigal son. Now what?"

"What, what?"

"What do we do?"

"We take Mom home, get some food into her, and there will be lots from the church. I'll tuck her in with a sedative, and you'll sleep in Nick's room."

"Then what?"

"Can you stay in the moment?" She was off the wall, her hands in flight. "You saw what just happened, Irvin—my dad! He took me to baseball games. He pitched to me and worked on my swing and taught me to ride a bike and roller skate and how to bait a hook and I hated that." She was crying again. "I had my first slice of pizza in the back seat of their car in the dark, and I was six, and I didn't know what it was—a drive-up pizza place."

He nodded. "Sorry. Did you like it? The pizza?"

"I loved it. The smell filled the car. Pizza was never as good as that first slice in the dark, and listen to me. It's like I'm talking about doing it my first time with pizza."

"I was going to mention that."

"Some of his friends were in fraternal organizations—funny hats, membership cards, and lots of drinking. Maybe Dad was a bit of a nerd—he wasn't a joiner. In his head it was just him and, 'Suffer not the little children.' Am I blithering?"

"Yes. But he did pretty well raising you." Irvin searched the ceiling like he was in the Roman Forum and raised both hands to the cheering crowd. "Arguments, please?"

"He once drove a blasphemer from the church. In the middle of his sermon, an indigent man stood up and yelled, 'John, 3:16 my ass!' Dad said the man wouldn't shut up. Stood there scratching his arms and yelling, 'John, 3:16 my ass.'"

"Sorry, but I'm seeing your dad with his homemade potato cannon under the pulpit. He pulls it out, aims and lands a two-pound spud on the guy's forehead. Knocks him out."

She stared.

47

Spit It Out, 1997

Detective Nettles also came to Pennsylvania. She held Miriam's hand at the funeral. Miriam hadn't expected that—that she'd show up and that she'd hold her hand. It was sweet, and she'd never forget.

Irvin stood right behind them, his hands on Miriam's and her mother's shoulders and blocking the view of some attendees. As the congregation was breaking up after the service, the detective told her she had to "skedaddle" back to the city, but she'd check in with her in a few. She hugged Miriam and her mom, gave Irvin more than a glance, and left.

It wasn't long after that Miriam felt she should say more to the detective. She weighed suspicions and the right-and-wrong of it all for the next couple months, but she didn't call. When Detective Nettles called to check in with her, Miriam was awkward on the phone, and she could tell the detective sensed it.

Miriam tried baiting the conversation with the charming little Jewish deli she'd discovered for lunch—and if the detective was ever out this way, she'd take her there.

The detective wasn't biting. "You have something stuck in your craw, Miriam. Spit it out."

Miriam swallowed. "I'm not myself, today. I'm sorry. It's hard being here. Mom and all."

Early black-and-white photos of Mom show her vacationing at the beach in Atlantic City with girlfriends. Radiant smiles. Eyes bright. Skin supple and smooth, their hair wind-tossed and free. She and her buddies away from home and finding their place. I don't see photos of her with boys. Those likely disappeared when she met Dad. As a kid, and helping her core and peel apples for sauce, I'd hear of those early good-times as she circled back around the same sanitized stories. Her posture changed describing those Friday nights, the bands, the lights, and how she just loved to dance.

48

She Gets a Clue, 1998

Miriam's mother wandered the house without a compass those first months after her husband's death. Miriam found her standing in front of the open linen closet.

"What, Mom?"

Her mother shuffled around to face her, hands at her sides. "I don't know, Miriam."

She found her mom at the workbench in the garage a couple times and once sitting in the dark at the kitchen table at three in the morning, fully dressed, her purse in her lap.

"Come back to bed, Mom."

Miriam tried to get her mother onto a schedule. Waking her at seven, she made her mom's breakfast. Lunches were a short walk away at Lee's Diner and their house-made bread pudding for dessert, and each evening Miriam prepared a unique meal from one of her mom's Moosewood cookbooks.

Six weeks into it, her mom drifted—room to room, out to the mailbox several times a day, lethargic laps around the garden. Miriam had an idea.

"Let's go to Moosewood, Mom."

Her mother closed the refrigerator door, turned like she was being poured, and slid her hands into the pockets of her cardigan. "Say again?"

"Moosewood. Let's go for lunch. Road trip."

"It's in New York. Ithaca. No." Her mother sighed, checked her sweater buttons, and opened the fridge.

"It's a short trip, Mom. And what are you looking for?"

"Chocolate milk." Her mother bent low and peered into the lower shelves.

"We don't have any."

"I thought we did. I just got some."

"We haven't had chocolate milk in years, Mom, but I'll pick some up."

"Why?" Her mother closed the door and turned to her.

"I thought you wanted some."

"No, I just thought we had chocolate milk. 'Moosewood,' you say?"

"Road trip to the source. You love their cookbooks and you've never been. Leave early tomorrow, stop at the Turkey Ranch for your coffee and rolls, and head north. You and me."

"Tomorrow, then?"

~ ~ ~

They had been seated at long-worn, arrow-back chairs at a table for four in one of Moosewood's resonant, high-ceilinged and provincially adorned rooms—a former high school classroom. It wasn't until they'd ordered that Miriam unfolded her napkin, placed it over her lap, and relaxed. Gently interrupting her mother's rambling oral history, bringing her back to the present, and negotiating her out of the car, up the walk, and to their table had required concentration.

She let her gaze travel. There was art on the walls—art that one might call "local" without giving it further thought. But she did. *Why local?* Done by artists from the county art guild? Dedicated amateurs? Would Larry Poons be called a local artist? No. But wasn't his studio just east of here?

Her mother had the tofu-feta scramble. She had crab cakes.

Maybe it was the strong coffee from the Turkey Ranch that had sprung her mother's memories. Since leaving, and heading up Route 15, her mom had been telling the story of meeting Miriam's dad—the handsome young divinity student on a hayride on a cold October night, skating at the pond that December, and warming their hands at the barrel's fire. A Valentine kiss, May flowers, and the first love she'd known. Then the ring—the one she was wearing.

Miriam heard little of this. She was in shock. She had seen Nick.

She had seen Nick, his back to her, in the Turkey Ranch dining room and, across from him, a guy who she thought to be the bartender from the Ramona. The heavier and a bit scragglier former bartender, and, there, he pulled a toothpick from the corner of his mouth, and that was him. Cash.

The first time they'd seen him at the Ramona, he'd introduced himself to Irvin and her as J-Money, but they should call him Cash. Her immediate impression had been that he was masquerading in Manhattan, in that bar, in that haircut, in those clothes.

At the Turkey Ranch take-out counter, she'd stepped aside until her order arrived, then left in a rush and, she hoped, unseen. She had crossed the parking lot to her car and, there, a few rows back, was Nick's truck. And next to it sat a low, red Corvette with New York plates.

As they pulled out of the lot, her mother continued with the newlyweds moving into their first cottage across the river, unpacking, and she'd wished she'd labeled her boxes.

Miriam nodded, not listening. The image of Nick and Cash laughing over their Bloody Mary breakfasts burned into her. Nick, so cocksure at the funeral with his shiny red truck. And that there had been a new bartender at the Ramona was hardly worth noting, but Cash here in rural Pennsylvania—and, surely that was his Corvette—having breakfast with Nick?

49

He Sacrificed His Tie, 1996

It was a little over a year before the Moosewood lunch that Miriam and Irv, his hand in a cast, had been chatting over a drink at the Ramona when he nodded past her shoulder toward the door. "The new sheriff."

She turned.

"Don't look!" he whispered. "What the hell's the matter with you?"

She faced forward. "Sorry." There was a ruckus behind her.

"You're good. The young, party staff's here. They're swarming him—trying to get him to join their table."

"We should say our 'hellos,'" she said.

"Go for it. The Whitney's new director seems to enjoy the attention. I'll hold your seat." He nodded to the bartender for another round.

"I'll be right back." She left her purse on the bar.

The director was being swept to the large round table in the Ramona's cramped side room. The associate curators and interns were fueled and rolling. One of the women was already wearing the director's tie as a headband, and someone slid a shot his way. He was going under.

"Miriam!" the tie woman raised her glass. "Miriam!" the rest of the table echoed.

Miriam spread her arms, "My lovelies." Then, sympathetically to the director, "Would you like to join us at the bar?"

He appeared hopeful as he shifted and slid his chair out an inch.

"Nooo!" yelled one of the staff.

"Oh please," Miriam said. "Let us have some time with him, too." The director squeezed out from the table post-haste and, a bit flushed, followed Miriam to the bar. He'd sacrificed his tie.

Irv and her purse were gone. Only their drinks remained. The bartender, Cash, was at the far end of the bar fawning over a young woman. When he moved up her way, Miriam summoned him.

"Have you seen my purse?"

"Oh, right. Thought it should be back here with me til the Irvster got back from the john." He retrieved it from the side of the register, winked, and placed it in front of her.

"Thank you. And may I buy our new director a drink?"

50

She Finds a Friend, 1998

In this small Pennsylvania city Miriam had dated. Tried dating—gave it a good try—and it was discouraging. Men who seemed smart, accomplished and charming proved to be full of themselves and desperate. The head of the chamber society, the dentist, the divorced attorney. They had gone to movies, concerts, and events at the library, and these men could not stop talking about themselves in the car on the way to dinner, during dinner, and driving her home. And they were horny. Dropping her off—and no way was she inviting him in—the dentist had stretched across the console, opened his lips in a contorted way he must have thought to be sultry—something was going on, there, with his hand beneath the seatbelt—and, with the dental work he was flashing, she was about to be snatched by *The Alien*. Startled, she jerked back, hit her head on the window, and she may have been semi-conscious for a moment. Regaining herself, she opened the door, got out, and addressed the man. "Please, don't! Don't call, don't . . . and please . . . Just don't." She closed the door.

She'd met interesting women at the college events. At her first, an open-bar gallery reception, she'd met a woman from admissions who seemed a bit tipsy. The woman shared that she was reluctantly living with her husband, she hated him, and, as soon as she could afford it, she was getting a boob job.

Well alright then.

Later that evening, she met a young revered English professor—Victoria Merritt. Miriam was taken how the woman chose and timed her words and by her sardonic humor. Victoria couldn't care less about the childish posing of the President, or the endless drone of talk radio and professional sports. Well, except for *The Yankees.* Now *there* was a happy coincidence! Otherwise, politics and mainstream culture she categorized as, "plastic transistor noise." Her life's mission was to instill literacy, responsibility, intellectual curiosity, self-awareness, and manners, and nothing would bump her off course. They spoke of parallels in poetry, music, and the visual arts—about meaningful global movements and The Great War, Prokofiev's *Classical Symphony*, and zeitgeist. Twenty minutes later, they'd exchanged contact information and made a coffee date.

They met at the quaint, storied tearoom not far from where Miriam planned to open her gallery. Great light from two large windows to the street, new-age music from the ceiling, and a corner table. Victoria had coffee and a cinnamon scone. Miriam had tea.

"No wonder you're so trim," Victoria said. She bit into the scone and swept cinnamon sugar from her jacket.

"I'm afraid my life has become small and uninteresting," Miriam said. "I don't seem to need or want much—a cup of tea, conversation with a friend, a good book."

"That sounds delightful. It's how we drift on weekends, Bill and I. Sunday mornings are coffee, bagels, Mozart, and *The Times* strewn about the house. Then, Monday morning and everything's back in gear—both of us in suits. So, how ever does a Whitney curator find her way to our small city?"

Miriam pushed her cup to the middle of the table and folded her hands. "I told you I left, but I was forced from the Whitney. There was a theft from a show I curated, and I was indirectly involved." She took in a long breath and let it out. "It was a year ago. Maybe you read about it."

"Brigitte Bardot and the Warhol."

"Yes, Brigitte Bardot. It is she who gave the story legs."

"But you had nothing to do with the theft."

"The Whitney lost an irreplaceable piece of art and gained a worldwide demerit in stature. Changes had to be made."

"Politics. It sounds like the college with all of our inter and intra-departmental grievances and jealousies. The temperature rises every budget cycle.

So why here?"

"I grew up here. Mom lives in town—alone. Dad died this year. I moved in with her."

"Rough year," Victoria said.

“Yes. A bonfire—Dad, Mom, my brother.”

“Your brother.”

“Estranged. He’s here, too. Somewhere.”

“Your father—I’m so sorry. You’ll be back on your feet. The hurt won’t go away, but curator at the Whitney? That doesn’t happen to everyone.” Her eyes lit up, “Will you help us at the college? With our new gallery?”

“I’m opening a small gallery a block from here,” Miriam said.

“Perfect. I’ll ask our director to contact you. She’s looking for someone to head her advisory council, and she’ll be thrilled to meet you.”

“What I mean is, I don’t think I’ll have time. I—”

“She’ll be in touch.”

Meeting Victoria was my good fortune. She is a friend with whom I've enjoyed hours of winding conversations at the little tearoom up the street from the gallery. We're a book club of two, we've worked on multiple shows at the college gallery, and, together, we've driven to the regional airport to pick up her guest speakers. She has a full life.

51

Kushala Means "Safe," 2007

Miriam and Detective Nettles stayed in touch the next ten years, and they'd lunch together whenever Miriam was in the city. Miriam shared her small wins at the gallery, told her about attending events with Victoria, and they laughed over her date with the dentist. And Kush, as Miriam had come to know her—*It's Apache. I'm named after my grandmother, Kushala. It means safe.*—also attended Miriam's mother's funeral.

The morning after the funeral, Miriam entered the historic hotel's formal dining room. She heard Victoria and Kush in animated back-and-forth as she approached their table.

"Then I guess you don't have time for the gym," Kush said.

"If I *wanted* to go to the gym, I'd *make* time," Victoria said.

"Yeah, I guess with all that reading, y'all don't have the time."

Miriam sat next to Victoria. Kush reached across the white linen and laid her hand on Miriam's. "I hope you slept, and you done good. Your mother got her best friend back when you left New York."

"She doesn't mean you weren't *always* her best friend," Victoria said.

"Well, thank you for clearing that up for us." Kush caught the waiter's eye. "Shall we order?"

"I'm not hungry," Miriam said. "I thought I was prepared. I wasn't."

"There's something with mothers and daughters," Victoria said.

~ ~ ~

Victoria pushed back from the table. "Not one more bite."

"Mom was never the same after Dad." Miriam had been sharing her mother's story through breakfast. "It was as though each year she got smaller and less able—withdrawing from life. Like she was watching a movie—our little trips, the meals, our walks—but the reel in her head had all the color removed." She picked at her plate.

"You've probably thought about what's next?" Kush said.

"I'm staying here. It's familiar and easy."

"You'll keep the house?" Kush asked.

"No."

"Mmm . . . How's that going to work with Nick? After he was done doing his heinous-prick thing with you at the funeral, I watched him climb into his truck. He broke down before pulling away. Kept the windows up, his head on the steering wheel, and just bawled. You were talking with the church ladies."

All this time, Miriam thought, Mom was the one who would never let him down. Deep in his black heart, she was all he had.

"Nick can have the house, but he won't want it. He hates coming to town. I'll sell the place and give him the money. I have to be done with it—with him."

"Come visit me in Texas anytime—both of you—and stay as long as you like. I'll be the little, tan fox sitting tall in the saddle with the shit-eating grin."

"Texas?" Miriam asked.

"I've retired."

"But . . . You're young. And, I mean, congratulations."

"Yes, congratulations," Victoria said.

"Twenty-and-out. Goodbye NYPD, and goodbye New York. I'll be back on the ranch in a couple days, and that's where I'm staying. Clean air, big skies, honest work, and lovin the horses. There's fishing, too, if the elderly Labs don't insist on following me into the lake. And I'm buying a truck, and I mean a big mo' digger. She scooped up another fork of home fries and held them as she spoke. "I just hope the Warhol thing doesn't whip back and slap you."

"Why would it?" Victoria asked.

They waited as Kush chewed.

"Suppose Interpol stumbles across a less-than-discrete collector in, say, Japan, or wherever our inside man unloaded it."

"Inside man," Miriam said.

"Maybe Irvin. Or the director, now that he's missing."

"He's missing?"

"About a year after the theft he disappears. Boom. Up and left lock, stock, and barrel. Can you picture him in a private jet on his way to Tulum? Maybe a cottage high in the Andes? Anyway, wherever *whoever* got rid of that print, someone's going to come across it and talk—a jealous ex, a friend of a friend, a friend of a cop—and it'll surface. Then, I'm sorry to say, you're back in the news, and all the finger pointing starts again." She picked the last piece of bacon from her plate and clipped off a bite.

Miriam pushed her breakfast aside.

"And I mean that about coming down and spending time with me. There's plenty of extra rooms."

"I hear there are scorpions," Victoria said.

"Flick em aside with your boot. Harmless little critters."

"Probably why they're called 'scorpions.'" Victoria folded her arms.

"Spiders and snakes, too, but who's counting?" Kush said. "You know what there isn't? Snow. Also I've never seen a cab at the ranch, go figure. Might make y' all homesick—no snow, no cabs."

Victoria turned to Miriam. "Is she always like this?"

"I—"

"And I'm not saying it was the director," Kush said, "just that he's missing."

PART 2

Nick

I'll never know exactly what made Nick what he is. The last time I saw him—spoke with him—it was so painful, and I think it brought closure to our relationship. And "relationship" sounds too positive. I've given up. Forgive me Mother. I'll not take another step to see him again. Nor will he to see me. Sometime before he came to live with us, before my parents adopted him, his die was cast.

52

In the Upper Room, 1967

His earliest memory is of lying on his back on the floor, country music, and people stepping over him and yelling. It probably didn't happen exactly like this, but he sees a woman in a dress straddling him. She looks down and says, "What are *you* looking at?" He's scooped up like it's his fault he's on the floor, and he doesn't remember what happens next, and everything's tight and small, and he thinks it was probably a trailer they lived in. Then there's something about broken glass, and he thinks it was a green Coke bottle, and a lot of blood, and more glass being thrown and breaking and screaming. He was crying, and he was shaken hard—rattled.

To this day, he avoids carnival rides.

He thinks it might have been a couple years later when a woman said, "Wait til Mason gets home, then you'll see what's what!" He ran to his bed and buried himself in the blanket. It was inevitable, his beating, and waiting for it got worse by the second. Then he was a discarded sock monkey in the divorce.

There was a flurry of in and out of cars, and in and out of buildings, and standing in lines with other kids, and then he was in a house with strangers, and he was afraid of them, and they had a dog with one eye, and it growled at him, and the whole place stunk. It was day and night, and there were more rides in back seats, and there were long tables and paper plates, and it was fish sticks and ketchup.

There was a very large woman and her cats, and she ate with her hands, and he saw her pick up a whole roast chicken and bite into it and keep biting until it was all bones.

The last couple he remembers in his shuffling through the foster circuit was Tingle and Rick. Looking back, he thought Tingle was the nicest of all of them, and she probably meant well, if she meant anything at all. They owned a motel, and Tingle cleaned the rooms while Rick did the outside work, and nobody fucked with Rick. The first time Nick whined about his food, Rick picked him out of the chair by his neck and held him close to his face. "Say that again!" Nick was six. He thought foster parents were awful.

Another move, and they said he should be glad because this was the last time, and he'd be with these people forever—and that scared him. What if this new guy was like Rick? Or his wife was like the Chicken Lady? The new people weren't like that, but equally screwed in their own way. The new guy tried to torture the hell out of him with prayer. He was a preacher.

"We knock at your door Jesus. We pray for Nicolas, that he may have a better life." The preacher hugged Nick to his chest, held him out arms-length, drew him back in, and kissed his cheek. "We humbly wait, and ask that you open to this child born of wanton sin." The preacher was huge. Then again, Nick was pretty small. At that moment, that first night in their home, the preacher knelt, his heavy hand pressing down on him, and Nick was on all fours. He wasn't exactly sure what the preacher was going on about, but it was loud and tearful. The big man seemed sorry and angry and scared all at the same time, and Nick wasn't sure why—except it sounded like it was his doing. He hadn't seen someone act this crazy since . . . well, that time with the Coke bottle.

Meanwhile, there was more weight and calling out, and there was his name again, and he'd soon be flat on the floor. "Uh!" Now he *was* flat on the floor, and the guy was like a radio running out words with no one in the room, and it was, "blessed," and "in your name," and "child of poverty and degradation," and "humble servant, Amen." The preacher struggled to his feet. He was wet, and he smelled a little like that one-eyed dog. Nick took in his first full breath in quite a while.

It was like a hook came out of the sky, and he was lifted off the floor by the back of his shirt, spun mid-air, and he faced the preacher eye to eye. "There is an upper room for you, and you and I are going to that room to pray for your soul until you fall asleep." He carried Nick up the stairs, into a small room, and lowered him onto a single bed. He removed Nick's shoes, kissed him on the forehead, and switched off the light. The mattress sagged as the preacher sank on the edge of the bed, and Nick rolled into him. Nick scooted back up to the other side.

“Let us pray that Satan leaves you tonight, Nicholas. Let us pray that you don’t burn in hell.” The preacher mumbled his parting prayer, rose, pulled the door shut with a slow *whump,* and left.

Nick was alone in the dark.

The room shook as the preacher thumped down the stairs.

Burn? He was going to burn in hell? Quiet, now. Quiet and dark. He had to get out of there! He felt his way to the door, walked his fingers up along the molding, and found the switch. Light. Orange room. He tried the door. No go. There was a window. He tried it. Nope.

The walls were bare except above the little bed—a picture of Jesus praying.

A small chair and a green dresser, and he opened the drawers. Some clothes he recognized, the rest belonged to someone else.

He had to pee. He tried the door again. He twisted and pulled, put his foot against the wall, and yanked. The door popped open. Just stuck, he thought. Maybe the window, too? He turned off the light and left the door cracked behind him.

Across the hall was a dark, open doorway from which it was a short distance down to what must be the bathroom. A sliver of light beneath the door—someone in there and taking forever doing stuff at the sink, and he was getting close to losing it. Knock-kneed and quick breaths, he backed into his room and watched the hall—prayed to the hall—for someone to come out of that bathroom.

The water stopped. A couple seconds later the light blinked off, a shadow came out, went into the other room, and shut the door.

Nick raced to the bathroom and let go a full-bore piss in the dark and all over the place. Some sounded like it splashed into the toilet, and the rest on the floor. Phew. He unrolled a huge wad of toilet paper and wiped up the seat, and threw the mess into the toilet. Another gob of paper for the floor, and he probably wasn't getting all of it. He threw that gob in, too, and flushed. Ah, so much better.

He'd go back to his room and, maybe, sleep.

Water. Cold running water, and his feet were wet. Soaked. The toilet. Now what? Run! He spattered out to the hall and shot back to his room. He forced the door shut with his shoulder, fumbled to the bed, peeled his socks, hid in the covers, and prayed the preacher wouldn't find out.

He didn't know the toilet was right above the preacher's bed.

When he was nine, my little brother hid a perforated shoebox of what may have been his own excrement in our parents' closet. A few years later, he spiked the tires of our car on a Sunday morning to keep us from going to church. On my way to my room that night, I passed his open door—his light on. He lay on his back on top of the covers, naked, his erect penis clutched in his grip, and he grinned at me. It was when I came home from art school that first Thanksgiving, that I found he had gone through my things. He had crudely and obscenely altered my life drawings.

53

Cash is Back, 1996

It's Friday, and Nick sits on a stool behind the counter with his back to the Earl's Performance Components calendar. His is the slump of a buzzard. He is thin, unkempt, and wears his waist-length Members Only jacket regardless of the season and temperature. Long thick nails terminate his pale fingers as he thumbs a hardware catalog most would peruse only on the john, and as a last resort. On the other side of the counter, a few motorheads in Ford, Chevy, and Mopar hats carry small, brown paper bags and troll the aisles of drawers and bins in search of the special fasteners their boat, bike, or car projects require—nylock nuts, rubber washers, fabric, nylon, stainless, and copper washers, stainless machine bolts, hex heads, torx heads, standard heads, phillips, heat-treated, and virtually every size and pitch. It's silent in the shop but for the occasional *tink* or *plop* of a fastener dropped into a bag, and one of Telemann's fugues barely audible from a small FM radio.

None of his customers know his name or anything else about him, except that's gotta be his curdled-milk-and-rusted-out '63

Falcon out front. Back home and gathered around the engine they're overhauling, the clutch they're replacing, or the go-cart they're glomming together for one of the kids, they refer to him as "The Screw Shop Guy."

He doesn't look up when a customer approaches the plywood counter to pay. He takes the bag from the customer, dumps it, sorts the fasteners into groups with one hand, and punches keys on the adding machine with the other. Total tallied, he rips off the receipt, shoves it across the counter and scrapes the fasteners back into the bag. Payment taken, change made, and not a word.

He props the "Closed" sign in the barred window promptly at three, dead-bolts the inner oak door, and clicks the rusted security door shut behind him. Ice on the step, his movements are cautious. The Falcon starts on the third try.

He negotiates the slush between his shop and the fish market and heads thirteen miles north. During his hours at the shop, from seven until three, he doesn't think. There, he keeps the past out with his catalogues, customers, and classical radio. At home, on his hidden and untended wooded lot along the creek, in the twelve-wide with the shades pulled, he shuffles from the fridge to the TV and back blurring any reflections with whiskey and water. It's when he's in the car on the way from the shop to the trailer, on the way from sobriety to inebriation, that memories seep in—of foster homes and the adoption and the clusterfuck of public school and the Army—memories like contaminated backflow. The Army is where he met Cash Hazzard, and now, twelve years later, Cash had found him. Something was up.

Late Saturday afternoon, Nick sits at the window with a smoke and a whisky and watches the creek. The Army—that was a fresh start. He was anonymous. He and the other seventy-nine guys in the training platoon of strangers. Which ones came from money, who was smart, who would succeed, and who would wash out? Those first few weeks, he was as rich and smart as the next guy, and nobody knew the better. Then, as the weeks and months passed, everyone found their level. The privileged and smart rose to leadership of course—the cream—and they were goddamn comfortable with their stations. Like they'd known it was only a matter of time until their entitlement would be noticed. Everyone else filled in the gaps below. Many just accepted it, knowing this was their lot in life, and they followed the orders, mopped the floors, cleaned the toilets, and marked the time. Others, like him, said, "Screw it," and cut every corner, and snatched up anything that wasn't locked up or nailed down—watches, loose change, rations, ammo, and no one ever found out who fucked up the Gunny's spit-shined boots—though they all paid dearly. He was out of the Army in two years, back home and good riddance to the uniforms and push-ups and orders and waiting in line and plane flights and the desert heat. From the day of his discharge, life would be steady, on his terms, and more of the same—day after day til the end.

He refills his glass with less water, more whiskey, each trip to the kitchen. He'd be asleep by seven. There had been times he woke in the chair at three in the morning, the TV on and the glass toppled between the cushions. TV off, it was a blind passage down the hall past the extra bedroom, the bathroom, to the back of the trailer, and a face-down flop on the bed.

Sunday morning, coffee, cigarettes, and Cash would be showing up at the shop in an hour. The Falcon starts on the second try.

54

A Regular Gig, 1996

Thirteen-mile drive to the shop and Nick's thinking, Sundays were the worst—his stepdad, the stepmom, his stepsister—Miss-perfect-nose-in-a-book Miriam. Thought they were going to save him, did they? He'd made them fight for it since that first bloody paddling for the goddamn toilet flood. Sunday suit and tie? The spankings, the yelling, the threats just fueled him. He'd gotten away a couple times when they stopped at the intersection—bolted from the car— and one time they were late and had to go on without him. They quit trying when he was in high school. He'd escaped that, too—high school—as soon as the Army would have him.

It was after returning from desert training that he and Cash got drunk, stole an MP's Jeep, and went out on the town. Cash kept the motor running while he went into the store for another pint. There was an altercation, the cashier's gun, a scuffle—he stepped back through the large display window—and the burglar alarm. Cash split. Nick had taken the heat, done stockade time, told the colonel he'd acted alone. Cash liked him for that—said he was a goddamn psycho.

Been some time since he'd seen Cash. On the phone, he sounded pretty much the same—same laugh, but more years of smoke and booze and a hint of New York in it. A Pennsylvania boy, Cash said he'd settled in New York after the Army cause of a little Puerto Rican girl. Said he was alone now. In the Bronx, two rooms to himself. The Puerto Rican girl had moved back to the island—took the daughter with.

Cash said he'd bumped around—worked in a tire shop and he'd worked a couple gas stations and, the last few years he'd worked his way up to bartending in Manhattan. "A regular gig where the smart and swell go, and whodaguessed?" he laughed. He also said he'd come onto something big—a no-questions-asked opportunity—and he needed a partner. Said he'd be at the shop Sunday—that they should meet at the shop.

No cars on the lot, the fish market closed, and it was plain weird coming to the shop on a Sunday. Nick opened both doors, then closed only the steel-mesh security door. That was weird, too, and it took him back to his confinement at Fort Knox. It had been a long shot from hard time—more like goddamn daycare, if you asked him. But the doors were steel mesh. He did his time and got the hell out.

All these years, he probably wouldn't be able to pick Cash out of a crowd. Probably put on some weight. Maybe bald. Beer gut. He wouldn't surrender to his weekday routine of turning on the lights and the radio. He cranked up the heat and planted his butt on the counter in shadowed silence.

55

A Red, White and Black Nike, 1996

A well-tuned rumble, and the front end of a white, '97 Trans Am with a New York plate poked up to the front of the shop, revved a couple times, and shut down. Nick watched the driver's door swing wide, and a red, white and black Nike step onto the lot. Now the other shoe—and above the door, it was older Cash, and his hair had thinned, and it was black—like, dyed black. The toothpick. Yep, there it was. Cash pulled it from the side of his mouth and tossed it. He approached the door. "Anybody home? That's your excuse of a ride? A geriatric *Falcon*?"

Nick slid down from the counter and leaned his butt back against it. "Fuck's wrong with my car?"

Cash opened the door and stood there with the wet and cold all around him. Still built like a cowboy, he grinned large. "Well, why don't we come out here and contrast and compare—your car and the one I'm driving."

"Shit if that's your car," Nick said.

"Didn't actually say it *was* my car, now did I?"

"Stole it, ain't."

"Let's call it a loaner—and that monster's got a 5.7-liter V8. It stomps, my man! Nearly three hours flat, and here I am."

"I got no need for speed. Why'd you come?"

"Well, what say we close these doors and talk about that?"

56

Cash Had a Gun, 1982

They'd been bunk mates at Advanced Infantry Training, and their first confrontation had been over who got the bottom bunk. Nick said no fuckin way was he takin the top. Cash didn't know Nick had a knife, and Nick didn't know Cash had a gun. But neither drew down, and they settled the whole thing with the flip of Cash's two-headed nickel.

Following that month of training, their unit was put on hold before deployment, so there was down time to be filled with busy work—inspections, PT, classes on hygiene, and a lot of grab-ass in the barracks. Paydays saw cutthroat poker, and, the nights off, the young soldiers scattered in search of custom-fit and made-to-order guilty pleasures. With few exceptions, those involved fake IDs and a lot of drinking.

Danger was Cash's sport. How much danger and how close to death he came was the measure of a night out—and he pulled Nick into it. They'd start off at a locals' bar—one where they'd never been—and, "Let's see where this leads, my man." Getting tossed out for drunk and disorderly hardly rated on the scale of good night. But if they were busted up and kicked to the curb by Junior and his cousins—well, that moved the needle.

This night, their bent-for-hell antics attracted the generous attention of a middle-aged local with money. “Buy the boys a shot on me,” he’d told the bartender. “Whatever they like.”

Nick had wondered what all that was about. They didn’t know the guy, did they?

Cash said not to look a gift horse, and roll with it. A few minutes later, two more shots appeared. Cash scanned the bar for their benefactor, and he was gone.

“Mind if I join you?” The guy rolled up behind them. Cash rattled his stool a couple inches to the side, and Nick followed. The big man squeezed in next to Nick and asked, “So where you boys from?”

The guy smelled like cinnamon. Nick didn’t flinch—stared straight ahead at himself in the mirror behind the bar. Cash leaned across Nick and said that they were from the base up the road.

“Far from home, then, I suspect,” the man said. “Hey!” he called the bartender. “A couple more for my friends and another one of the usual for me.” The shots arrived and a few minutes later the man’s drink—a stemmed glass with layers of red, yellow and clear, with a cherry on top. The man raised his glass. “To a beautiful sunrise, boys, and I hope we can enjoy it together.”

Nick had that dilated, WTF look, and Cash could tell that Nick’s motor was spinning up. Time to intervene. He slipped the toothpick from the corner of his mouth and placed it on the ashtray. He told Nick to switch places with him. Nick gladly did. Cash settled in next to the guy, leaned into his shoulder—soft and friendly like—and asked, "Come here often?"

The guy laughed. He super-laughed. He wiped his eyes and put an arm around Cash and pulled him in closer. "You're okay. You're a good one. What say we have another drink, and then I take you boys home to a fine supper? I'm talking game hens and rice, asparagus, and some of the best Kentucky bourbon money can buy. My treat."

Nick had ordered a beer. He was out of Cash's freak circle and could finally breathe. He scanned the mirror. Lotta military guys in civilian clothes—dressed-up, sexy, and way-out-of-their-league women all among them. Somebody had just dropped a quarter, and the jukebox blared, *"War! What is it good for?!"* A sweaty muscle-bound guy in a messed-up uniform danced and stumbled alone with his beer in front of the jukebox. He was bumping into tables, and it appeared no one was up for stopping him.

In the far corner, a band was taking to their platform. The drummer moved his pieces around, two guitar guys plugged in and screwed with their amps, the music shut off, and colored lights lit the band. The muscled guy slumped alone in the dark in front of the dead jukebox. He stared at the floor, and it looked like he was going to cry. But he didn't. He raised the bottom of his longneck to the low ceiling, took a pull on his Bud, and lumbered over to his stool at the bar. Nick noticed he wore the ribbon of the Silver Star. The guy was a hero.

The bass and drums started a slow, funky beat. A tall black man entered from a side door and approached the platform. Slicked hair, his suit glimmered in the dark, and as he approached the lights, it glowed iridescent blue and green. The other guitar player moved up to the mic and announced, "Ladies and gentlemen, put em together for Elizabethtown's own—and world-renowned—Slipper Piston!" The man was on the platform in one skinny-pants leap, grabbed the mic stand, clicked his head left, then right, and snapped a finger. The rhythm stopped. He grinned at the bar, and there was a shining gold tooth. "One, two—*Mustang Sally*, . . . " And they were off—a big-cammed, syncopated, 350-horsepower Wilson Pickett feathering the clutch at intersections, and cruising that block in second gear.

In the mirror, Nick saw that Cash and the weird guy were up to something. Then Cash pushed back, and yelled, "I gotta dance!" Next, Cash was dancing with a woman easily a foot taller than him with a three-foot braid, and the heavy guy was moving over onto Cash's stool. "You gotta dance, too?" the guy asked. Nick felt for his knife. The guy went on about a lot of stuff—some of which Nick didn't hear, didn't care to hear, didn't fucking *want* to hear. And when was Cash gonna be done dancing? The guy's relationships, his childhood, betrayals, his mom, and blah, blah, blah.

Nick slid off the stool, made his way through the mass of undulating, sweat-licked couples, and wedged between Cash and the tall dancing woman. Over the music, Nick yelled that this was screwed—that he'd best get that guy outta his face, or he was either going to stab the sonofabitch or start a fire.

Cash apologized to his blond partner, and it was occasion for tender and mournful regret that they must part. She leaned down, they held both hands, and he said he didn't even know her name, but he was sure he loved her, and she was probably starting to get motel thoughts for him because he had a great smile and danced like James Brown—if James Brown didn't know how to dance.

57

The McIntosh Amp, 1982

"I own rentals all over town." The big guy had been bragging about himself ever since they got in his car—goddamn white, nineteen-sixty-something, cherry, two-door, top-down convertible Caddie. Nick rode in the backseat and let the cow pile blather on to Cash up front as they cruised the broken lanes between soybean fields beneath the summer moon—past random rural cottages, some dark, others ghostly lit with late-night TV and the kids in bed. They turned onto a dirt road, slowed, pulled into a drive, and a garage door opened. In the thick heat and stray light, vinyl, leather, and shoe polish is what Nick smelled.

They were out of the car, and Nick trailed Cash and the guy through what looked like a small shoe factory—leather scraps on the floor, empty water bottles strewn around, and about a dozen sewing machines. "This is where money is made, boys. My little Mexican ladies show up again at six tomorrow to make some of the world's most desirable purses while I'm upstairs making deals. You know what it costs me to make a four-hundred-dollar purse? Nine bucks. No shit, right? C'mon."

The man led them up a long, narrow, flood-lit flight. At the top, he fumbled the key, and opened to his apartment. Cash was first in behind the man and said something about how cool the place was with its high ceilings, the art, books, and furniture. Nick followed a few feet behind. The man adjusted the lights and a/c and went out to the kitchen to fix drinks.

Cash sat on the sofa and told Nick he was taking "that fucking expensive" McIntosh amp. Nick countered saying he was taking that other thing.

Cash said it was a goddamn preamp.

The man was back with the drinks. "How about I put on some music?" He carefully placed an album on the turntable. "I'll be in the kitchen for a few. You guys unwind and let me know if you need anything. The powder room's down the hall."

"Chances are

I wear a silly grin

Whenever you come in a room . . . "

Nick said he had to piss.

Cash told him to go for it.

Nick said he wasn't going near that fuckin powder room, and he'd rather stick it out a window.

Cash told him to hold it, then. He went over to the stereo shelf, unplugged the amp, and started to the door.

Nick snatched the preamp.

The man called from the kitchen, "Hey, what happened to the music?" He appeared in the doorway. "Hey, what? I mean, what're you guys—?"

Cash told Nick to run. Nick stood stunned for a moment and watched Cash set the amp at his hip like a stack of schoolbooks and draw his little automatic. He aimed at the guy's chest.

Nick ripped down the stairs. He heard, *crack, crack, crack!* He skipped the last three steps, was outside, and sprinted under the moon. Mown field on his left, five-foot weeds on his right, and it was a dirt road. He took to the weeds and squatted.

Where's Cash?

Blood pounded in his ears. This was big. This was fucking big. He couldn't get enough air into him. Cash killed the guy, and this was total fucking big! Where the fuck was Cash?

He heard a car—*the* car. The Caddie—and it was driven by a maniac, and sliding in the dirt, and swerving this way through the weeds, then back to the road. A shotgun blast not ten feet from him as the car passed. It was the big guy and he yelled, and he was fucking pissed. Another blast and he was going to kill the little cocksuckers. Nick backed deeper into the weeds.

He heard the car powerslide on the dirt, and it was headed back his way. Another blast. Pellets ripped the weeds a couple feet from his shoulder. Damn! Where was he? Where was Cash? *Fuck* Cash! Stooped low, Nick held on to the preamp and barreled blind through the weeds. Gullies, holes, sticks, and rocks—the field had no end. Weeds and more weeds. He tripped, and again. He sucked in dust and bugs and, "Accgh!" His face! He blinked and choked.

His lungs heaved, his legs burned, and—no shit and goddamn—he crashed out onto a road.

A breeze. He lowered the McIntosh to the heated blacktop long enough to take an emergency leak. He was shaking. Sweat ran from him faster than the piss. Another twelve-gauge blast, muffled by the field behind him.

The route sign said this was the road they came in on. Soaked, bladder relaxed, he zipped up, grabbed the preamp, caught his breath, and began a slow jog back to town.

58

All Warmup and Bullshit, 1996

Cash entered the shop, slipped behind the counter, and straddled the stool. "Nice place you got here, and whodaguessed anyone could make a living selling screws? Your own boss, too, I'll bet."

Nick came off the counter and closed the doors. He moseyed over to one of the cabinets of little drawers, leaned back against it, folded his arms, and waited. Cash would beat around the bush before diving in and telling him what the hell this was all about. Nick knew he wouldn't have to pay attention to what Cash was saying for the next few minutes—all warmup and bullshit. It had taken Cash forever, back in the day, to tell him how he could have missed that expensive-purse guy from four feet away—and all three times. It was blanks. He'd loaded the gun with blanks. It startled the guy—scared the shit out of the guy—long enough for Cash to make it down the stairs and into the night. He ran the opposite direction as Nick.

The next night, exiting the barracks to hock the equipment in town—they'd probably get a hundred bucks—the lieutenant saw them leave the building. He cut them off before they made the bus stop.

"Nice-looking gear, there, privates."

"Yes sir," Cash said.

"Looks expensive. McIntosh. How'd you maggots come to have it?"

"My uncle, sir."

"Your uncle."

"Yes sir. Passed away, bless him. My aunt said he wanted me to have it, sir."

"Crock-a-shit."

"No, sir. Honest."

"Tell you what. I'll give you what the pawnshop's going to give you, and we call it a day. Otherwise, I take you two dipshits to the O.D., and we find out if two thousand dollars' worth of McIntosh gear has been reported missing."

They took the deal and caught the bus.

Cash was finally coming around to the subject of his visit to Pennsylvania and The Screw Shop. Nick grabbed at his forehead, wiped down his face, and began to pay attention. Goddamn headache already.

"So I told you I was tending bar in a high price joint, right? Cultured clientele? Cultured pearls? Oyster puke? People who never did a day's work—and maybe they started out with all the marbles or maybe not—but they sure as hell ended up with all the marbles? Well a couple of the regulars at six-bucks-a-drink work at a museum up the street where they have some expensive shit—and we're not talking in the thousands or tens-of-thousands, here. Nick, you following this?"

Nick was deciding did he want to roll his sleeves up or leave them down. He had rolled them back down and was buttoning them at his wrists, and the buttonholes weren't working. They were horizontal, or something. He looked up. "Yeah, I got ya."

"I overheard some shit, and I'm proposing a score, Nick. Life-changing shit, and I thought you might want in. I want you in."

"Change whose life?"

"My life. Yours. Theirs, too. Fuck em, right? I got some inside security info. It's perfect. Like the old days, Nick. Boom! In and out. Only this time you make two hundred grand, and thank you very much." He folded his arms, puffed up, and showed off his teeth.

"And you get?"

"Three hundred, okay? It's my deal, and I gotta figure this whole thing out—like notes, and diagrams, and what to wear, and the weather, and figure the time of day, and day of the week—the whole thing."

Nick worked the button at his wrist.

"You hearing any of this? I drive all the way over here for the one guy in the world I can count on and he's, like, fucking comatose?"

Nick fumbled his button. "Two-fifty."

"Fuck *what?"* Cash sprang from the stool and paced behind the counter.

"Same's you, if I'm in."

"You heard that you're a late arrival, right? That I started this whole thing, made some connections, figured everything out, and *invited* you to score two hundred thousand dollars just because? We got history, Nick."

Hell with the buttons. He rolled his sleeves back up and stared at Cash.

"You're breakin my heart here. You see the sacrifice I made—tracking you down? Obtaining this car? Working for months on this plan and building it all around you? Don't tell me I can't depend on you."

"Two-fifty."

"Christ on a shingle!" Cash grabbed the stool and slammed the floor. "So *you* get two-fifty, and *I* get two-fifty, is what you're saying?" He dropped back onto the stool like a bag of rocks.

"I get what you get."

Cash folded his arms and lowered his chin to his chest. He mumbled to himself, and it involved a lot of swearing. After a couple minutes—"Ahhgg, goddamnit!"—he exploded off the stool, gave it a good kick, and sent it flying. He stood exhausted. "Okay." He nodded. "Okay. Two-fifty."

The corners of Nick's eyes wrinkled so slightly that only Cash could have seen that he was in. Nick shoved off the cabinet, approached the counter, and they shook. "What, where, and when?"

59

Bonnie and Clyde, 1996

"And the only thing standing between us and the art is the passcode to that little gallery—and I got it." Head up, chest expanded, Cash stood behind the shop's counter and examined his fingernails like he'd just won the Pocono Miller Genuine Draft 500.

"Yeah? What about the guards? The alarm?"

"Element of surprise. Surprise and speed, and glad to see you still resemble a ferret. Far as the alarm—let er ring. We'll be outta there before they know what hit em."

"Uh, huh." Nick nodded and twisted *what-ifs* for a couple seconds, and none of this was helping his headache. "And how'd we get into that building?"

"Well, now you cut to the crux of things and why I'm here and how we're such a winning team—like Butch and Sundance, like Bonnie and Clyde."

"Bonnie and Clyde."

“Okay, bad example. But like the legendary partners in crime and Jay Gould and Jim Fisk and totally screwing the gold market and the robber barons and Black Friday and 1869. Think of it—pulling the wool over Ulysses S. Grant?”

Nick rubbed his face with both hands and took a deep breath. “What were we talking about before Bonnie and Clyde?”

“Bump keys.”

“Bump keys.”

“Yep.”

“That’s what this comes down to?”

“Well, I’d be remiss not to speak to the incredibly bullet-proof feeling I get in your presence. If anyone was to look back at the places we’ve been and the things we’ve done, they might be convinced of our invincibility regarding dynamite and the law.”

There he went again. Nick lit a smoke and thought he could probably check out for a few.

“You are the bump key genius, my man. No one knows how to make that work like you, and there’s a Knox box, and that’s how we get in.”

Nick was getting hungry and thinking maybe hit McDonald’s and bring back a bag of food. Cash was probably hungry. He’d bring two Big Mac Meals. *And what’s a Knox box?* “What the hell’s a Knox box?”

"It's like a little safe installed in the side of the building by the loading dock. It's got the keys to the building inside for police and fire. The cops have keys to the box."

"And now we're safe crackers."

"I know a guy who knows a guy who used to work at Knox. Says a bump key will open their boxes. Bump, bump, bump—open the box, and there's our key to the magic kingdom."

"Huh." Nick snuffed out his smoke on the sole of his shoe and stuck the remains in his shirt pocket. He folded and unfolded his arms, jammed hands into his pockets. "Then we go in and wander around looking for some goddamn painting in a museum full of a thousand goddamn paintings while the alarm's ringing and all the lights come on?"

"My man, have a little faith. I know another guy who knows a guy, and I got a map. We sprint through that place like Carl Lewis, and we're outta there in ninety seconds—speaking of 'need for speed.' You see why I should be making the bucks? You see why it shouldn't be fifty-fifty? You see how much has gone into this while you're selling a buck-thirty in screws? And, oh, would you like ninety-cents-worth of washers with that? Paper or plastic?"

Nick turned his back to him and landed his butt on the counter. His gut hurt and maybe it was from all the booze or thinking about a Big Mac. Or maybe from Cash showing up and being such a know-it-all prick as usual. Hard to tell. Maybe he was just hungry. "Then all we gotta do is run an ad in the classifieds and see if anyone's interested in buying stolen art for five hundred grand?" His head was pounding and now he was getting an awful bad stomach. This was a screwed plan, and they'd be left holding a half-million-dollar bag.

"Got it covered my man. We got a no-questions-asked-and-money-back-guaranteed fence. *Good Housekeeping* seal of approval."

Whenever they'd gotten into deep shit in the past, Cash had introduced his plan with, "No questions asked." It was a red flag. That and, "My man."

60

Route 80 to New York City, 1997

Nick was going to take the bus to New York, and he didn't like it. He didn't like opening his little suitcase with the dull brass slide-buttons and spring-tripped latches. They flipped open, and it was the hollow sound and empty smell of moving again. He threw in a pair of jeans, a couple shirts, socks, and underwear. His toothbrush and razor lay on top, naked as orphans—and they were going to New York, and it made little sense. Brush his teeth in New York? What was he going to do with two hundred and fifty grand, anyway? Maybe a new truck, was all he could think. A pint of Old Grandad was last into the suitcase. It was 4 a.m. and pitch-black when he locked the door to his trailer. The Falcon started on the first try.

Highway into town was empty but for a big rig with Tennessee plates that passed him about fifteen miles-an-hour faster than he was going. At four-thirty, he backed the geriatric Falcon into a space in a sleeping neighborhood without street cleaning, grabbed the little suitcase from the passenger side, stepped out, and locked his door. Three blocks to the bus station, the mist had strengthened to drizzle, and it was trying to snow. This was a part of town that should have its own flag—a flag for police-targeting, domestic troubles, rundown houses, teen violence, and broken sidewalks. He tripped twice. At the station, he paid cash for his ticket and checked out the exhausted lobby. Plenty of places to sit beneath bug-specked florescent tubes where four strangers—two of them looking as hungover as he was—slumped on orange plastic chairs. He went outside for a smoke. Opalescent, black pools, skimmed with oil and diesel fuel in the three empty bus slots. He checked his watch. Five o'clock, and he heard the approaching bus slow, shift gears, and make the corner a block away. The rain had increased. The cold soaked through his shoes. He had less hair these days and was glad he'd grabbed his hat. It was an adjustable truckers' hat that puckered in back on the last plastic dot, and it was too big on his immature Catawba head.

He checked inside his jacket for the ticket. He patted the back of his jeans, and he had his wallet. Keys in his front pocket. Good to go.

The bus pulled into the bay right in front of him, and he was temporarily blinded. Then it appeared the bus was intent on permanently blinding him—its motor running, its lights six feet away and heating him and the front of the building. *Turn off the lights, you prick.* Probably some dipshit who lived with his mother. Probably wore his goddamn bus-driver uniform at holiday meals, and his mom thought he was something special—a man in uniform. For sure, he was a dick, blinding him, and he could have at least switched to low beams. It's not like it's an airport with international safety regulations, right? Like, there were numbered gates for United Airlines and little guys in jumpsuits and flashlights directing them?

He moved a few yards into shadow. He imagined entering the bus, presenting his ticket to the driver, and pulling the prick out from behind the wheel—down to the street by his shirt front, and dragging him out into traffic. He'd watch from the medial strip as the shit got run over by fifty-mile-an-hour commuters and a delivery van—his body flipped and splayed like a crash-test dummy. He'd have the uniform cleaned, pressed, folded, and sent to the mother. "Happy Thanksgiving." Driver didn't know how lucky he was.

The four passengers came out into the blinding glare—two with big roller suitcases and two with backpacks. Immediately, the bus lights dimmed, confirming this was between him and the driver. The driver—and he was a wormy little slick—was polite and accommodating with the two women with big suitcases. He helped load their luggage into the side of the bus, took their tickets, and helped them up the steps. Next, he welcomed the two kids with backpacks. They entered the bus like water running uphill.

Now, his turn. He told the driver, "Don't touch me."

Nearly empty bus, he shuffled down to near the back and chose a window seat in front of the roller bag women—on the side that would be looking to the fence lines and hills. He watched through his reflection as the bus station backed away in the rain. Dark and miserable, he settled in, lowered his hat, and closed his eyes.

Cheek pressed against the window, he woke. Rain like cold gray hell, warm air pushing up from the defroster. He decramped, straightened his hat, stepped down into the aisle, and stretched. Behind him, the two women were collapsed into each other and snored. Both dressed in black, it was hard to tell where one ended and the other began. He bent, and, out the window, there went a sign for Stroudsburg. Damn, he'd slept half the trip. He pulled his little suitcase down from the rack and extracted the pint.

61

Lost in NYC, 1997

Nick stood outside the Port Authority where Cash had told him to stand and watched the endless flow of depressed delivery trucks. He was a little fucked up, shoulders scrunched, and freezing. He wished he was home in front of his TV. He also wished he hadn't gone into the men's room in the terminal—there was some weird shit going on in there—but he had to piss like Secretariat. He lit another smoke. He'd been standing there for half-an-hour and was starting to think about finding a bar. Where the hell was Cash? If anyone was watching, Nick looked like a mid-thirties guy from rural Pennsylvania here for the trout fishing. A young woman approached. Slender, scarf, high-heeled boots, and, over her shoulder, a big-bag purse. "Like a date?"

"Yeah?"

"Let's go then."

"Where?"

"I know a place."

"They got TV?"

The woman backed away. "Where you from?"

"Here."

"I never saw you here before. Where you from yesterday?"

"The sticks."

"The sticks."

"So, they got TV?"

"Yeah, they got TV."

"Awright."

"Walker, Texas Ranger!" The TV screen filled the room with living color and the theme song, and Chuck Norris was jumping onto the roof of a car. Nick was on the slumped dog-bed-of-a fold-out sofa having a smoke. Crystal Ring—that's what she said her name was—was regluing a purple fingernail. "So you come here from Pennsylvania with a hundred and forty bucks and buy some whiskey, get a handjob, you're nearly broke, and you're watching TV. Shit, man, I bet all *kinda* women want *your* number!"

"Uh-huh." He pointed the remote at the TV and turned up the volume.

"Has anyone ever suggested you're one crooked piece of work? Like your ass was put together with non-union labor?"

"Uh-huh."

"You know that's not my real name, right?"

"Huh?"

"Crystal Ring. That's not my name, and we gotta go."

"Wha—"

"Somebody else gonna need this room." She crossed the linoleum and switched off the TV.

~ ~ ~

Nick was lost in New York City. Cash hadn't shown, he'd blown his bus fare home, and as night approached, he didn't know which way he was walking. It seemed he was moving farther away from the commercial part and into a residential part—narrow streets, less traffic, and now what? *The Ramona!* He remembered that Cash worked at the Ramona. In the next block, Nick ducked beneath a torn green canopy and into the warmth of a hotel—not like the mega chrome and glass towers earlier, but a much smaller, older building. He checked around for a phone. The deserted lobby opened to a small, low-ceilinged bar. He chose a stool, put his suitcase on the floor in front of him and ordered a whiskey, rocks. He tapped out a smoke and asked the bartender if she knew of the Ramona.

"Oh yeah, the Ramona. Of course," she said. "Everyone knows that place, but nobody goes there. Ya can never get a seat." She smirked, went down to the middle of the bar, and poured a quick one for a cop who had just come in. The cop peeled out of his gloves and earmuffs. In the mirror behind the bar Nick saw a guy squeeze out of a phone booth in the back. Nick left his drink and suitcase and went to the booth. The phone book was on a hinge contraption that made it nearly impossible to use, and you had to be in the seat to use it. He wedged in, pulled the book from its slot, and used his knee to help hold it up.

R . . . Ra . . . Ram . . . Ramona. *Shit!* There were three of them. He tore the page out and returned to the bar. After another quick one, the cop left, and Nick summoned the bartender. He pointed to the page and asked if she knew which Ramona was near a museum.

"You tore a page outta my fuckin phone book?"

He said he'd put it back.

"Hell right you'll put it back!" She went down to the cash register and returned with a roll of tape. "And you'll do a good job of it."

He asked again about which address might be near a museum.

She pointed. "That one. Now fix my goddamn book."

It was a long cab ride, and he was down to thirty bucks, and he'd be sleeping somewhere on the street tonight. He hated New York. He entered the Ramona.

Contemporary, expensive—Frank Sinatra on the sound system—clean, and just one other customer at the far end of the bar. The bartender came his way and nodded. Nick stood holding his little suitcase. He asked did the bartender know Cash.

"Course I know Cash. Whatta ya drinkin?"

Nick pulled out a stool and sat. He said he'd have a short beer. He asked if he had Cash's number.

"Yeah, I got his number—unlisted—and I'm not givin it out, if that's where you're headed."

Nick said he was a friend from out of town, and Cash was supposed to pick him up at the bus station and hadn't shown.

"Go figure. You have great taste in friends." The bartender went back down to the taps, drew a short one, and placed it on a coaster in front of Nick. "Two bucks."

Nick stood, had a little trouble pulling the ones from his jeans, and dumped some on the floor. Bending to pick them up, he knocked the stool over. "Sorry." He righted the stool.

The bartender leaned back against the counter, hands on hips. "What time d'you start drinkin today?"

Nick shoved two dollars across the bar and got the rest stashed away. He sat and asked if Cash still worked here.

The bartender checked his watch. "His weekend's about over. If he shows up in forty-five minutes he does."

Nick downed the beer and thought, okay, then. He shoved the glass forward and said he'd have another and a side of whiskey. He downed those, ordered another pair and said he was moving to a table.

"You want a map?"

Nick moved to the back of the room and noisily to a corner table. It took two trips—suitcase and drinks. The bartender seemed good with that. Nick lit a smoke, laid it on the ash tray and signaled for the bartender. The guy came out from the bar with a glass of water. He placed it on a coaster in front of Nick and picked up the empties.

"You can sit here and wait for Cash, but I'm not serving you again. That's it. And you fall asleep, I call the cops. You get loud, I call the cops. You get *anything*, I call the cops."

Nick nodded and slumped in the chair.

"I'll call the cops."

Nick sat up, collected his shit, and took a breath. Probably thirty minutes to go, and it was going to be a long thirty. He'd sit here and smoke—eyes wide open and smoke—and wait for Cash.

Chain smoking helped him stay half alert, and, about two hours ago, he'd bought a new pack at the liquor store with the hooker. She didn't smoke—said it was bad for you. She drank, though, and they'd shared hits on that fifth before and during the handjob. He'd asked her to stop for a second as he took a hit. Then he'd pass the bottle to her idle hand as her business hand resumed business. Probably how she lost a fingernail, passing the bottle back and forth.

He looked up, and Cash was behind the bar, and the other bartender wasn't. The place was nearly full. "Yeah, I missed something," he told himself. It wasn't the first time he'd fallen asleep with his eyes open. Behind the bar Cash was busy, and Nick didn't know if Cash even knew he was here. He remembered that "call the cops" stuff and decided not to yell across the bar. As he lit another smoke, a soft-focus, movie-version of a tall, beautiful young woman approached his table—big blue eyes and her good old Wisconsin daddy's farmgirl peaches-and-cream complexion, her smile was genuine.

"Hi, Nick." Hand on her hip. "Cash sent me. He said I should get your dead ass into the office and fuckin padlock the door."

She held his suitcase and waited outside the men's room while he took his last whiz as a free man. Then she showed him to the office and fuckin padlocked the door. As pressed out as the bar was, the office was not—no windows, low ceiling, tiny john, government-issue desk, and a file cabinet. That and a sagging leather couch. "Call the cops, my ass." He adjusted a cushion at one end and stretched out.

62

To Infinity and Beyond, 1997

It was like his brake pedal wasn't working, and it kicked back every time he pushed it. Why had he pushed it? Because he was in the wrong lane, and traffic was headed his way, is why. He hit the brakes again, and this time they kicked back harder.

"Nick. Nick!"

Nick opened an eye, and it was awful. The glare from the ceiling, and one of the florescent lights stuttered and spit. He slowly opened the other eye, and Cash had been kicking his foot. Already, Cash was ripping through his opening monologue. ". . . case of mistaken identity and they had to let me out." He rolled the toothpick to the other side of his mouth. "Seems anytime something goes missing and the suspect's a slender, good-looking white guy, they come lookin for me. They got no imagination. Otherwise, my man, I'd have been there to pick you up. Not lookin too worse for wear, now that you got some sleep. You ready to—?"

"I gotta take a leak." Nick was coming around.

"Right on, my man. Let's get you to the swell's pissoir."

"*Where* we goin?"

"To infinity and beyond! You, me, and about five hundred K, if you're hearing me right. C'mon." He tossed his toothpick into the can. The couch creaked and wheezed as he pulled Nick to his feet.

Nick stood, as for the first time. His eyes were heavy. His head was like someone hadn't read the recommended inflation pressure. His ears were ringing. Hell, his teeth were ringing! Nick said, "Infinity and beyond?" *Like Toy Story?* There were a lot of hinge-and-pivot joints between his head and feet. Which ones would make his shoes move?

"C'mon, Nick. This way." Cash pulled his sleeve.

"Don't."

"Yo! C'mon."

"Gimme a minute."

They walked a couple blocks to the 77th Street Station and took the train up to the Bronx. Way up. They got off at Bedford Park, then backtracked four blocks to Cash's place—a third floor walk-up. Cash had been talking pretty much nonstop since they'd left the Ramona. "And, not that you'd see it cause we were on the train, but we passed Poe Park, and they got the little cottage there where Edgar Allen Poe lived, and everyone must have been about four feet tall in those days cause ya have to duck in every doorway. Over there's the place makes the best pizza."

When they arrived at Cash's door, he had unlocked two of the three locks, then remembered another story. "You know that pizza place? The one I showed you, well—"

"Hurry up. I gotta piss."

Cash pointed. "End of the hall. If the door's open, it's available."

Cash lived in two rooms—a bedroom and a kitchen-and-everything-else room. Three-thirty in the morning, and he pulled a noisy frying pan from the drawer beneath the stove and set to grilling up a couple burgers. Nick sank deep into the couch and turned on the TV.

"Five days from now, and at nearly this very hour, we'll be streakin through that tunnel and on our way to new lives, my man."

"Uh-huh."

"What're ya gonna do with all that money, Nick? Close The Screw Shop? And your place by the creek's paid for, right?"

"Right." He changed the channel and it was *National Geographic* and something about dung beetles. He turned up the volume.

"Ya wanna guess what I'm gonna do?" Cash flipped the burgers. "Nick?"

"What?" Nick glanced over, then back to the TV.

"You wanna guess what I'm gonna do with all that money? Guess the very first thing?"

"No."

"Brand-new Corvette! Yellow if they got it. Red if they don't."

"Whatta ya have to drink?" Nick asked.

"Whiskey and Coke."

"Gimme a whiskey and water, ice."

"Ketchup or mustard?" Cash slid the burgers onto white bread.

"Both."

Cash put the drinks and burgers on the cluttered table in front of the couch and plopped down. "We gotta watch this while we eat? Balls of shit?"

~ ~ ~

Nick woke on the couch, and it had to be the middle of the day. His back hurt, and he couldn't breathe right, and it was like somebody'd been sitting on him. Through the closed window, there was a jackhammer right below them. Cash flip-flopped in from the hall wrapped in a towel, hair wet. "He wakes." Nick watched him heel-slap to the bedroom. Hangers screeched on a steel pipe, and he heard the bed springs collapse.

"We gotta make a list," Cash said from the bedroom. "Everything we're gonna need. Then we spend the rest of the week getting it. Also, we gotta do a drive-by run-through. We'll do that the night before, so's there's no street changes we gotta be aware of. You got sneakers? Like, running shoes?"

"No."

"There's a place near here's got em cheap. Get some today, and get used to em. Can't afford to be tripping when it matters most. Tell the guy you want the fastest ones he got."

"How we doin a drive-by without a car the night before? I guess I know how were doin the actual job the next night."

Drawers opened and closed, then the bed springs again. "I'm borrowing a car."

"Borrowing."

"For the run-through and, yeah, borrowing. First we drive by the museum, check it out nice and slow-like. Maybe take a trip around the block to get another look. Then we head for the tunnel and scoot straight through to Jersey. By then, you'll have your new shoes broken in from our practice sprints at the park."

Cash came into the room dressed like a bartender and ran a comb through his hair. He pulled a fresh toothpick from his shirt pocket and replaced it with the comb. Toothpick in his teeth, he moved a pile of table clutter and exposed a large diagram. "And you'll have this floor plan and the gallery code memorized."

"*That's* the place? The Whitney Museum? I think my sister works there."

"Well no shit? Nice that we're keeping it all in the family, right?"

"I don't know about this." Nick scratched his head. It was his friggin sister and Mom and all.

"She work there at three in the morning?" Cash asked.

"No."

"Alright then."

"Yeah, I guess. What the hell? Practice sprints at the park?"

"Huh?" Cash said.

"You said, 'Practice sprints at the park.'"

"Right. Two hundred yards from the truck dock to the gallery. A few seconds to punch in the passcode, ten seconds to grab the art, and a two-hundred-yard sprint back to the street. We gotta be clockin about eighteen miles an hour. Get you some fast shoes, and we time ourselves at the park."

"This is bullshit. 'Time ourselves at the park.' Fuckin grade school." Nick creaked up out of the couch, half-mast-and-wonky boxers, and went over to the little kitchen window. It was the shits out there—worn out, overcast, crowded, and it could have been anywhere. Everything busy in both directions and for what? He opened the single cabinet above the stove. "Fuck's the coffee?"

"Downstairs. Little bakery next door. Indian guy—his name's Peet. Get your pants on."

~ ~ ~

"Those are your shoes? I mean, they got batteries and glow in the dark?" Cash said.

"The guy said these were the fastest."

"How much?"

"Ten bucks."

"Shit, man."

They were at a far end of the park, on a double-wide diagonal walkway bisecting the place. Cash wore a whistle around his neck and held a stopwatch. He handed Nick what proposed to be a Christmas wreath box but heavier.

"What's this?" Nick asked.

"A prop."

"Prop."

"It's the approximate size and weight of the thing we're after, and you gotta be able to run fast while holding it. Don't drop it."

"This is such crap."

Cash had his thumb on the stopwatch. "Assume the position."

"*You* assume the position."

"Nick, we gotta be fast, and for starters we gotta assume the starting position. Like this." Cash turned sideways and crouched. "Then, I blow the whistle, and we race down the sidewalk to the tape."

"Tape."

"Yeah. We cross the tape and I stop the watch. We're aiming for thirty-five seconds."

"Tape."

"I put duct tape on the walk, okay?"

"Tape on the walk, and why not chalk on the walk, and we could invite kids to help?"

"Right." Cash said.

"Right."

"Ready?"

They assumed the position.

63

Badda-Bing, Badda-Boom, 1997

They hadn't slept. Cash had taken Nick to work with him at 6:30, given him a beer, and, at the shift change when he had to go on duty, he conscripted Nick to the office with a six-pack, two sandwiches and a few DVDs—*Angels in the Outfield, Beauty and the Beast,* and *Reservoir Dogs.* Hours later, bar closed, everyone gone, Cash came into the office and closed the door behind him. He bent down, touched his toes, then stretched wide-armed backward. "Time to boogie!"

"Now what?" Nick asked.

"Now you and me take a walk in the neighborhood and find the ride that matches this key." He showed the key.

"Whose key?"

"Lady who shouldn't have left her purse in the restroom. Customer found it and brought it up to the bar. Clueless and one-key-less lady lives around the corner from here."

They'd parked up the block, bump-keyed the Knox Box, got the entry key, and everything went as planned with the alarm ringing its ass off. Nick's fast shoes worked. So did the code, and the print was in a heavy frame, and he didn't drop it, and they got it to the end zone with no trouble. Once they were outside, Nick slowed up, and Cash ran up his back.

"Fucking run, Nick!"

At the car, sirens were blocks away and coming out of every crack. Cash flipped the inside trunk release, Nick got the art wrapped and into the backpack, slammed the trunk, and they headed for the tunnel.

"Badda-bing, badda-boom, my man." Cash stretched back, arms straight, both hands on the wheel and a fresh toothpick. "Rob from the rich and give to the poor. That'd be us, for about another couple hours—the poor. Whatta ya think, Nick? Do I know what I'm doin, or what?"

"What?"

"Didn't I say, 'Piece of cake?'"

Nick slumped in the passenger seat, arms folded, eyes closed.

"You goin to sleep over there?"

"I'm listening to the car. It's quiet. I never been in such a quiet car."

"Well yeah, it's a Lexus."

"Hot Lexus with New York plates," Nick said.

"We'll be changing that soon. New plates. Everything'll be different soon."

“It’s different already. We broke into a museum and stole shit, and now we’re in a brand-new stolen car, but we still ain’t rich. And who’s this guy you’re meetin anyway?”

“You don’t want to know that. Him and me, we sit down for a cup of coffee, we switch backpacks, and I’m outta there.”

“Where am I?”

“You’re in the parking lot takin a nap in this here quiet car.”

~ ~ ~

A *tap, tap* on the window. Again. Nick roused from the dream where he’d been at the ocean—sun, wind and kites, kids running around, a young woman. He’d never been to the ocean, and now a cop. He raised up slow to the window and smiled. Smiled and nodded. He showed his hands.

“You okay?” the cop said, all uniformed up and badged and proud in his Smokey hat.

“Yeah, I’m good.”

“Step out of the car, please.” The cop had his hand at his side like on a gun, but it wasn’t a gun. It was mace, and this was a shopping mall rent-a-cop.

Nick opened the door slowly and stepped out.

“Now I gotta see some ID” The cop pulled a note pad and pen from a flapped shirt pocket.

“ID? Like how come?”

"Cause I said's how come, and I gotta report on respondin to a situation."

"Situation."

"That's right, situation."

"Look, I'm sorry for sleepin on your lot." Nick passed him his license.

"Pennsylvania," the cop wrote. "Car's got New York plates. This ain't your car. Looks like some lady's car."

"Yeah, uh, it's my brother's car, and he's in there shoppin somewhere. It's been a while."

The cop relaxed his stance and handed back the ID. "Hell, I knew it. Your brother's car. Probably a city boy, ain't? This ain't your kind of ride, am I right? You look more like a jacked-up-truck guy. I'm trained in this, and you got that look. Yep, truck guys—you and me. No problem, friend. I hope he's done his shoppin soon." He contorted his neck and spoke from the side of his mouth into to the little radio at his shoulder. "Red Dog One, stand down. Repeat, Red Dog One, stand down. Over."

Nick nodded, dropped back into the car, and the goddamn alarm went off.

"Fuck, and he has the keys!" Nick sprung up and out of the car.

"Pop the hood," the cop said. "We disconnect the battery." He produced a Leatherman multitool from his belt. "When your brother gets back, we can reset everything."

We?! Goddamn smart car.

The alarm was deafening, the hood was open, the cop leaned into the engine, and here came Cash. Cash adjusted the pack's shoulder straps—his face screwed up. Nick shook his head and shrugged. Cash slipped between a couple cars and re-approached the Lexus from the rear. The alarm stopped. The cop poked up out of the engine bay, "Got er done." Cash appeared next to Nick.

"What's goin on, boys? Was that my car mouthin off?"

"I guess this'll be your brother," the cop said.

"Yeah."

"Your brother somehow set off your alarm, so I loosened the battery cable. Fancy car. Meant for a woman, if ya ask me."

"Why, thank you, officer. We'll put it back together now. Then we gotta get going. I'm already late for my . . . " He pulled the toothpick from his mouth and tossed it. "Stylist." He winked at Nick.

"Stylist, huh? Lady's car and spendin the day shoppin. Lost track of time doin all that shoppin, ain't? Nothin to show for it though."

"Oh, I found a few things. They're in my pack." Cash peeled out of the pack and brought it around front.

Nick wasn't believing this.

"Maybe I should have a look in that pack," the cop said. "Been to the sporting goods store? You see their guns? Friggin hollow points? They'll blow a man in half. You pick up a piece? You got a license?"

"Well, now that you ask, I was in the men's department, and I'm all, 'Decisions, decisions.' Boxers or briefs? My brother, here, he thinks I should go for boxers, but I'm a brief man. Keep em snug." He grabbed himself. "Which way do you swing, officer?" He continued to hold himself. "It was simple when we were kids, right? The colors? Underwear was white. Now it's mauve, persimmon and armadillo. Mid-rise, low-rise, microfiber-butt-enhancing-package-boosting, and I can't wait til someone comes up with something aromatic and edible. Persimmon Smoke? Yum." He hiked his crotch again, released his grip, and smiled.

"You fellas have a good day, now." The cop spun and slipped to the next row over and disappeared.

"Edible," Nick said.

Cash grinned large. "Let's get this tub wired and go count our pay."

They ditched the NY plates, and the Lexus was now tagged Jersey. A short hop across the state and they entered Pennsylvania. "So no surprises with your guy at the coffee shop?" Nick asked.

"Smooth as silk."

"You still thinkin underwear?"

"Easy as pie, then."

Nick nodded. "Who paid for the coffee?"

"I did."

"What the hell?"

"No biggie."

"It's his deal, right? He should cover expenses."

"It was three bucks. Maybe he only had hundreds."

"So, easy as pie," Nick said.

"Yeah, til I thought my guy's having a heart attack right there in the middle of Starbucks. He gets that shit-or-go-blind look, staring past me, sweating, he chokes on his coffee. I check behind me, and there they are—two cops at the counter, and they seem concerned."

"Concerned."

"Yeah, my guy's, like, all red and his eyes teared up, and one of the cops asks if he's okay?"

"Damn."

"Yeah. My guy gives a two-thumbs-up and nods—couldn't talk. I didn't look back again, but the cops never came over. We waited for em to leave is what took so long."

Cash pulled off a forest exit on Route 80 and pulled the car onto a dirt lot behind a small abandoned market. Out of the car, he snagged the pack from the backseat and swung it onto the trunk lid.

"I know it's all here. I already seen inside. But let's get a better look." He opened the flap wide and they peered in. "Ain't it beautiful?"

"Yeah. Little packages all wrapped up like that."

Cash pulled out a stack. "Fifty little bundles of one-hundred-dollar bills, my man. Twenty-five for each of us."

"Fuckin A."

Cash closed the pack and stashed it in the back. "Now we go to your place, get the Falcon and drive to Ithaca."

"The Falcon to Ithaca."

"You follow me, we take the plates and leave the Lexus. You drive me back to your little burg, we divide up the money, and I catch a bus back to the city."

"You could fly."

"Too many complications."

64

He Was More Hungover Than Usual, 1997

Two weeks later, a brand-new, four-wheel-drive-and-raised Ford F-250 was parked outside The Screw Shop, and Cash had a shiny red Corvette. They didn't make them in yellow that year, but to hear him tell it, it was the most beautiful goddamn red you ever saw. He called The Screw Shop. "You oughta hear the stereo in this beast!" And he'd moved to a nicer place in the Bronx. "Got my own bath and a view of our practice park, Nick. Oh, and by-the-way, your sister *did* work at that museum, but she don't now. Got fired, according to the TV."

Yeah, well, Nick thought.

The geriatric Falcon was moored in the deep forest beside his trailer, and Nick was thinking on what to do with it. Twenty years later, some of it would still be visible as vines slowly consumed the car, as they would have his trailer, if there hadn't been occasional traffic to refill heating fuel oil at the back, exchange propane tanks at the front, and set the ladder along the side for shoveling snow off the roof. The winters were tough in his trailer. Not much insulation and there were leaks. Flat, tarred roof with seams that baked and got more brittle every day of summer, and now there were cracks in the roof and drips in the kitchen. Also things froze, expanded, and disconnected—electrical things, plumbing things, and fuel oil things. He'd had to call a plumber in the middle of winter nights over the years.

~ ~ ~

It might have been six months after the heist when Nick answered the phone. It was the funeral director, and he was sorry to convey that his father's service and burial would be taking place on Monday.

He was sorry to convey. Nick dropped the phone. It unwound itself on the kitchen floor. Fuckin funeral director. Wasn't that his goddamn job? To convey? Isn't that how he made every buck he ever made? Conveying? He buries the dead sonofabitch and moves on to the next one? Sometimes two at a time? Dressed up all pretty in polished shoes that he probably just tied up after getting out of rubber boots, and hosing down the steel table, and sliding his father's body, whose "*service and burial would be taking place on Monday*," into a cold drawer. What'd they do to the old man before they put him in that drawer?

He hated his father. He loved his father. No one made the commitment the preacher had. It had been a long shot, and the old man was willing to take it cause he probably thought he had God on his side. Leading him in prayer, reciting the same Bible verses over, and over and trying to get him to memorize them? "Blessed are the meek . . . Yea though I walk through the valley . . . " In the car, fishing on the lake, before each and every meal. Yeah, sure, the old man kept him fed. And he was supposed to thank God for that? He was expected to kneel and give thanks for that? He hated him for being a preacher, and the preacher hated him for being a sinner. "Fuck you!" he told the old man. The preacher nearly said it back and caught himself—but there it was on his lips. Instead he slapped the sinner's face hard, and it made his ears ring. God, he hated the preacher.

Miriam called the day he died. She was pretty broken-up over the whole thing. Said Mom was sedated. He listened, said, "Uh-huh," and that was that. What the hell was he supposed to do about it? Miriam the artist. Miriam the college student. Miriam the whatever-she-was at that fat-ass museum. It was mostly her job, directed by Mom, to convince him that Dad wasn't a prick. Mom. Caught between the preacher and him, and she always had to take the preacher's side cause he had her by the nuts. Each time Miriam would start in about it—about why couldn't he act like a normal human being and how he was making their lives miserable—he unleashed his counterattack. He made her pay for days after—laying booby traps in her room, contaminating her make-up. He'd once cut a great hunk of her hair as she slept. He hadn't exactly meant to cut her neck like he did, and the goddamn bleeding went on forever. Miriam. So perfect in their eyes—dressing nice, smelling nice, reading books, drawing, keeping a diary, and he'd read every bit of it, and she was boring as shit. He'd go downtown and buy a suit.

~ ~ ~

He was more hungover than usual—technically, drunk. He put a note on The Screw Shop door, "Closed. Open tomorrow." He climbed back up into the truck, and everything smelled new—the truck, the cowboy boots, and his suit which didn't make climbing into the truck any easier. The guy with the measuring tape said a tight fit was the style, especially for trim guys like him. He wished the guy'd given him a one-size-larger shirt collar. He checked his chin in the mirror and carefully removed the wad of toilet paper. Don't shave drunk.

He'd taken a wrong turn, not so familiar with the east end of town, and arrived late. All the cars lined up behind the hearse and about a hundred people under and around a white canopy. A lot of heads turned his way as he pulled up. Yeah, the exhaust was loud, and—go t' hell—he liked it that way. He buttoned the three jacket buttons, strolled over, and stood at the edge of the gathering. His mom and Miriam sat right up front. There was a small New York-looking, foreign-kinda-woman on the other side of Miriam and holding her hand. Some tall, blond, smarmy guy stood behind them. The fat bald guy conducting the funeral seemed awkward reading the Bible and telling everyone to pray and all. Maybe a last-minute stand-in, now that the preacher was gone. The guy asked if anyone would like to say a few words. People shuffled around like no one wanted to, then a lady in the back spoke up. "The reverend was a fine man, a caring man, and he helped our family through two days like this one. I don't think I could have gone on living if he hadn't been there."

"Here, here, and Amen," someone said.

"He could appear to be hard on the outside, but he had a soft center," another someone.

Fuckin-A hard, Nick thought. His dad sure as hell never showed *him* the soft center.

"He wrote a fine letter of recommendation for our daughter, and she's a doctor now."

"He put so much energy into those food drives for the poor."

"Amen. And blessed are the meek."

There it is, Nick thought. The gathering bowed heads, and the leader guy was praying again. All those times his dad had him on his knees and praying for forgiveness for the cruel things he'd done to his sister, for flattening their tires, for the flaming bag of shit, for breaking into lockers at school, for, well, a lot—he'd done a lot. Now, it sounded like the guy was finishing up.

". . . comfort us in our grief, Lord, and give us your assurance of your promise of eternal life. Through Jesus Christ our Lord, Amen."

Yep, Nick thought. Amen.

The crowd moved away from the grave. Nick lagged, then approached the headstone and blanket of AstroTurf. "I guess you can be glad I stayed outta your hair all this time, right, Reverend? Must'a been pretty quiet around the house, just you and Mom. Did you keep fishin at the lake after I was gone? I liked bein out there. But you sure as hell weren't any good at fishin. *We* weren't any good at fishin. Great at arguin, though. Scared the fish away, yellin at each other, all alone way out there in that little boat. Mom ever get you that lectric razor? I stole a Norelco and almost gave it to you. Hah! Then we had a nother fuck-you flare up, and I threw the whole thing in the crick—wrappin paper and all. Man, the shit that went down between us. I didn't understand you, and you sure as hell didn't understand me. Well, that's all over and done. No second chances. Sleep tight, Reverend."

The crowd had gathered over near the cars beneath the trees. Hands in his pockets, he started that way and said back over his shoulder, "You oughta see my truck."

Church ladies. They were clustered around Miriam, his mom and the tall guy, and most of them looked like his mom. Most were medium build. There were a few skinny ones, a couple plump ones, and they all probably cooked a lot. Damn, his mom could cook. Her meals and desserts were the best things in his young life—not that he'd tell her. It probably showed at the table as he wolfed his meals, and he was embarrassed by that. But he couldn't help himself with her candied ham, and scalloped potatoes, and rosemary chicken, and rhubarb pie. The woman glowed, and, looking back, he thought it might have been from the heat of the kitchen. She was also a woman who smiled for no apparent reason. She was Norwegian and blond, and she had great bright teeth in that smile. As he approached his mom and Miriam, he had no idea what to say. Like, you're supposed to say something, right? "Yo. What's up? Sorry bout the preacher?" Hell, let Miriam do the talking.

The church ladies and their men had moved on, and now Miriam saw him coming. She hustled Mom into her car and closed the door. She said something to the tall guy and he moved away down the drive. As he approached her, she turned to face him. Pale. Small. Another gun fight, he thought. She took a deep breath and two steps his way. He didn't mean to speak first, but he did.

"Finally."

She went off on something about him blaming Dad for everything and wishing he hadn't shown up and her typical Miriam and holier-than-thou crap. It was like a day hadn't passed between them. As kids, it was his nature to tune her out when she started in like this. It was always basically the same message. Now she had that smug, calm-and-collected look she always got near the end, and, if Mom wasn't watching from inside the car, he might have reached across and slapped her. Instead he leaned his head to the side and spit. She'd always hated that—him spitting while she was telling him off. Then he let her know he knew she lost her fat-ass job, and he wanted to tell her how much money he had squirreled away just to see the look on her face. But he didn't. Instead, he went over to the car. He opened the back door, and their mother stepped out. She looked so old. Arms at her sides, she stared level with him. He moved closer, the tips of their shoes touched, and he embraced her. "Mom."

Back at the trailer, he was taking a long-needed piss. He watched himself in the mirror over the toilet, and it was like his eyes were on fire. Screwed from the neck up, bad skin, and it had never been good. Suit and tie, and, from the neck down, it was like he was looking at somebody else. He flushed the toilet, un-noosed the tie, opened the goddamn collar, and threw the jacket in the tub.

The first thing he'd done returning home was turn on the TV. It ran like a hamster wheel in the front room. He stepped from the bathroom, bounced off the wall, and aimed at the kitchen. The whiskey. Dad.

65

Dolly, 1998 - 2008

Nick returned to the cave of his life and his daily drive through the morning haze to The Screw Shop. Days filled with nuts, bolts, washers, and the little FM radio. The painfully sober drive home, and the hum of the television, and alcohol oblivion. He'd be closing the shop one of these days. Didn't need it anymore, but it was about all he had to fill his time. It would be ten years later that he'd throw in the towel.

~ ~ ~

The truck was ten years old, and it suited him fine. He mainly just drove it to and from the shop, and he changed the oil himself every five thousand, so it was in pretty good running shape.

This day, he stopped halfway home at a motel's restaurant because the day's protracted hours of sobriety had made him especially crazy. A guy had come into the shop to return a dozen obviously used bolts that The Screw Shop didn't carry.

"Didn't buy em here," Nick said.

The guy insisted that he had and engaged the other two customers and rallied for their support.

Nick told the guy, "Get the hell outta my shop."

The guy amplified his rant and Nick said, "Now you're trespassin." He pulled a Louisville Slugger from beneath the counter. "Is it worth it?" he said. "A broken arm for twelve fuckin bolts?"

The motel parking lot was jammed. He pulled around behind the building and parked on the grass.

The restaurant had an oval bar, it was nearly full, and, by appearances, everyone knew each other.

"Whiskey," he told the bartender.

"Water? Ice?"

"Whiskey."

The bartender placed a shot in front of him. He reached for it and—

"Okay, who's having the prime rib?" It was a large blond woman, her hair a mess, an apron and a huge knife. She held the door to the kitchen open with her heel.

Half of the bar raised their hands, and she counted with the knife. "One, two, three, . . . " The knife swung past him, then stopped and returned. "Is that you, Nick? But older and less hair?"

All the bar looked his way. He threw back the shot.

"Damn, it *is* you. Have yourself another drink, and don't go nowhere while I get this roast carved. We got some catching up to do."

The bartender was back with the bottle. Nick nodded, the bartender poured.

"So how do you know Dolly?"

Thumb and forefinger, Nick slowly turned the shot on the bar. "I used to run with her brothers. Long time ago."

"Didn't know she had brothers."

"It was a long time ago." Nick downed the shot and placed the glass back on the bar. "One more'll do'er."

The bartender poured and moved on to other customers. He laid paper mats, and forks and knives wrapped in napkins in front of those who'd signed on for the prime rib. It was ten minutes later that Dolly made trips from the kitchen delivering three steaming meals at a time.

~ ~ ~

They'd run trap lines. As winter approached, he and Dolly's brothers—a couple years older than him—stood around a boiling tub on an open fire and watched steel traps bubble and churn as they were rid of human scent. Once the water cooled, the boys slipped into long rubber gloves, pulled the traps out by their chains and laid them on beds of leaves. From then on, until the traps were set according to the mammals the boys were after—fox, weasel, raccoon—the traps would be handled with rubber gloves.

Packs on their backs loaded down with boiled steel, the boys trekked up what was referred to as Frey's hill over acres of fallen corn stalks to the edge of the forest. Deep inside, moist, soft earth, dark, and, "What's that noise?" They set the traps near what they thought to be fox dens, pathways beneath tree roots and at ends of hollowed logs. It was especially important they remember where the traps were set. Over the next months, they'd awaken before dawn to check the sites daily. During the last weeks of the season it was in snow.

Weekends and some evenings, he'd hang out at Mark and Billy's house. Mark, the oldest, was eighteen, Billy, seventeen and their adopted sister, Dolly, was his age—fifteen. The only times the four of them were together was if he stayed over for supper, and the suppers were never calm. Their mom yelling up the stairs, "And don't make me call again!" When she *did* call again, it was, "And this time I fuckin mean it, Dolly!" Dolly stomped down from her room at the last second and took her spot at the table.

Supper would start out quiet and slow—no eye contact. The potatoes got passed, and the beans got passed, and the meatloaf got passed, and the tension built as the boys bypassed Dolly. You could feel her irritation damming up, and it was going to burst any second. When it did, and her swearing at them, and their laughing at her, and her grabbing a knife and about to lunge across the table, and then their *dad* got involved, and the shit *really* hit the fan! The boys hated her, and she hated them.

It was a slow summer morning when they shared a joint, and Mark and Billy were talking about the girls at school, and which ones did it and which ones surely didn't. In the course of their discussion, Mark was inspired to ask Billy and Nick if they wouldn't like to see Dolly's tits. He had a plan. He'd tell her he was offering a truce—that he and Billy were sorry for all the shit they'd been pulling on her all these years, and, now that they were older, they saw how wrong they'd been. Could she forgive them? Wouldn't she like to hike up to the spring with them today? He'd even pack her lunch. Then, up there and all alone, Mark would say, "Now!" and Billy and Nick would grab her, and he'd pop the buttons of her blouse, and he had a Polaroid.

Billy was all in.

Nick wasn't sure.

Mark asked him didn't he want to see Dolly's tits?

"Well, yeah, of course, but not that way."

Mark said it wasn't going to happen any other way, and what the hell, it wasn't like anybody was getting hurt, or anything. It was always Mark who clubbed the animals caught in their traps.

Dolly was hesitant, but Mark was a great actor. If things hadn't gone the way they had, he might have made it in Hollywood, is what his mom said for years after. "Such a handsome boy."

The four youths slogged single file up the narrow dirt road between fields of tall corn in congealed August heat. Mark and Billy, packs on their backs, talked baseball. Dolly and Nick brought up the rear, and it was Dolly's on which he fixed. Sweat rippled down her back leaving transparent, flesh-toned trails streaked through her white blouse and soaked deep into her pink denim shorts. She had filled out nicely these past few summers, and it made him itch.

In the forest, the shade was a relief and ten degrees cooler. Mark and Billy fell silent. The four slowed their steps and checked back over their shoulders. They had entered a dark and ferocious place where the rules changed. Bears, bobcats, snakes and panthers, and sometimes you saw scattered bones and hunks of fur. Things got torn apart and eaten here. A half mile in, they came to the spring, a landmark where the boys had drunk beer, smoked joints and slept under the stars. Mark and Billy dropped their packs. Dolly, her back to them and on her haunches at the spring, cupped her hands and drank. Mark pulled the camera from his pack. Dolly stood and faced them.

"Group photo?" she asked.

"Now!"

Billy lunged and seized Dolly's arm and wrist.

Nick froze.

Dolly yanked away, ripped at Billy's shirt, and spun him.

"Now!" Mark yelled at Nick. "Now!"

Nick couldn't move.

Mark snagged Dolly's collar and ripped her blouse open. She screamed and Billy came loose. Now all three were flailing on the ground. Scratches, sweat, and kicks, Mark yanked at her bra and yelled at Billy, "Hold her down!"

Dolly screamed, "Nick, do something!"

Billy pressed all his weight onto her shoulders.

"Nick!"

Nick's senses came crashing back. Three strides and he straddled two sets of legs. He reached in from behind, got Mark in a headlock and squeezed.

"What the fuck's the matter with you?!" Mark choked.

Billy was up and both hands dug into Nick's scalp.

Nick squeezed harder. There was a loud *crack*, and Mark went limp. Blood. Lots of blood ran down the side of Mark's head and over Nick's arm. He pulled Mark's dead weight off Dolly. She scrambled backwards on her butt, a rock in her fist. He dropped Mark face down and fought for breath. Billy fell to his knees.

~ ~ ~

Dolly came out to the bar and took the stool next to him. She'd brushed her hair and wore fresh lipstick. "So. What have you been up to, Nick?" The bartender slid a pint in front of her, and she took a sip.

"Not much."

"Where you living these days?"

"At the creek."

"Full time? That old trailer?"

"It works."

"You got a woman?"

He shifted on his stool. “Not exactly.”

“What would be ‘exactly?’”

“Got a handjob in New York one time.”

She choked on the beer and laughed. “That don’t count, Nick.”

“How bout you?”

“Did I get a handjob? No!”

He nodded.

“I’ve been alone eight years, now. Donald had second thoughts about his sexuality and left me for a man. A clarinetist. I hear they play beautifully together.”

“Clarinet.”

“Uh-huh.”

“Kids?” he asked.

“None.”

Nick motioned to the bartender. He arrived and poured.

“You see your brothers?”

“Fuck them. Billy’s long gone. Out West, I hear. Detroit. Building cars. And, Mark, well, he’s in the home. You couldn’t drag me there.”

He nodded. They drifted, silent—knives and forks clicked on plates, a game on the big screen, random words around the bar.

“You ever think of me? Of that day?” she asked.

"Few minutes ago."

"That's it?"

"I guess other times. Times I was sober."

"Did you wonder what became of me?"

"I guess."

"If I moved away? If I was married?"

"Dunno. Maybe."

"You saved me that day, Nick."

He glanced at her, then back to his glass. They went quiet again. He downed the shot. "It was you with the rock."

"You saved me."

A young couple came in and sat across from them. Probably college kids and at the edge of love, the way they bumped shoulders when they laughed.

Nick placed both palms flat over his eyes and rubbed his face. He let out a long breath and stepped back off the stool. "Nobody was saved. I gotta be goin."

"Ride me home?"

"Where?"

"It's about six miles out of your way. I have to wait for him to get off." She motioned to the bartender. "That's two hours from now. I got no car."

"Awright."

They went around back to his truck. Nick unlocked her door, and she climbed in.

"Thanks for doing this, Nick. Riding me home, and all."

"Yeah." He pulled onto the road and switched on the stereo—*The Rite of Spring*.

"What do you listen to?"

He made the turn off he never took—toward her place. "This."

"Why?"

He watched the road, unfamiliar. He went off on a decreasing radius turn—slow, but off.

"You okay?" she asked.

"To the nines."

"Kinda weird music."

"Weird."

They were quiet for the next ten minutes as the truck followed the slow spread of its lights into Stravinsky's sudden dips, irregular rhythms, and blind curves.

"Oh, right here. Turn past the post."

She lived in a trailer among five others perched on a rise above an ancient Amish farm. He put the truck in park. She opened her door, and the cab was infused with the smell of pig shit.

"Damn, Dolly. How long you lived here?"

"You get used to it. Want to come in?"

"Why?"

"Wash the stink off."

"You got cable?"

"Not exactly, but I'm high enough here that reception's good. I get a movie channel. Old movies."

"You got whiskey?"

"Damn, Nick. What else? Yes, I have whiskey."

"Awright."

66

Sundays at Dolly's

Nick and Dolly enjoyed knowing each other once a week for the following years, always Sunday nights at her place. Nick kept mum about the Whitney and his great bounty, and Dolly continued to work at the motel cleaning rooms during the day and cooking in the late afternoons and evenings. A few years later, Dolly had *her* windfall. She and three others from the motel split a winning lottery ticket. She got cable with all the premium channels and bought her first car—a Black Cherry Miata—and its stereo was much better than in Nick's truck. She loved the smell of her new car and sat in the driveway those first few weeks for an hour-at-a-time snuggled behind the wheel in her little bucket seat—shoulder belt and all. Some people get larger with age. Dolly got smaller.

It was about ten years after they'd started seeing each other that some out-of-stater T-boned a truck at Trout Run. Early to the scene, Nick snooped in the out-of-stater's wrecked car, and, damn, there was an envelope with ten thousand dollars in unmarked bills. Dolly never heard about that, either.

In spite of their financial good fortunes, money got thin. That's when Nick hired out across the road from Dolly's throwing hay bales onto the wagon with the farm boys in the fall and cutting top wood left by loggers in winter. Hard work didn't bother him none—made him sleep good. But he refused to shovel shit. So when it was time to do that, the farmer paid Nick to keep an eye on the two youngest of the nine kids while the women—Grandmother, Mother, and the older girls—did the shoveling. Truth be told, and he eventually told Dolly, he liked taking care of the kids.

"What? Nick, I never knew you liked kids."

"Gotta say as I do. Them kids, anyway." They were funny and a little out of control, and falling all over each other and the cats, and he made farting noises, and made them laugh.

"Did you ever want kids, Nick?"

He scratched his neck. "Nah."

Over the years, Dolly also heard about the Coke bottle and the blood, and the chicken lady, and the preacher wars, and Cash, and jail, and the Army. Nick's mind went unfettered after sex, and they laid there on top of the sweat-soaked sheets in the summers and beneath the quilts and their breath-in-the-air winters as his stories ran free.

At first, she figured they were mostly lies—Nick's stories—but hearing them repeated for years to come and with little variation, she decided they were probably true. His life *had* been screwed up. He was better now. With her.

PART 3

Irvin

When you have worked with someone for thirteen years and stayed in touch for the next twenty, you probably know them pretty well. As well as you're going to. Though we worked closely during our time at the Whitney, Irvin and I, for the most part, had separate private lives. I do know that he required little sleep, so if it was as little as four hours, and adding his seven-hour days at the museum, that gave him another thirteen hours to fill each day. Idle hands . . .

67

Valedictorian, 1975

Irvin sprained his ankle in PE, and it was the talk of the school. It had been during the indoor badminton unit, and his new sneakers didn't slide as the old ones had. Racket extended, he rushed to the birdie, and he was sure to make this play and drive the plastic projectile right down his opponent's throat. His forward momentum and the weight of his lingering, prepubescent chubbiness, inherited from his father and grandfather and generations of Rappaports before him—and that stuck sneaker—bent his right ankle farther than it had ever gone. He went down.

Racket extended, he sprawled out larger than he had seemed standing up. Another humiliation!

A sophomore photographer for the school paper heard the raucous laughter in the boys' gym. She stepped in, quickly got the shot, and headed for the editorial desk. It was noted beneath the wide, excellent, above-the-fold front-page photo that Irvin was in contention for valedictorian, had stolen the show as Mortimer Brewster in *Arsenic and Old Lace,* and was president of the chess club.

During his convalescence, Irvin submitted the final draft of his graduation speech. He'd had plenty of time while his ankle was raised, iced, heated and iced again, to focus on how to eliminate the other two valedictorian contenders. This consisted of sending hat-in-hand drafts of his speech to the head of the selection committee, in which he flowered her name. An intimate student-teacher correspondence developed between them, and as thick as his waist and heavy his thighs was the flattery he lathered on the lonely woman.

He delivered his speech leaning on the cane he'd come to use with great theatricality—a valuable prop that had kept him out of PE for the remainder of the year. He'd be seen later that summer dancing elegantly with Cheryl Troglitz Friday nights at the YWCA. He'd taken lessons at the Arthur Murray Dance Studio above the butcher shop.

68

The Saudis Were Loaded, 1976

It was as a Stanford undergrad that he discovered his great talents for poker and drinking, and he came to find he needed little more than three hours' sleep a night. With nearly twenty-one hours a day at his whim, he was able to keep his grades up, fatten his bank account—some of the students, especially the Saudis, were loaded—and have a hell of a good time doing it.

All the while, his baby fat melted away, his shoulders and chest filled out, he'd shot up nearly a foot, and he was damned good looking. *Übermensch.*

69

Stanford, 1983

"What is it you want, Irvin?"

He was in the pipe-tobacco-and-redwood office of Dr. Banta, the program director. Irvin was being interviewed for placement in the Doctor of Philosophy studies.

Across the desk from the director, Irvin leaned back, fingers woven behind his head, and he grinned. "I want to win."

"Care to expand?"

"My old man says talent, smarts, and good looks should be fueled by ambition."

"Your father does what?"

"Philosophy, Harvard. He also writes and directs plays."

"He sounds like a rich man," Banta said.

"Hah," Irvin laughed. "He struggles with perfection—the finite in parched pursuit of the infinite. He told me to go beyond the summit, fly with the raptors, swing from a star."

"And your mother?"

"Genius mathematician. Also Harvard, also an actor. Film society, medieval music group, and their theater—The Janus Players. I was in a few of the productions. Played the tragic Hap in Miller's *Death of a Salesman.* They say I was brilliant, a natural."

"Your mother also says, 'Good looks should be fueled by ambition?'"

"Nice. No, she says, 'Keep your head down and fall into line. Do your little part for the grand equation.' It's a math thing."

"What do you expect to accomplish in pursuit of your Ph.D.?" Banta asked.

"I've always been at the top of the game, and I want to keep it that way." He raked his fingers through his hair and shook out blonde curls.

"Yes, top of your game." Banta referred to the CV on his desk. "Undergrad honors, film awards, Assistant Program Director at the Cantor Center, master's residency in Paris, and now, here we are. What do you see as the top of the art history game?"

"I want to curate, be the great decider."

"Curate what? Where?"

Irvin sat back, folded his arms, and watched the two-way parade of students pass Banta's window—engineering, architecture, pre-med, and strings of future VCs and CEOs. "At the Whitney."

Dr. Banta laughed. "You've set a very high and highly specific goal, Irvin, and I think we can help with your trajectory."

70

After the Fall, 1997

Irvin landed at SeaTac and took a cab into town. Raining like hell, and it was perfect for his mood. It had been a bad five years. What he thought to be his Destiny had left him. Miriam and he washed out of a possible romance, then the Jersey guys, and friggin Detective Nettles, and now he was fired from the Whitney.

Was this a tail-between-the-legs moment? Not if he didn't want it to be. Make adjustments at halftime. Change up the defense every play, and go to a quick-count offense. Keep em on their heels.

He asked the driver, who sounded like he was from a sub-Saharan country, "Does it rain every friggin day?"

The driver glanced up into the mirror and nodded.

The cab came to rest at an angle suited for a missile launch. The rain had stopped, and the new challenge was gravity. It took two tries to open the door. He grabbed the back of the driver's seat and engaged feeble core muscles to rise and climb out of the cab five blocks up the Pike Street hill.

Damn, there's a sidewalk? Who walks this?

The driver kept his foot against the precariously stacked train of Irvin's roller luggage, and Irvin paid the guy.

The driver asked, "You got this?"

Irvin assessed the situation and determined—no. He tipped the driver a twenty and asked could he help. The driver kept his palm out. Irv gave the guy another twenty.

They huffed the luggage through the lobby, into the elevator, and up to Destiny's floor. Long haul down a long hall and they arrived at 622. Irvin knocked and the driver was already halfway back to the elevator. "Thanks," Irvin called. No response. He knocked again.

"Yeah, yeah. Keep your pants on." A chain slid and two locks clicked. "Irvy! I thought it was tomorrow at six." She stood in bare feet and sweats and held the door. "You said the ninth."

"Hi, Des. Yeah, today—the ninth. Maybe I should wait out here until tomorrow? Maybe tomorrow you'll be glad to see me?"

"C'mere, creep." She pulled him in by his jacket collar and closed the door. She wrapped much of her young, smooth self around him and locked onto his lips. Deep, soulful, and blood rushed to sleeping parts. She pulled back and took a breath. "I gotta dance tonight. I switched with someone cause I thought you were coming tomorrow, and I haven't changed the sheets."

"Do we have to change the sheets? My luggage."

"What?"

"It's in the hall."

Irvin was tired from travel. He sat at Destiny's small kitchen table and heard her in the shower—the whole place smelled like whatever she was sudsing.

Big continental move away from New York, and he'd promised himself he'd clean up his act. The gambling, the drinking—well, the gambling. He sipped scotch.

The Whitney. Hah! They didn't have a bit of proof. He'd told the director exactly—exactly—what he thought about that, and he and Miriam had left the borough. Miriam home to her parents, and he'd called Destiny. "You finally grow up? You in love with me, Irvy?" is what she'd said.

Run out of luck and now he was in sockeye Seattle? *Was* he in love? This was it?

No.

So why was he here? How about this was the best hand he was going to get, and did he want to fold?

No.

Things had majorly changed, and from some perspectives, he was somewhat screwed. His parents had called. A lot. He hadn't answered. They were retired and had plenty of time to dig deep into *The Times* articles and replay the network news. He'd be the talk at breakfast, lunch, and dinner, and he could hear his dad. "He should have gone to Harvard. We told him to go to Harvard. If he had gone to Harvard none of this would have happened." Here, in friggin Seattle, he had more than enough money to stay in play. But play what?

Destiny seemed happy that he was here. She seemed happy period. And she lifted him, warmed him, and he knew she was real. Maybe without all his game on, he'd relax some—give the two of them a chance.

A waft of damp heat pushed up behind him, and she came into the kitchen wrapped in a towel.

"Shall I go down there with you tonight?" he asked.

"Aww, Irvy. Thank you, no."

"Why?"

"Cause I'm going to be dancing, and flirting, and I don't want you to get chewed up in all that jealousy. It's my job."

"How long, I mean—"

"I'm old for it. In stripper years, I'm a hundred and twenty-seven." She scrubbed her hair with the end of the towel.

"You don't have to keep doing this. I can pay the rent. We can buy a place."

"I'm not doing it for the money. It's for me. It's empowering. I take off the armor, rip it up, and I own the room. I control those sorry freaks." She spun away and into the bedroom.

He poured two fingers over ice. They had history, he and Destiny. Sixteen years ago, he'd come out of the high-stakes room at Jimi's Filipino club in San Jose, and there she was—G-string and hanging upside down on a brass pole. Mirrored walls showed nearly all of her, and the sound system pulsed Elton's *Benny and The Jets*. He was smitten.

"You did well tonight, Irvin." A short man and bodybuilder, Jimi's voice was soft as the morning breeze. Otherwise, he was solid as a vault. His hand rested heavy on Irvin's shoulder.

"Huh, wha—?" Irvin said. He stared at the new girl—and did she just, like with slightly crossed eyes, wink at him? Upside down?

"She's got electric boots, a mohair suit

You know I read it in a magazee-eene

B-B-B-Bennie and The Jets"

~ ~ ~

Back then, he'd been working for Jimi the past three months as Jimi's poker avatar. His first time at Jimi's table, he'd beat Jimi with a bluff—beat him bad—and he shouldn't have done that. Jimi was The Man, and Jimi was convinced Irvin had cheated. Four a.m. and Jimi had asked him—told him—to remain at the table while the others left the room. Jimi's bartender, César, stood with his back to the door.

"You win big. Worse is you embarrass me. I watch you close tonight. You only lose when you decide—to fuck things up. I don't see what you do, but it is something. Now fate has made us personal. We are together in life and death. This is what I think. Do I remove you? Do you disappear, because everyone knows, 'Don't fuck with Jimi?'"

Irvin backed his chair from the table and rose. Both palms out, "No, listen, I—"

"Sit!"

He sat. Fuck, and why was he here? Not for the money, for sure. He'd played smaller tables all around The Bay for the past six years and made way more than enough for school and any car he wanted. But to be invited to Jimi's table was being asked to play with The Bigs. He should have held back some, but he couldn't. He just couldn't.

"The money is something, but that isn't it. If I put this bullet in you this morning," Jimi touched his jacket pocket, "it is not over. I have my money, and you are dead. But I am still in shame."

"Listen—the money—it's yours. And here you go." Irvin reached for the Nike bag on the floor.

Jimi flicked a look, and César whipped a Glock from behind his back.

Irvin froze.

"I take your bag, then we decide," Jimi said.

César crossed the room and kept the gun at Irvin. He knelt slowly, pulled the bag from the floor, went around the table, and back to the door.

"It is my game, my table. But you will sit in my chair. You will represent the house. Word will travel about Jimi's blond gringo bitch. There will be many challengers. Sometimes you will lose—when I tell you. Good for business. This way you will pay me back. When I am happy, I reconsider our relationship."

That early morning that Irvin had first seen the new dancer, Jimi said, "You did well. Here's your two percent of the table, and I will see you here tonight. In some months, then we talk."

"Yeah, right, Jimi. Thanks." He took the ten grand and slipped it inside his jacket. "Mind if I stick around a while? Get a drink?" His eyes on the dancer.

Jimi grinned. "Her name is Destiny, and don't fall for the white-trash stripper. I must leave. If you don't go with me right now, how will you get to your car?"

"I'm good. People see us talking—that we're friends."

"We are not friends. But, one drink. Then get the hell out before you find yourself in panganib." He added a warning grip to Irvin's shoulder, then left.

Irvin wove through tables of women and guys and their eyes, and it was obvious there wasn't a lot of Asian love for him here. He took the only empty stool, and César appeared.

"You don't drink here."

"Jimi said, 'One.'"

"I give you one—quick one. Then you go."

"Okay, Manhattan."

Joan Jett and The Blackhearts pounded out of the speakers. Destiny slid down the pole and uncoiled like a python on the raised, polished blue floor, and the floor came right up to his elbow at the end of the bar. Alternate thighs and elbows spread, she was a serpentine slather of passion and sweat. She writhed and bellied toward him and rolled onto her back. She was three feet away—and he felt her heat, and the heat of the lights, and the hate in the room—and now, her weight on her shoulders and heels, she quivered and heaved, and up onto her hands, and her back arched, and the ripples in her belly and thighs, and the supple contours of her lovely breasts. He was trapped in her stare, and it was just the two of them alone now, and she was upside down, and she pursed her lips into a kiss. She opened them ever slightly to a secret of white, perfect teeth and stuck out her hungry tongue.

Oh-My-God! He'd never seen the underside of a naked woman's tongue! Her hands and face within reach, his fingers crawled as in a trance.

"No!" César clamped hard on his wrist. "You drank. You go."

"But—"

"Now."

The music had changed to a Filipino singer, and some of the women next to their guys at the tables were seat-dancing and singing along. Destiny had strutted from the stage, through the glitter curtain, and his time was up. The room was about to devour him. Jimi had said he could only do so much to keep him safe here.

César came from behind the bar. "Now!" He escorted Irvin out.

It had rained. The small parking lot was shoulder-to-shoulder with jeweled-and-tuned Japanese cars. To his right, smoking beneath the roof's overhang, three guys as sharp as switchblades leaned against the wall and went quiet as wolves.

Jimi had said it, "How will you get to your car?"

He had ten grand in his pocket, and he knew the weak adrenalin rush of fear. Game on. Fight or flight—and, like the lamb, there was only one option. Or could he maybe try his generations of entitled, inbred, Rappaport smarts—a little humor, and wiggle away?

Hey, you guys hear the one about the tall white guy and the three handsome Filipinos?

How many drinks had he had? He didn't remember how many at the table, then the Manhattan. Damn, he wouldn't be able to perform for this crowd.

Flight. Square up like you own the place, and walk straight to the car. He lit a smoke, nodded to the guys, and headed out. He was nearly to the street when he heard, "Puki!"

He didn't look back, just waved in the air.

"Hey pussy, get the fuck back here! We gonna talk!"

Talk to the ass! He sprinted to the Beemer and—shit and hallelujah—peeled away with three shivs in the mirror.

~ ~ ~

The apartment door eased shut, and he was alone for the next, what, ten hours?

Another drink, or sleep?

He rolled one of his bags into Destiny's bedroom—*their* bedroom—and found his gray flannel jammies and toothbrush. Now that he'd given in to it, he was thrashed.

Out of the shower, into his jams, and lights off, he slid into the covers and closed his eyes. His eyelids were acid. He blinked a dozen times to clear them, and the pillow smelled like her—her hair, her shoulder, her dreams. In Jersey, she'd burrowed her face into his neck, then, turning away, snuggled her butt up against him.

Man, it had been a long day.

Sirens terminated a couple blocks away. *Must be near a hospital.*

He rolled to his side and tried a second pillow to silence the street. Breathe deep and steady—in two-three-four, out two-three-four.

Empowering. She said the dancing was empowering. Didn't her day job empower? The senior center? Doing work that meant something? Directing staff, bringing the love to forgotten seniors? She had her master's, for chrissake, from Stanford no less.

One hundred and twenty-seven in stripper years. In dog years he was two-eighty.

He rolled to his other side. The Whitney. He'd made it. Write-ups in *The Times*, receptions, interviews, and the talk of the avenue.

Fuckin guys in Jersey had no humor. Fuckin hand. Most of it healed, but it hurt like a mother on the plane—cabin pressure.

Detective Nettles, the tweed terrier. Master of distraction. "How'd y'all come across someone who just had to have that Warhol? Nice shoes, by the way. Italian?" Then she goes into what she's read about the international market for stolen art, and what a hotbed Japan is. "Y'all know any Japanese collectors? Hey, and I checked out your old address in Montclair. Place you sold six months ago? Is that place really listed on the National Registry? Phew. That had to be expensive—built in 1908. What'd you pay for something like that? Not what you make on a curator's salary. Perhaps you have a second source of income?"

She made his skin crawl.

He rolled over, tugged at the blankets. Released a calming breath.

His dad. Had he accomplished as much as his dad? His mom? Was curator right up there with tenured professor? Damn right.

Do the sirens never stop?

They'd been disappointed in him, that he'd totally screwed up the family DNA and rejected Harvard. "It's free, Irvin. And you can live at home."

"No." They were smothering him. Cambridge was smothering him. Gray winters, gray summers, and humidity was smothering him. California was a blue-skies beach, little deuce coupes, and he wanted a tan.

"You're on your own, then," his dad said.

"Promise?" he'd said. That was stupid. It hurt his dad, and it was a hair-trigger response. Could he lay off the sarcasm and not jump at the bait every goddamn time? He was a cynic. Everybody taking this shit so seriously—the academics, politics, the news, personal relationships, their children, the oxygen-sucking NFL and their first-round draft picks. His father chasing the subtleties of "or" and "and," trying to get to the root of it all. And if he ever got to the root of it all, then what? Start back at the beginning looking to disprove what he'd spent his life proving?

The serpent swallowing its tail.

It had all come easy to him—the math, the science, the language—while everyone seemed to struggle. Those years in school, he didn't get it—why everyone else didn't get it. He'd glance up at the white board, and the error would light up like the Fourth of July. Calculus came to him like breathing.

He should just get up and be done with it. He rolled onto his back, palms flat on his chest. That lasted ten seconds. He rolled to his stomach, punched the pillow twice, and settled back in.

In Texas Hold 'Em, he knew what the other players held with deadly accuracy. All of it—too easy. So, he'd gone rogue now and then to keep things interesting. Then taking Jimi's money at Jimi's table and coming close to taking Jimi's bullet at Jimi's table.

There had been one little slip-up during the first Detective Nettles interview, but she didn't catch it, and it warmed him, now, thinking about it. Gotta pay attention to what's being dealt, Nettles. And *you* gotta cover your cards, and watch your mouth, Irv-boy.

Here he was, a couple thousand miles away in a beautiful woman's sheets. Destiny. He sure caused her some heartburn while he was keeping himself amused—running around on her. "Sorry baby, my bad. Won't happen again. Sorry baby, I'm only flesh and blood—it's you I truly love. Sorry baby. Sorry." Until he pushed her over the edge.

Destiny. One side so soft, sensitive, nurturing—the other side wanting to burn the house down. She never came out and said she'd been abused as a kid, but she had. Raised on the moisture-wicking surface of the moon in California's hardtack, just outside the metropolis of McKittrick, and, "Do you want gravy on them fries?" Oldest of five kids and pretty much mother, father, and county sheriff to the other four. All she said about it was that at nine she had a life-changing event, and she got real smart—bore down in school, read ahead, and got her ticket the hell outta there. Got a full financial-need scholarship, but that doesn't buy ramen and pay the rent. She said she met a senior who was dancing two nights at a little club in East Palo Alto and making more than enough to live on while her mix of scholarships and grants paid tuition. The woman told her, "But, you gotta be damn good, honey. You ain't *damn* good, you're still gonna starve." The woman gave her the owner's name and told her to show up at three if she wanted to audition. "I'm not givin you a reference though. Maybe you can dance, maybe you can't, and if you can't, it ain't stickin to me."

Destiny said it took a couple more days of ramen bowls and Wonder Bread for her to screw up her courage and put a tape together. She said she was nervous as hell during the first number. That when it was over, the club owner—and he looked a lot, and talked a lot like Danny Glover—invited her to sit down at the bar and gave her a beer and a shot, and said, "You got it in you, girl. You could be the main attraction at this club, but you gotta be comfortable in your skin. You gotta take it to em. Now, try again, and, this time, let it all out."

She moved to Jimi's bigger-bucks San Jose club a couple years later when she was a senior, and she was making good money when they met. Not what he made gambling—nowhere near—but good.

Tomorrow was Saturday. He'd take Des to lunch, visit a few galleries, see what's happening on the street, get into the Seattle art vibe.

Okay, he wasn't sleeping. He tore the covers off with a windshield swipe, wall-tapped to the kitchen, flicked the light switch, and made coffee.

I'm up.

71

Reflecting in Seattle, 1997

He found half-and-half in the fridge. Destiny could afford the calories with all that dancing. Miriam was probably asleep in Pennsylvania right now. Probably a simple life there. No Broadway, for sure. Not much to do, he guessed.

Broadway. He'd scored two tickets to *The Phantom of the Opera* and asked Miriam if she'd like to go.

She would.

They'd been working together for eleven years and, lately, he'd sensed they were seeing each other a bit differently—department meetings with lingering glances and he finding excuses to hang out in her office. Little more than a block from the Whitney was the Ramona, his watering hole. She'd been a few times with an intern or two, but now she walked over with him all the time—well, weekly. She wasn't much of a drinker, and, while she was at the bar with him, he restrained himself—way restrained himself—and it was maddening. But, he figured, it was worth it. He had always been drawn to her smarts, her calm, and her skeletal frame with flesh of finely shaved butter. Her fingers moved with the wind, and he was fascinated with how the light flickered between them when she talked.

There had been other women—edgy women, gambling women, that bawdy Mother-Earth singer with the big feet, actors, and, of course, Destiny. Destiny should have been a keeper—nubile, cunning, beautiful and rapier sharp—their nocturnal habits and questionable associations perfectly synched. She'd followed him to New Jersey when he snagged the Whitney position, and it wasn't much later that she'd promised to love him forever. "All in," she'd said, and he snatched that up like a hall pass. Home free with her unconditional love, he dropped her so many times her Superball lost its bounce, and she left for the other coast. Never said a word. Packed up and gone. For a while, there, he didn't know if she'd moved across town or been abducted. Go to the cops? No thanks. Don't get on *that* radar. He'd ask around, see if anyone knew anything. Whatever.

It was two months later the envelope arrived with no return address—postmarked Seattle. Her account of how things had gone down between them was rational, organized, and well-written.

He was her kryptonite, and she needed distance. She had a new life, ran a senior center and was dancing in a couple clubs. She recalled some of their good times and hoped that, given enough space, they'd be able to be together again. She'd even included life coaching advice because she really did love him, but didn't like him, and he had a lot of life ahead of him, and she wanted to give him a hint as to how to be a complete human being, because right now he wasn't. It gave him pause, made him sit back and think—

the letter in his hand. Maybe he'd been a shit. Of course he had. Did he love her? Maybe he should drop everything and go to Seattle and find her.

Whoa! Don't get all commando on me!

She should come back here! She's the one who left. She could have stayed, and they could have had this talk. Well, they *did* have this talk—frequently. But *she's* the one who left.

He'd determined he'd have to shape up if he planned on getting anywhere with Miriam. Yeah, it was time. Abandon the nocturnal bad habits, shoulders square, surrender to a normal life—in bed by ten and oatmeal in the morning. He hated oatmeal.

So he laid off the poker. He still placed sports bets—horses, baseball, soccer—but they took little effort and didn't interfere with his Miriam ambition. And, those couple times they went out, he deferred from wine at dinner, seeing how she'd barely finish one glass, and without his leash he'd have cracked a second bottle and then some. Best to not start.

72

Late Night Buffet, 1995

Phantom had been huge! After the show—a crisp, clear night—they strolled up Seventh Avenue nearly to Carnegie Hall and stopped into a little karaoke bar he knew.

"Best karaoke in the city because the performers stop here after rehearsals," he crowed.

Realizing the night was on a roll, he'd allowed himself a martini or two. Miriam sipped a chardonnay. The raucous singers were on fire, and—young, hot, and bohemian—they nearly blew out the sound system belting Gloria Gaynor, Tom Jones and Cindy Lauper covers.

Out on the street, the night seemed slo-mo and quiet. He'd waved down a cab, and, back at her address, she asked if he'd like to come up and see her place?

"Sure."

It was a five-floor walk-up. He hadn't breathed so hard since that first night with Destiny. God, she was athletic!

At Miriam's door, her key in the slot, she looked back over her shoulder. He knew what she was thinking—*911?* Bent over, elbows locked, he gripped his thighs. It would take a few minutes to recover—the gushing in his temples subsiding, his breathing dropping below the threshold of projectile vomiting. He wondered how Mrs. Greene did this—five flights? Primitive, tottery legs, and, lo and behold, he was in her apartment. Vision clearing, the chainsaws in his ears abating, he was in a pocket of repose. Nearly silent. Soft lights. She said something about freshening up and disappeared. He was alone, panting and sweating profusely in a well-kept space somewhere in Manhattan. The relatively little alcohol he'd had raced tight laps through him, and he needed to refuel. "You have wine?" he called.

"I beg your pardon?"

In the kitchen he chose a delicate linen towel and dried his face. There was a bottle of Bailey's on top of the fridge. *No thanks. There has to be more.* He was deep into a cupboard when she came in.

"Irvin?"

"Hey, what's this? Single malt?" He pushed a few things aside.

"My uncle. Dad's brother brought it back from Scotland."

"Scotland." He admired the sealed cylindrical package.

"A gift, and I didn't know what to do with it."

He pulled the bottle from its box. "Want to see?"

She put water on for tea.

Her living room was small and Spartan. The few things she had were nice things—tasteful, simple, the way she dressed. She came back in, lowered an album onto the austere turntable, and sat across the room from him. He closed his eyes and absorbed single malt.

She said she hardly knew anything about him aside from work, the drum majorette, and the sheep. Also his brilliance and fearlessness attacking difficult projects.

"Bull in a china shop?" Eyes closed, he took another sip.

She nodded and said he appeared that way at times, but his success rate was impressive.

"We're a good team," he said.

She said this evening had her wondering what kind of team.

He emptied his glass. "Who's that singing the love songs? Interesting choice." He gestured toward the turntable. "Classy." He rose, went to the kitchen, and returned with a refill.

She said it was Chet Baker, and she'd been collecting fifties and sixties jazz vinyl for a couple years. She was taken by those troubled souls flashing moments of genius despite upside down, surreal relationships, addictions, the law, and their Jekyll-and-Hyde lives.

"Jekyll and Hyde?"

She cited Charles "Bird" Parker as an example of one having such dedication to his art, practicing up to fifteen hours a day, and beset by struggles with opioids and alcohol which would end his life at thirty-four. She said the attending physician estimated Bird's age to be fifty or sixty.

"The fast and the furious." He headed back to the kitchen. When he resettled, he asked, "So if you weren't chief curator, then what?"

She placed her cup on the saucer next to her and asked what he meant.

"You know. If the cards hadn't been dealt as they had." He sipped and closed his eyes again.

She said she could have been a writer.

He nodded. "Nose-in-the-air Pulitzer pulp? Sci-fi? Chick lit?"

She said she might have written travel books.

He opened his eyes. "I didn't know you travelled. I always had you as a stay-at-home girl." He ought to bring the damn bottle in here.

She said she hadn't traveled, but if she had a chance, she thought it would be fun to write about her experiences. She rose, went to the turntable, and flipped it to the Gershwins—.

"They're writing songs of love, but not for me

A lucky star's above, but not for me

With love to lead the way

I found more skies of gray

Than any Russian play could guarantee"

"Damn, that's depressing!" he called from the kitchen.

Back in his chair, "So where would you travel? Your first book?"

She said she was fascinated with Cuba, and someday she hoped to go there and write about it.

"Friggin communist Castrito banditos. Great cigars, though."

She agreed that the Castro experiment had been colorful, challenged, and had a tragic legacy. She related how Cuba had suffered violent revolutions led by poets like José Marti and other artists following their hearts, and how Cuba was a spawning bed for the birth of governments shedding their European influences in Africa. She spoke of the sacrifices and the passion and the food and the music and of the lovely people.

His eyes were closed again, and he wasn't listening. Half a bottle of single malt, and he was at the warm entrance to inebriation's full buffet of lost inhibitions.

He was thinking, comfort foods—creamy macaroni and cheese and he hoped it had a dripping, buttery crust, and steaming enchiladas with salsa verde and just the right amount of bite. That and something with a sweet breakable shell—like paper-thin dark chocolate cups filled with milk chocolate mousse that would melt on his tongue.

He chose a plate and stepped forward. "Is this going to be a sleepover?"

She stared at him for a long half-minute, then said, "No. I'll call a cab."

73

Was It the Scotch? 1995

Maybe he'd moved too fast. Of course he had. But a nearly-perfect hand—*Phantom*, long walk up the avenue, tiny kick-ass karaoke bar, and ending up—and hell's bells and hallelujah—in her apartment for the night? Okay, that hadn't worked, and she called a cab.

Here they were, Monday, in fine suits and great shoes, and a meeting scheduled at ten. The director's meetings always started precisely at ten. This was going to be embarrassing for both of them. He'd wait until the last minute to enter. She was always early.

It was a fishbowl conference room, and there, on the other side of the four glass walls, were the director, the director's assistant—an overachieving kid full of testosterone, and ambition, and straight off the grad school farm—the chairman of the board, a new board member, two strangers, two of the curatorial staff, and Miriam. A few were at one end filling cups and small plates with provisions to sustain them through what might be a heated conflict, or, more likely, a protracted campaign of polite suggesting, deflecting, deferring, and acquiescing.

He entered, found a seat, and opened his small leather binder. The director tapped his pen on the table.

Irvin had briefly scanned the agenda a couple weeks ago when it first showed up—something about public art for the new library. Another design by committee, he thought. So he hadn't invested much in the subject. He was sure that Miriam had gone at it tooth and nail and would have put together a presentation detailing international public art installations and what made them so successful.

If called upon, his contribution would be obsequious reinforcement and, "Whatever she said."

The director's assistant, Todd, was reciting the minutes from the last meeting as if this was the reason they had convened. Irvin watched the kid and wondered if *he* had ever been so full of himself. Todd's hair with that glistening, messed up, right-out-of-the-shower look, full, rich, and alive with whatever it is that makes young hair look so—what—post-sex virile? Todd's shirts, though—Macy's for days.

Had he ever been so full of himself? Well, perhaps when he was younger—but justifiably. He had been high school valedictorian, after all. And look at him now—friggin curator at the Whitney, living in a Montclair mansion, and who fit better in a suit than he did? Okay, he *was* full of himself from time to time, but not *that* full.

The director asked for approval of the minutes, there were a couple "ayes," and, "The purpose of this meeting . . . "

The director introduced the library strangers who paid glowing homage to the chairman who introduced the new board member who also paid glowing homage to the chairman. Irvin doodled in his binder and kept his head down.

He sneaked a glance across the table and two seats to the right at Miriam—her posture perfect, eyes fixed on the director.

There was a shuffling of chairs, and one of the library people went to the head of the table. The director moved to a side chair. Curtains rolled across the glass, the screen lowered, lights dimmed to near dark, and three-dimensional and animated floor plans and elevations appeared on the screen.

" . . . architect's vision . . . common areas . . . ingress and egress . . . "

In the cover of darkness, he again glanced at Miriam. She stared straight at him. He knew faces—could read faces—and hers was as stone flat as the best poker pros in Vegas. He lowered his eyes to his binder a few seconds, then did another take. Her eyes. It wasn't cold hatred in those eyes. Not quite. A bit of ice around the edges, like late fall in Upstate. But there was surely a hint of something worth noting.

Was her weekend a series of reruns of Friday night? Did her ire rise with each showing— visions of chanting crowds, pitch forks, torches, and grisly executions? Or were they sad reruns? Sympathetic black-and-white films from the forties drenched in violins, Gene Tierney, and diffused focus—did she regret calling a cab?

Had he come on too strong, too soon, and did she overreact and then get over it, as in, we're all adults, right? No, hers appeared to be clear-eyed, static-free intent, cleansed of yesterday's tangled emotions and wrong turns—and now a back azimuth pointed his way. For sure, he'd made his move too soon. He also drank most of her uncle's scotch. Was that it? The scotch?

The lights came up, and he was back to flourishing doodles in his binder. The director asked, "Miriam?"

As he called it, Miriam had handouts delineating successful twentieth century public art installations from around the world. She guided the table through the highlights of her report, then handed off to the co-curators of the Whitney's recent biennial.

Irvin flipped the page in his binder and, to the untrained eye, took copious notes.

Another twenty minutes, and the director again tapped his pen on the table. "Meeting adjourned."

The director and Todd left the room like being sucked through a vacuum tube. The co-curators and library people chatted with the electric crackle of a project launch not yet having lost a wheel and headed for the cliff.

Miriam paused at the door, turned, and nodded toward her office. How had she known he was watching?

She stood stiffly with her back to the shelves. Her eyes surrounded him. "Please, have a seat, Irvin."

He did. Soft leather folded around his thighs as he gripped the chair's chrome arms.

"Friday was nice, thank you."

"Ah, well . . . " He started up from the chair.

"Please."

"Sure." He dropped.

"We're friends, right?"

"Yeah, of course."

She pushed off the shelves, passed the parade of Barbies, and stopped behind the desk. Her hands rested on the back of her chair. "So why, after a lovely dinner, the play, and the fun bar, did you jump to 'sleepover?' Was I being set up? Had it been your goal from the start?"

"No, wait, I . . . " He pulled himself up from the chair and—

"Please." She pointed.

He sat.

"Irvin, you are a beautiful, brilliant man—"

"I—"

"And you have a screw loose."

He rolled his eyes.

"You do Irvin. You must be aware that you are kept here because of your inspirational and unblinking creativity. You are one of a kind. Any museum in the city might pay dearly to lure you away. What they don't know is they would then have to live with you. And, socially you are impossible."

He nodded and thought, Okay, I surrender, whatever. New game, and I'm in. Deal the cards and give me a chance and win back the losses. "I guess I was farther into our 'relationship' than you were."

"You were a little drunk."

"Yeah, that too. Sorry about your uncle's scotch."

"It went to a good home."

"Make it up to you? Dinner Saturday? Arcadia? Drinks at seven, move to a table at nine or so? I know the owner—Annie'll take care of us."

She chewed her lip. "Can I tell you tomorrow?"

"Once burned, twice shy?"

"Something like that."

The next day's good news was she agreed to a second date. The bad news was she insisted on a goddamn jungle adventure—a picnic on the lake, and she meant *on the lake*. What the hell do you wear to something like that? His weekends were slacks, a Polo, and Italian loafers, and that wasn't going to get it. A friggin boat?

74

Top-siders, 1995

There was obviously a side of life he'd been missing, Irvin thought as the salesclerk approached. The guy wore a kilt.

"What brings you into The Great Outdoors, mate?"

Irvin slid his hands into his pockets. "I'm supposed to go on a rowboat expedition this weekend—poison ivy, bugs, sunburn. I can't go dressed like this."

"You got that right. Follow me."

Irvin followed and wondered what you'd wear beneath a kilt. The guy led him to an area of the store that smelled like a stable.

"Top-siders." The guy pointed to a row of rustic moccasins. "Size?"

Four hundred fifty dollars later, Irvin left The Great Outdoors with two large bags of what the kilt guy assured him was the bare minimum for surviving his weekend.

75

Call Me Old-Fashioned, 1995

In the store, he'd looked the part surrounded by canoes, shotguns, camo suits, and men and women who could probably gut a fish. However, in front of his bedroom mirror he wondered how he was going to get out of his neighborhood and onto the train. This *Crocodile Dundee* bit was going to be an issue in Montclair. It might work if he had a tan, a rugged complexion, and a big knife. But soft hands, white legs, and museum curator? Not.

He wore pre-diet slacks over the cargo shorts and kept the bush hat in the daypack with the sunscreen and bug spray until he got to the park. Inside the park, the hat came out, the slacks went in, and he squared his shoulders. Bald knees strode off to find Miriam.

She waved—T-shirt, ball cap, shorts, and running shoes. Damn, she was cute.

"Hey," she said.

"Hey." They hugged politely. "You've got an honest-to-God whicker picnic basket," he said.

"Call me old fashioned."

"You're old fashioned."

"And you are striking in khaki."

He stood straighter. "Shall we?" He motioned toward the boats.

"Our craft awaits."

Miriam lowered into the rear of the boat, put the basket in the front, and sat in the middle. He wondered why she was sitting backwards.

The young attendant held the back of the boat as Irvin stepped in, and the boat was crazy unsteady and all off balance like there was something wrong with it. The kid sneered at him and said something crude. Then he gave the boat a shove, and they were headed out.

Miriam took control of the oar handles and began rowing, and now he saw why she was in the middle and backwards. He should have gotten in first. He checked out the other boats, and none of the guys were being ferried by a woman. They should trade places. He saw how she rowed, and he could do that, no problem. Now someone in one of the other boats was pointing at them. Across the water he heard laughter.

"Let's switch places," he said.

"Please!" she said.

Having his sea legs, now, he stood and started toward her.

Boom! From out of nowhere they were viciously rammed by another boat. He lunged to shield her from harm, she moved abruptly, the boat tipped, and he was forced overboard. You should never move abruptly in a small boat, and she should have known that. This sucked. Miriam looked so alone and panic-stricken. But the lake, this close to shore, is, of course, shallow, so, standing there up to his waist, he told her he was okay, and he'd simply wade ashore and meet her back at the boathouse.

The offending boat rowed away quickly.

76

A Visitor in Seattle, 2018

Irvin closed the door to the gallery's shop. Lights off in the back, and, adjusting his hold, he hefted a case of wine out to the front to close up for the night. There was a baked goods and BINGO affair at the senior center, and he and the wine would be joining Destiny there in half an hour.

It had been twenty years in Seattle, and he and Des were settled into domestic comfort, and, these days, she pretty much called the shots. Sure, he had the high-visibility gallery, his picture in the paper, and all, but she was driving their car, and he was better-than okay with that.

A large man entered and closed the door behind him. Irvin slowed and stretched a patient smile. "Good evening." He lowered the wine to the floor by the desk.

The guy looked to be seventy-something, and you never knew, especially about people of a certain age, who would make the next big acquisition. He'd told Des that each sale these days was crucial to keeping the doors open. When he'd first established the gallery, the world was emerging from its crippling recession, during which art was purchased only by the one-half-of-one-percent—and at huge discounts. In the following years, he'd seen sales increase slowly with each new quarter. He'd learned long ago to read collectors versus tire-kickers and artists.

Hands in his coat pockets, the gentleman toured the gallery downstairs and up, and he had that hungry look. Irvin checked his watch. He'd better call Des.

"What the hell, Irv? Where's the wine? You're supposed to be here right now!"

"I'll be there, Des, a little late. I've already shut down the back, and the wine's right here next to me. Last customer of the day just came in. He looks serious."

"Get up here."

"Be there soon. Love you."

Silence.

The big man held the rail and came down the stairs slowly. He pointed to the leather sofa. "Do you mind?"

"No, please. Be comfortable."

The guy took off his coat, folded it, and placed it on the sofa next to him. Flannel shirt, gray wool slacks, and comfortable shoes—probably Rockports.

"Sorry I'm so late. You were closing up."

"Not at all." Irvin rested his butt back on the desk, arms folded.

"It takes a while to get here, and I didn't count on rush hour from the airport."

"You just flew in? From where?"

"New York, and I should have left earlier, but this was the best I could do."

Irvin crossed the space and offered, "Irvin Rappaport."

The man reached up and they shook. "Brian Beaufalont, NYPD retired. Brian patted the open side of the sofa. "Can we chat?"

A surge came up in Irvin. "Of course." He nested in the corner of the sofa and faced the man.

The man scooched around toward Irvin. "Folks have been looking for someone like you for a long time. Recently, I have, too."

Irvin rewound and replayed. He chuckled. "Someone like me?"

The guy didn't look all that comfortable. "Yeah, someone smart and skilled. Someone who knows the odds, can read people, and gets things done when the lights are out."

Irvin smiled. "I should be flattered?"

"You'd agree you're smart and skilled? That you know your subject, and you're well connected in the international market?"

"It's my job, and, 'Kids, don't try this at home.'" Irvin laughed. His phone buzzed. "I'm sorry. This will just be a moment."

"Hey, Des."

"Why aren't you here?!"

"On my way."

"Get up here. These people want wine."

"Right, okay. Soon."

Silence.

"I'm sorry." The man rose. He pushed a hand deep into a coat sleeve. "You were closing, and you have to be somewhere. I can come back tomorrow. It's already past my bedtime back East." He opened the door.

"Please, I can stay a while." Irvin checked his watch.

"Ten tomorrow? You open at ten?"

"Yes, but—"

"Good. I'll see you then. We have a lot to talk about. G'night."

He closed the door and disappeared beyond the front window.

77

Is This Guy Writing a Book? 2018

Goddamnit, Irv, can I count on you anytime soon?" Destiny took the case of wine, set it on the floor behind the table, and pulled a few bottles. She handed him a corkscrew. "Start opening." There was a thirsty line waiting. "What took so long?"

He popped a cork and started on the next bottle. She poured and handed a glass to a petite, frowning woman in a cardigan.

"Guy from New York. Flew in to talk to me. He's coming back tomorrow, first thing."

"Who? Why?" She passed out glasses, two people at a time.

"Hell if I know." He sat another bottle in front of her.

"One glass, Ronnie," she said.

"Retired NYPD," Irvin said.

"Jersey? Gambling? But you were done with that a long time ago. Right?"

"Right."

"So what then?"

"I guess we'll know in the morning. He said we have a lot to talk about."

"Is that good?"

"Maybe he's writing a book." He set another bottle out. "That first lady in the sweater's back in line."

~ ~ ~

Destiny snored. He liked her snoring. If snoring could be called amusing, hers was. But that's not what had him awake, lying next to her.

NYPD retired.

What's *that* about? First of all, statute of limitations, right? So, if they're still trying to pin this on him, good luck. *Retired.* Remember that little nugget.

Maybe he *is* writing a book and exposing Nettles and Ciccone and sloppy investigations. What ever happened to Ciccone? Crude ways and shortcuts probably caught up with him. Probably had to leave town. Probably living in Norway. Maybe this cop will include how Brigitte Bardot came to New York and was heartbroken about the theft and made the papers with her mission of saving the animals.

If he *is* writing a book, he'll get an earful here. Goddamn fat-ass board. And the director. Did anyone else know the director was a flaming speedball? They will now!

78

Retired New York Police Detective Brian Beaufalont, 2018

Irvin had been up since three. The back pain—the growing old—was a bitch. At daybreak, he went down to the market for breakfast.

It was great to be at the market before the crowds arrived. Streets and floors liquid mirrors from the rain and early morning hose downs. The sea air, a volume of cool plasma gushing through empty aisles, everything fresh and tidy, dramatically lit—the fish and meats on ice, the produce, the flowers. In another hour the place would be shoulder-to-shoulder with the insistent patter of commerce. Upstairs, the café was quiet, and he was the first to arrive. He took a table by the window and the latent clang of a buoy somewhere in the mist. Coffee arrived. Did he want the crab cake Eggs Benedict this morning or the yogurt, granola, fruit bowl?

"Which is it today, Irvin—happy or healthy?"

"Why, thank you for asking, Donna. This morning's blood pressure was close to normal. I think I'll go for the eggs."

She patted his shoulder.

Looking out across the water he recalled that night in Prague—then that *other* night in Prague. Brigitte, at sixty, had the lithe energy and blithe spirit of a twenty-year-old, hustling Anna and him through the crowd. Mick's people had informed security, and they had a pass and they met Mick, and he was delightful, and they stayed for a few numbers, then left early.

It had all happened so quickly and effortlessly. Now, a dream.

~ ~ ~

Seattle's damp and cold washed into the gallery with the big guy and his coat. He held a to-go carrier with two large, covered cups.

"G'morning. Brought you a latte from across the way. They say you take a double shot."

"Good morning, and thanks."

"Mornings are calm here? Can we talk?"

Irvin spread his arms. "You're looking at it."

The man handed him a cup.

"I'll take that." Irvin dropped cardboard carrier into the basket behind his desk, and returned. "Shall we?" He motioned to the sofa.

A repeat of last night, the man folded his coat and eased onto the sofa. Irvin took the opposite corner.

"A lot to talk about?" Irvin opened.

The man rustled around slowly in what appeared to be unrelated movements. He leaned most of his weight on a hand sunk deep at his side, scooched sideways, reached down and across, grabbed a shin, and pulled his knee and calf up onto the sofa. He continued to hold onto his shin, and, somewhat settled and out of breath, said, "Twenty years later, and here we are."

Irvin raised an eyebrow. "Later than what?" He took a sip.

"I've met Miriam. Nice lady. I bought a watercolor from her. She shipped it to our home in Brooklyn—free."

Interesting starting point, Irvin thought. He crossed a leg. "Yeah, Miriam," he shook his head, "she can be a pushover. We keep in touch—she sends me handmade birthday cards. *Her* hands. What took you to her gallery? Kind of off the beaten path, there in the middle of William Penn'syltucky." Yep, he thought. Definitely something about Ciccone, Nettles and the Whitney.

"The short version is that my coming here starts with Ronald Cash Hazzard, his partner, Nick—Miriam's brother—how they got her code, and who put them up to the whole thing."

"Her code. Miriam's?"

"That's right."

"The Whitney theft?" Both eyebrows this time. "You're going way back—speaking of the beaten path. That was a long, long time ago. I'm sorry, your name again?"

"Beaufalont, Brian Beaufalont. I represent the insurance company."

The man scrunched around some and winced like he might have back trouble. Irvin had read that a lot of big guys have back trouble.

"So Miriam, you're saying—and her brother. And another guy."

"Ronald, aka, 'Cash,' Hazzard."

"Damn. It looked bad for Miriam back in the day. But her brother, too, you say? You've talked to him—and the other guy?"

"Cash. Cash died in an auto accident eight months after the theft."

"Huh." Irvin uncrossed his leg and crossed the other. "Then you're saying, 'Crime doesn't pay?'"

"Miriam is involved. But she didn't know Cash the way Cash knew 'The Irvster.' You were a regular at the Ramona, where he worked."

"Everyone went there."

"Your buddy, the bartender, was Nick's pal from the Army—and didn't they get into a lot of off-duty trouble. Petty larceny, possibly grand theft, general mayhem, and something coming close to manslaughter. Starting to see how this kind of comes together?"

"No."

"The insurer would like the print back, and you and Miriam know where it is. We would like to return the Warhol to Ms. Bardot and recoup the six-million-dollar payout. Any assistance you can offer will be generously rewarded."

"Generously."

"Ten thousand dollars."

"Really." Irvin lifted up from the sofa, went behind the desk, and tossed his cup into the basket. He came around front, rested his butt back on the desk, and folded his arms. "For a six-million-dollar print? What are you guys smoking?"

"You have a nice gallery. A lot of serious collectors, repeat business—Japanese, Russian, Chinese."

"You left out Jersey. Yesterday I sold a Burton diptych to a nice couple from Livingston."

"However, it's unlikely a stolen Warhol would end up in Livingston, New Jersey or anywhere else in the U.S. Your international customers, on the other hand—"

"You're reaching, Brian. And where's the FBI and Interpol in all this interstate, international drama?"

"The car Nick and Cash stole in Manhattan was found in Ithaca, a couple hundred miles away. No interstate drama."

"Then why come all the way to Seattle? So far, you have Miriam, her brother, and Cash cold, so to speak. Why are you dicking with me?"

"Miriam and her brother benefited from the theft but wouldn't have a clue how—or where—to unload the print. You did."

"In your dreams. Look at me here. You see a guy hanging out at the country club?"

The man moved painfully around, both feet on the floor, and leaned, elbows on knees. He gazed up at Irvin. "It's a cover."

"What?"

"Your modest lifestyle, this gallery, your whole underfunded shtick. Six-million-dollar print and you already had a buyer. Russian or Japanese and looking at your record in the Japanese market—I'm going there. You get an advance, pay off the two goons, and you and Miriam come away with at least a two-million split. Possibly double that.

Smart, you both keep it in cash and subsidize the rest of your lives on opposite coasts. You build up this small gallery and an international reputation. Everyone in the city loves Irvin. Your buddies at the lunch counter can't wait to see you come through the door each day. Your celebrity wine and jazz openings are the talk of the town. My guess is your longtime girlfriend doesn't have a clue. Help us out, and the status quo remains status quo. You get ten grand and we part as if we've never met."

"Or?"

Beaufalont sat back and folded his arms. "Or it makes a great story for my old college roommate at the *Seattle Times*. The other night at dinner, he mentioned their Sunday readership is more than seven hundred thousand. I didn't tell him precisely why I'm here, but he was damn curious."

"And?"

"The revelation of your role in this—a big human interest angle. Their Sunday magazine. The fact that twenty years later you had a chance at redemption and said, "No," will severely impact your relationships. Do you want to go through that—start over? Again? Where will you move next? You're sixty, Irvin. Is this what you want?"

"I thought you got here last night."

"I've been here a week."

Irvin came off the desk and went over to the front window. The usual delivery vans had driven up over the curbs and lined up side by side on the bricks of the square. A break in the clouds—heaven's rays lit men and women pushing hand trucks into and out of the few restaurants, shops, and the kitchen showroom. In his pockets, his palms were wet. What is this guy? Friggin super cop? He thinks he's different? Five or ten percent of missing art is recovered, and he thinks he'll beat those odds? He thinks this is it? That I'll give him a name, an address, and plane fare to Osaka or Minsk?

Irvin heard his pulse in his ears and felt that boost as the adrenalin tap opened, and now the delivery people appeared pixelated, color enhanced, and in slow motion. He was awash in the white rabbit of good vibes. He hadn't felt this in a long time—the beat, the juice, the game on and, damn, he was on fire! Like the night he'd bluffed Jimi. Like the night the big-ass Jersey guys broke his hand.

But twenty years had passed, he was sixty, and it was getting late. What more was to be lost—or gained—by wiping the slate and being done with it?

Why not tell the guy what he wanted to hear? Game over. You win. Why not? Because he was back at the table with a straight flush!

He spun around. "Sorry, Brian." He grinned. "All you're holding is a pair—Miriam and Nick."

79

Detective Nettles Was Right, 2018

Clouds streaked past Detective Beaufalont's window, whipped around the corner, and dragged along those lagging behind. Between wisps, he had a sunset view of the Pike Place Market lights, the Ferris wheel, and white ferries on the bay. The afternoon shower had left surfaces deep hued and reflective—everything washed clean. He'd be leaving in the morning.

Irvin was right. He had nothing. Nettles was right. This was beyond Miriam. The director? Probably. He'd surely made a big deal of deflecting everything to Miriam and Irvin. Funny how people *can* disappear. A year later, he just doesn't show up one day? It was like he walked out of his condo one morning taking nothing but his passport and the clothes on his back. Living comfortably in Paris? For all anyone knows, he's sleeping on the streets and spreading Hep C. The few notes Nettles and Ciccone left indicate the guy was definitely deep into metabolic accelerators.

80

The Coming Dark, 2019

Given that he was nearly sixty-two, Irvin couldn't seriously say that his condition had come on quickly—it had been, after all, sixty-two years—but it seriously seemed to come on quickly. Maybe he should have listened to Des—of course he should have listened to Des—and gone in for annual checkups. But, until a few months ago, he was getting around pretty well and chalking up his increased clumsiness and progressive backache to the Pike Street hill and the ticking down of years.

Now he had returned the paintings, the sculptures and prints to his artists, closed the gallery, and he was well known in the neurology wing at the hospital. It was a mouthful, his condition—an advanced intramedullary spinal cord tumor, known among insiders, and he was an insider, as ISCT. When he slept, he slept sitting up. By all reports, this next bracket of weeks and months would alternate between spasms of significant discomfort and the blur of narcotic drips.

"Another of Irvin's genetic anomalies," his parents would have said, had they been around to see this. Both parents were still frisky and conspiring to make something of him right up until their very ends. A month apart, they'd simply dropped over mid-scene, and fade to black.

So this was it? What it all came down to? Stanford honors, beating out the other fools, the winnings, the losses, the games—and then a game that *nobody* wins? Who thought of *that*? All this time there was never an honest deck and the house totally stacked against you? C'mon, someone deal one more hand. Win back the losses.

But one more wouldn't be enough, would it? No, he'd want another one more, then another. Yeah—maybe bringing an end to the absurd was okay after all. Let the game clock run down. But he still had some things to square with Des. So—put a little time back on the clock?

He'd settle up with Des after he talked to Miriam, and she'd be arriving tomorrow. He told her she needn't come. They'd been in frequent FaceTime contact ever since his diagnosis, and FaceTime was as good as being there, right? But she insisted.

He'd kept all of her birthday cards.

~ ~ ~

From the bed, he heard Des answer the door.

"Miriam! Finally, we meet."

"We've waited too long, Destiny. Or—and I'm sorry—do you prefer Des?"

"These days, it's Des," she laughed, "Destiny's a little much for my current line of work. Here, let's take your bag to your room. Love your jacket."

"Des. Bring her in here."

"Keep your pants on, Irvy! The woman just arrived."

Des led Miriam to the guest room. "There's a part of him that's enjoying this despite everything. 'Des, bring me chocolate. Des, change my pillow. Des, I need a pill—and a good one this time.'"

Miriam laughed. "Please, not our Irvin."

"Uh-huh."

~ ~ ~

There was an immediate connection with Des—solid. Until now, she'd known her only as a character in Irv's tales. In the next three days, perhaps she'd come to know the real Des. As she unpacked a few things, she thought it wasn't as if she was here for a holiday meal with friends. Hers was a sad arrival, maybe an intrusion—she hoped they didn't see it that way—an intrusion into these last months Irv and Des had together. She was steeled for what she'd see at his bedside. He'd propped up a good act on FaceTime but had faded noticeably these past weeks.

She slipped the silver frame into her blazer pocket.

~ ~ ~

"Irv." Miriam crossed his room to the hospital bed. Thin arms raised to her. She bent and kissed his cheek, and just that quickly the miles between them, the years, . . . and now this. His fingers combed her short hair, and lingered. She nearly purred. She raised from him, tears in their eyes.

"I didn't think you should come, . . . I'm glad you did."

She sniffed. "Me too."

He moved slightly—squinched in pain. "It's been quite a trip until now."

"Yours has been a big life."

"And yours isn't? You're still beautiful, . . . by the way."

"You never told me I was beautiful."

"I thought you knew."

"It would have been good to hear. I wasn't very self-secure."

"You're more assured now?"

"I do the best I can with what I have. But there aren't a lot of men looking for a sixty-two year-old woman."

"If Des didn't have me on this leash, . . . I might make a pass."

"I heard that, Irvy!" Des called in from the kitchen.

He winked at Miriam.

"I want to give you something, Irv." She pulled the framed Polaroid from her pocket and handed it to him.

"You and Shirley Chisolm. From your office."

"From back in the day."

"This is precious. Thank you." He handed it back. "But I'll trade you . . . for the Reggie Jackson baseball. I could get a thousand bucks for that."

What to say?

"Miriam. Please put it there . . . on the nightstand. Where I can see it."

She moved the glass and placed the photo next to it. She sat by the bed. "Are you being kept comfortable?"

He closed his eyes. "I sleep a lot."

"Caretakers?"

"Des has been incredible. *Always* has. Others come in . . . when she can't be here . . . or to spell her. A nurse. A priest. Episcopal."

"Are you kind to the priest?"

He opened his eyes for a moment, smiled, and closed them. "She has a sense of humor."

His breathing nearly disappeared—miniature waves licking a lake's shore. She scanned his face—some features sunken, others raised. His lips moved, white fingers atop the sheets twitched, and she knew he was dreaming. How quickly he had gone from here to there. Behind her, Des came in.

"How long?" Miriam asked.

Des held onto the back of the chair. “Days. A week. Not long.”

“He was a wild hair.” Miriam said.

“He’s perfect. Hasn’t always been, but he grew up, and now our colors match. He’ll sleep for the next hour—the meds. Come out to the kitchen? I have small plates, and we can have a drink.”

“Thank you, Des. I’d like to sit here a while.”

“Of course.”

81

Where to Start? 2019

It was the next morning, and he was at his strongest and best in the mornings. Des had shaved him and brushed his hair before running off for groceries.

"Well, you're looking fresh and smart," Miriam said from the door.

"Fresh is as fresh does, Forrest."

"Can I get you something?"

"You can sit with me."

Where to start? he thought. Twenty-two years later—and what part of his recall was real, and what parts imagined, carved, resized and shaped to fit his ego and these next coming moments?

He'd told himself the story a thousand times by now—had built a fine country estate on robust-if-recently-eroding delusions. That there were no options. Survival had been paramount. That they'd both come away with good lives. Not great lives like New-York-name-in-the-lights great, but reasonable and good lives. She had her gallery, right? Her friends, her enduring beauty—And what the hell?—her health. A few weeks from now he'd be a mid-sentence smear. She'd consider that before tearing into him, right? That in the end, and after all, *he* was the victim? He'd spin the tale, expose himself to her mercy, and tell her the remaining money was hers. And, bolstered by the money, she'd feel sorry for him.

Yeah? Keep dreaming. The money's not going to put a dent in how pissed she's going to be. And then, when Des finds out, he'll be needing that nurse and priest *full* time.

Shit, and here we go. Ready to rock? He took in as much air as he could.

"You've probably been wondering . . . how the Warhol came up missing. Who was behind the whole thing?"

Fingers woven in her lap, she cocked her head.

"Beaufalont was here . . . months ago. He thinks it was you or me. He's leaning toward you . . . your brother, and all. That was a surprise to me . . . your brother. You were . . . clueless?

Never mind. It doesn't matter. Cash, of course, our toothpick . . . white-bread-and-Kool-Aid . . . bartender. Petty thief. An easy mark. Tragic. He had a great car for a while." His eyes met hers briefly as they patrolled the ceiling fixture, the window, the bedside glass, her photo.

She shifted her weight.

"About the time I broke my hand . . . that my hand got broken . . . I needed money fast. A lot of money. Life and death."

She sat straighter. "Your reaction to the theft—to all of it. An act."

"Family of actors. Mom, Dad, . . . me. I never expected . . . to come out ahead . . . on the sale of the print, . . . but I did. Way ahead. Twenty years . . . I've burned through . . . a little over half. The rest is yours, Miriam."

Her breathing increased, knuckles white. A tear broke loose. "Why, Irvin? All lies. Twenty years, goddamn it."

"Luck of the draw. Your purse . . . on the bar."

She stood to leave, then lowered back onto the chair.

"Where is it, Irvin?"

More tears, and softly, now. Controlled. Nothing like he'd expected.

"Safe-deposit. All in hundreds."

"The print."

"Oh." He closed his eyes and whispered, "I have to sleep."

"Where is the Warhol?" Softly, still.

"Kyoto. Kondo family. Dangerous." He opened his eyes briefly, then his lids dropped. "There. Please close the door, Miriam, . . . behind you."

She didn't move.

~ ~ ~

Miriam came out of her room, pale, exhausted, and towing her bag.

"Hey Miriam—what's up? What's wrong?" Des had just come in from the hall hugging two bags of groceries.

Miriam stared at her. Weightless. "I have to leave, Des."

"Now?" She glanced into the bags. "I have dinner."

"Thank you for your warmth. Your grace. It's lovely meeting you, and I'm so sorry about Irvin," Miriam shook her head. "About all of it." She took one of the bags from Des and led into the kitchen. She put the bag on the counter, then the other bag.

"All of it?" Des asked.

She hugged Des. "He's asleep. I'm sorry." She left the kitchen, took her roller, and was at the door. She turned, "I wish it could be different. You're a special person. Irvin's been lucky." And she was gone.

PART 4

Miriam

We text frequently, and Kush is convinced I need to blow oxygen into the part of me that only she and Texas can ignite. I must sound tired and broken to her. I haven't told her about my trip to Seattle—about Irv. I keep turning it over—looking for resolution. There's been a crazy thought presenting itself since Seattle—his confession, the money. Something beyond me. It could involve Kush.

82

Holes In Her Socks, 2020

Miriam scraped toast crumbs from the counter and tossed them into the sink, rinsed her cup, and they washed away. She'd been up since four, and there was Victoria's *beep.* She worked the straps of the carry-on over her shoulders, grabbed the roller bag and locked up as she left.

"Hey, good morning, and thanks for doing this," Miriam said.

Victoria glowed red in the tail lights, and Miriam's bags went into the trunk.

"No holes in your socks, I hope." Victoria pulled onto the empty street.

"Pardon?"

"You're going to have to take your shoes off."

"Oh, right. No holes."

"Then how ever did you get them on?"

"Groan."

Twenty minutes later they stood at the curb and the front door of the region's airport.

"Promise not to come home wearing boots and a big buckle?"

"Depends."

"On what?"

"If it grows on me. I'm not sure what to expect."

"The unexpected then. Expect that."

"Sage advice."

"You know that little sidewinder is over the top right now. Making everything perfect for your arrival."

"I hope not."

"You owe me five bucks if the sheets are pressed."

"You're on. I guess I should be going."

"Got everything—ticket, phone, wits?"

Miriam nodded. "Next stop Philly, then Austin."

They hugged and Victoria watched Miriam disappear through the double doors. She checked her watch. "Dunkin Donuts is open."

83

Somewhere Outside of Austin, 2020

The ranch was greener than she'd imagined. Flat sandpaper scrub shaded with hundreds of live oaks and as many fragrant cedars. What she knew of Texas were the Houston art museums, the Alamo, Barbara Jorden, The Johnsons, The Bushes, *The Astros*, and she had it pegged as a significant part of the dust bowl. But here were flourishing trees and the lake.

Kush had picked her up in her raised, super-duty Ram truck. Kush, ten years younger, popped right up and in. They laughed as Miriam struggled. "You got this, Ke-mo sah-bee?"

She barely made it on her third try. Off the freeway, they followed a long, dusty, dirt road to the ranch and through the gate.

Eighty-something, Kush's dad had a lot of right angles to him—square shoulders, straight back, the lines on his forehead and mouth went flat as the southern horizon when he wasn't unwinding a tale. His large, rancher hands and swollen knuckles hung at the ends of cabled arms, and Miriam was sure he could reach her from that opposite end of the table if he chose. And there, he stretched across and passed her the basket of biscuits from over six feet away. Kush chowed down on ribs.

"Thank you, Mr. Nettles."

"Slather a couple up with butter and have a good time." It was his easy speech that had rounded shoulders.

"Great that you're here. Makes Dad sit and be polite. And you can call him Sam."

"Thank you, KK," he said. "When Miriam calls me Mr. Nettles, it makes me think my dad's in the room. Though, I have to admit, each glance at the mirror these days, I see his ghost. That guy was some man." His biscuit pointed at Miriam. "Can't think of a thing he couldn't do but fly."

Miriam smiled at Kush, "How did you end up my size?"

"The men are tall—Dad, my brothers. The women—my Apache gramma and Mom, my aunties—small people. Me, sis..." Her dad noisily adjusted his chair on the stone floor.

In the blistering Texas heat, the interior of their thick-walled adobe home was quiet cool. Sam's dad had built it with the genius of native and Mexican help and it was passively regulated. Hill Country history wafted off the lake and drifted in through screened windows and doors.

~ ~ ~

The young labs were outside dogs—one black, one blonde. Laurel and Hardy. One walked like he had gum on his shoe, the other like he'd lost his hat. At water's edge, Kush was bronze and fit, and Miriam was trim and city-white. Kush wove her fingers into Miriam's. "Beware the Alaskan Bull Worm!" A hand squeeze, and the women waded in. It was spring-fed freezing. Behind them, Laurel and Hardy followed. They swam slow, endless yards to the floating dock through the smooth translucence, and Miriam imagined fish with rows of needle teeth, and leeches, and snakes. It was farther than it appeared—the dock. The dogs had turned back. Another hundred yards and the women climbed the little steel ladder and puddle-landed. Miriam was spent, hair dripping and cold. She lay belly down on warm, worn wood and, within seconds, smelled the lake cooking out of her. She nearly slept. It could have been Pennsylvania, and she was fishing with her dad, and, "Glory be to The Father and to The Son and to The Holy Ghost . . . World without end, Amen." Their battered aluminum boat, the musky smell of aquatic life, the day at rest but for the shimmer of water and insects. That was over fifty years ago, and then came Nick and her ambition and the Whitney and Irvin and Prague and the pigeons.

Her stomach had boiled on the ride from Irv's apartment to the airport. Her eyes on fire, and, behind them, the miniature building blocks of reason collapsed. Following his confession, she had stayed at his bedside, and, as vision crushed in on itself, listened to him sleep. When she'd returned to her room, she closed the door, crossed to the bed, picked up a pillow and screamed into it. The scale! Her goddamned life, and twenty years of lies, and more lies, and she stood and cried. How had he seen what was happening to her—Because of him!—and done nothing? His very existence, his self-absorption, had swept her out to the street. Was he sorry?

That her future was squeezed from her? Her life reduced to has-been? Had there been even a hint of remorse? No. He offered money!

Midflight and unsteady, she'd held tightly to seatbacks and decorum as she made her way up the aisle and into the lavatory. She was violently ill. Returning to her seat and wet with sweat, she pulled the blanket over her and slept for the rest of the flight.

Kush—and should she tell her? About Irvin? How, even in death, he was using her?

The money? Of course he'd been desperate. But they were friends! His betrayal—"Nature of the beast," he'd said. All these years. Abusive relationships, and could she—why *shouldn't* she—hate her brother and her best friend? She'd, long ago, justified letting Nick wither in her past, and she was still pushing back on vengeful thoughts of Irv—his death.

Now, with the sun on her body, could she deserve this moment—accept this lovely companionship with Kush, and Sam passing her the biscuits?

Kush. A radiant, engaging woman. The only guys in her life were her father and brothers, as far as she knew. They hadn't yet talked of past romances, if any. Being around her again was so natural and easy.

Close the gallery? Stay here—Kush had invited her—and learn to ride? At this age? She'd been afraid of horses, but when Kush introduced them—her two Arabians and the three she boarded—her fear fell away. Each horse, its own disposition, friendly and smart, and, according to Kush, one a jokester. The dogs got along with them.

The money. She had the money, and she should turn it in. But to whom? And what would they do with it? They'd had plenty of time to find the print, and failed.

No, the money could be put to better use.

The dock bumped and rocked, then a splash. Miriam rolled to her side and propped on an elbow.

"Aren't you hot?" Kush called. "C'mon in."

Miriam backed down the ladder ever slowly. "It's ice." Head above the surface, she did a breaststroke to within a few feet of Kush treading water.

"You know what's been stuck in my butt all these years? Something I can't force out?"

"I'll try to decode that," Miriam said

"Irvin."

Must we? Now? "Oh? What about him?"

"Well, a lot. Big gambling habit, for one. Probably how he bought and lost that Montclair mansion."

Of course. "He had a mansion?"

"Not any mansion. Had to cost millions. On the National Registry and he dumped it lickety-split. Fire sale. About the same time he broke his hand . . . changing a flat." She grinned. "Imagine him changing a flat?" She took a deep breath and sank below the surface. Thirty-seconds and she popped back up. "I can't either. But the thing that keeps biting my butt is—I'm trying to remember when we saw that truck dock video for the first time. The one with the two yahoos running up the street and jumping into that car."

"The Lexus," Miriam said.

"Right. I didn't mention that in my notes, and it's really eating me. Did we interview Irvin before, or after we saw the video?"

"You told me it was a Lexus the first time we talked."

"Right, but that was a day after we talked to Irvin. When we talked to him the day before, he mentioned something about the two guys leaving in a stolen . . . and he didn't say, 'car.' He said 'Lexus.' I'm not sure anyone knew it was a Lexus at that point."

Miriam stared at her, took a breath, closed her eyes, and sank below. The cold so thick and complete, the warmth of her body welcomed here, and slowly slipping down. How lost and lonely the Earth in this dark universe, how short and small this life. The breathing world gone, she exhaled. The hollow sound of rocks in a barrel, and she touched bottom—the mud soft around her ankles. The pressure, her lungs bursting, everything speeded—her father, Mom, Nick and a loud truck. Irvin, Anthony, her body against his, and she had known love. She opened her eyes to the ache and the cold, her dreams, and the jazz, and she didn't need air. Kushala. It means safe. *You can stay. Just stay.*

~ ~ ~

Dusk's descent, the dogs at the stable and Sam in the house, both women quiet on the dock. They had treaded water as Miriam told Kush of her visit to Irvin, of his confession, and the money—how she was crushed and had left immediately. Over two million dollars, and she didn't want it. "Then, he put it in his will, and I heard from his lawyer. I gave part to Destiny and some to an education fund for inmates. There's nearly a million left."

Kush stared out across the lake and said she'd been leaning toward the director for a couple years, but the thing about the car kept following her around, which led her back to Irvin. That, and how, that Saturday, he was unaccounted for. She glanced at Miriam.

Leaned back on her hands, Miriam nodded and stared at the same distant shore. Was this the opening—the time to tell Kush what she'd been thinking?

"The money presents options."

Dark had fallen as they waded in from the lake, and, snugged in towels, made their way to the house.

"You can't leave this weekend, Miriam. Call Victoria, call the gallery. Change your ticket."

"I can't do that to them."

"You need more time. There's something unfinished—do this for yourself. Stay another week."

Unfinished. "I . . . "

Kush put her arm around Miriam's waist as they walked. "C'mon, I'll teach you to ride, we'll go out on the town. Cripes, we'll bake cookies."

Miriam cleared it with the interns and Victoria. "By the way, I owe you five bucks." She changed her ticket and stayed, sleeping on pressed sheets.

They shared belly laughs as Kush showed her how to saddle a horse and taught her the fundamentals of riding, which, in Miriam's case, involved a stepladder. The dogs followed them out at sunrise and into the purple crown sunset each evening—Miriam in running shoes and one of Kush's Stetson hats. A few times, Sam's long shadow of the Marlboro cowboy trailed behind.

84

Would She Like Her Brothers? 2020

Miriam slept late. She woke as Kush settled on the edge of the bed with tea and churros. Shorts and a T-shirt, hair damp, and her skin glowed—her smile. "Tea and sweets to start your day. Bring your cup, we'll tour my room."

Getting closer to Kush on the ranch, it was the "terrier in tweed" that had been so far from her element in Manhattan. Kush's bedroom furnishings were similar to Miriam's room—bleached wood and heavy. But this was Kush's sanctum sanctorum. Dozens of pictures on shelves and walls chronicled the woman's life. Black-and-white photos of rodeos, a young Kush with her mother and father, her sister and her sitting on the top rail at the corral and laughing. "See what I mean about my sister?" A photo years later of Kush between her tall brothers lined up on their mounts, backs straight and all business, and Miriam wondered if she'd like the brothers. "You will." A touching sepia studio portrait of a twenty-something Kush and her mother—two dark, beautiful women, and they could have been sisters—her mother eternally young.

There were action shots from her high school days—barrel-racing, soccer, and lacrosse—and more than a dozen trophies, and there were rifles on the walls. By the door, a small color portrait of the young, uniformed, and squared-away Officer Kushala Nettles—Graduate, New York City Police Academy.

85

There's more.

Table set, dinners plated, and napkins in their laps, the three ate while Sam was back to his polychromatic tales. "Like the time your mother and I—and she wasn't your mother yet cause we were just dating—and wasn't she the sweetest thing you ever saw. Anyway, she and I snuck off with Dad's '47 Plymouth, and, of course I thought Dad would never know cause he was already in bed and snoring like a John Deere, and we drove down by the river to find a hidden spot to be alone in the moonlight, and, . . . and, . . . " His head lowered. He coughed softly into his napkin, glanced at Miriam, then away. "It's like it was yesterday." He laid his hand on his daughter's.

With Sam in charge of dinners, it was the two women who did the cleanups and catching up shoulder to shoulder at the sink—one washing, one drying. Sam early to bed, Miriam and Kush repaired to the front porch and settled into the line of heavy, rough-hewn chairs. A light wind from the lake, a deep mulberry sky, and the staccato clutter of starlings coming to rest. Both women quiet, they were audience to a warm night.

An audible breath and Miriam began, “There’s more.”

“Mmm?”

“The two skinny guys. My brother.”

Kush turned to her. “Say again?”

“The video. One of the guys was my brother. Nick.”

Quietly, “Shit damn, Miriam.”

“My brother and the other guy. The other guy in the hoodie. He died that year. Nick’s friend from the Army—Cash. He tended bar at the Ramona. Irvin recruited Cash at the bar, then Cash recruited Nick.”

“Damn.”

“I’d more than suspected Nick for years. He knew I did, and he found it amusing. His betrayal was nearly silent. Irv’s hit like a storm.”

The birds had gone quiet, the trees to shifting silhouettes.

Miriam stared into the dark. “I’m thinking of leaving the gallery for a while. The kids can manage it.”

“Mmm. How long?”

“A while.” She turned to Kush, gave it a moment, and said, “You know how to get things from people. Answers.”

“Excuse me?”

“An observation.” The breeze picked up, and she moved into it. “Have you been to Japan?”

"What?"

A start, a stop, and whispers circled objections with barely a ripple. The two women stayed up late beneath stars never seen in Manhattan.

ACKNOWLEDGEMENTS

I am grateful for the time, incites and encouragement many have contributed bringing Miriam, Irvin and Nick to these pages. I should have kept better notes, and if you are momentarily rattling about in the dark space where once was my memory, please know that, sometime soon, your name will likely appear in the middle of the night, and I'll bite my hand.

I am, firstly, in ever-loving thanksgiving for Jane Burton, my wife and pilot, who holds my heart and hand, and lights our way.

And, special thanks to:

Bruce Allen, who listened, laughed and kept me rolling through the miles

Mitch Allen suffered a couple drafts and gave Miriam her Biblical name

Dave Borofka had kind comments and questioned Miriam's Mac

Steve Bower, from Williamsport, PA, painted the striking, enchanted trees

Julie Finney kept Beaufalont and Nettles on track

June Gillam unplugged Miriam's Saturday morning

Frederick Holmes & Co. took us to Seattle

Sacha Kawaichi was a week-at-a-time listener and laugher

Ruthie Kitchen wondered about Nick in an early draft

Deborah Lapp removed the calliope from Miriam's workshop

Jo Miele gave the nod of an odd Italian grandmother

David Pava was like a brother, we shared a birthday, and he inspired "Guzzi Mon"

Howard Rappaport organized and led the critical choir

Nancy Spiller somewhat sanitized Mrs. Greene's manners

Pattti Walker read, corrected, punctuated, and commented thoroughly

And remembering The Screw Shop Guy.

www.ingramcontent.com/pod-product-compliance
Lightning Source LLC
LaVergne TN
LVHW100508110826
845146LV00002B/556

9798996029303